SO-AUX-774

DOG

HEAVIES

Tor books by L. J. Washburn

Wild Night
Dead-Stick
Dog Heavies

L. J. Washburn

DOG

HEAVIES

TOR

A TOM DOHERTY ASSOCIATES BOOK ▪ NEW YORK

This book is a work of fiction.
All the characters and events portrayed in it are likewise
fictional, and any resemblance to real people or incidents is
purely coincidental.

DOG HEAVIES

Copyright © 1990 by L. J. Washburn

All rights reserved, including the right to reproduce this
book, or portions thereof, in any form.

A Tor Book
Published by Tom Doherty Associates, Inc.
49 West 24th Street
New York, N.Y. 10010

Printed in the United States of America

ISBN 0-312-93160-3

First edition: March 1990

0 9 8 7 6 5 4 3 2 1

To James, a true follower
of the cowboy way

ONE

Hallam could hear the shouting before he ever reached the office. The angry words, muffled by the thick wooden door, were so indistinct that he couldn't make them out, but there was no mistaking the tone.

Somebody in there was madder than hell.

Hallam paused just outside the door and leaned closer to it. He told himself he was just indulging an old man's curiosity, listening to the argument going on inside the office of J. Frederick Darby, the head of production here at the studio. Darby's office was at the end of a long, thickly carpeted hall, and all the other doors along the corridor were closed at the moment. It was close to lunchtime; probably most of the people in the building had already gone over to the commissary. The reception desk up front had been empty when Hallam arrived, so he had wandered back to Darby's office on his own, on the chance that the production chief would be there. Darby had asked Hallam to drop by sometime today when he called, but he hadn't specified a time.

From the sound of it, Hallam thought, this wasn't what they referred to as an *opportune* moment. He straightened as one of the voices suddenly got louder, indicating that its owner was coming toward the door in a hurry. Hallam had just stepped back out of the way when the door opened and a young man stomped out, his face red with anger.

The man barely gave Hallam a glance, just brushed past him and stalked down the hall toward the front of the studio's administration building. A few seconds later, another man appeared in the doorway of the office and called after the departing youngster, "You'd better go somewhere and cool off, Eliot. It's not going to do any of us any good for you to act like a stubborn fool!"

Without looking around, the younger man replied with a curt, obscene suggestion that made J. Frederick Darby turn pale. Darby stood there in the doorway for a moment, then seemed to notice Hallam for the first time.

It was hard to miss Lucas Hallam for very long. He was a big man, several inches over six feet, with broad shoulders and a powerful frame that age had bent only slightly. His craggy face could never be called handsome, but it had an unmistakable strength. His hair was gray and thick and usually a little unkempt, and a moustache of the same shade drooped over his wide mouth. He wore boots, a tan suit, and a broad-brimmed Panama hat shoved to the back of his head. With a grin, he said, "Mornin', Mr. Darby. Hope I didn't come at a bad time."

Darby gave an exasperated sigh and shook his head. He was half a foot shorter than Hallam and rapidly balding, with sharp, pale blue eyes behind thick glasses. Despite his unimpressive appearance and thin, high-pitched voice, he wielded more power than anyone else at this studio.

"No, Lucas, I'm glad you're here," he replied. He nodded toward the lobby at the front of the building, where the angry young man had disappeared. "That's my problem, right there. That's what I wanted to talk to you about. Come on in."

Hallam followed Darby into the office and took the seat the production chief indicated in front of his desk. Balancing his hat on his knee, Hallam waited while Darby settled down behind the desk and then sighed again.

The office was not overly large and was strictly functional, unlike some of the producers' sanctums Hallam had seen since coming to Hollywood. Darby was more interested in results than luxuries. Hallam could understand and admire that in a man, as long as it wasn't taken to extremes.

Darby leaned back in his chair, laced his fingers together on his small belly, and said, "That was Eliot Tremaine, Lucas. Have you ever heard of him?"

Hallam considered for a moment and then shook his head. "Don't reckon I have. He any kin to Pete Tremaine?"

"Eliot is Peter's son. I'm not surprised you don't know him; he's been back East with his mother for years. She got him a few parts in some of her plays when he was a boy, and he's done quite well for himself. He's had several leads on Broadway, in fact."

"What's he doin' out here in Hollywood?"

Darby closed his eyes in sheer frustration for a few seconds, then opened them again and said, "Peter Tremaine has decided that it's time for his son to have a movie career."

Hallam frowned. "Doin' what?"

Slowly, spacing out each word, Darby said, "Peter wants us to make him into a cowboy."

Hallam sat back in his chair, his frown deepening. He had no idea what his connection was with Darby's problem, but he had a feeling that he wasn't going to like it.

He had known Peter Tremaine for several years, had been a riding extra on several of Tremaine's pictures, including *Western Passage,* the epic that had put Tremaine up in the same class as Cruze and Jack Ford, directors who were given big budgets and a fairly free hand. Nobody in Hollywood carried as much clout as DeMille and, before him, Griffith, but Peter Tremaine was in the next rank. And at the moment, he was Darby's leading director. The studio counted heavily on Tremaine's efforts to keep them in the black.

So Hallam could understand why Darby had a problem. If Tremaine wanted his son to be in the movies, Darby was going to have to do everything he could to accommodate him.

Hallam mulled that over for a few seconds, then asked quietly, "Can the boy ride?"

Darby shook his head.

"How 'bout ropin', shootin' a gun, things like that?"

"He's never been further west than New Jersey," Darby replied bleakly. In a display of anger unusual for such a normally mild man, he slapped the top of his desk and went on, "Peter just doesn't know what he's asking! We can't take a boy who's never played in anything except drawing-room comedies and make him into a Western star. It just can't be done!"

Hallam wasn't so sure about that. He happened to know that Gilbert Aronson had never even been on a horse until he became Bronco Billy Anderson. For every real-life cowboy who had gone on to a career in moving pictures, like Art Acord and Yakima Canutt, there were others like Bronco Billy and Tom Mix who had had to learn the required skills—or at least learn enough to fake it for the camera. But Darby had a point. It was a hard thing to pull off, especially when the actor didn't want to learn.

"Looked and sounded to me like the boy wasn't too sold on the idea," Hallam commented. "I reckon that was what the two of y'all were wranglin' about?"

Darby nodded. "When Eliot's father wired him to come out here, the boy thought he was going to act in the same sort of material he had been doing on the stage in New York. He didn't find out until he got here that Peter wants him for his next film."

"He wants to cast the boy in *Sagebrush?*"

"That's right." Darby looked puzzled. "How did you know about *Sagebrush,* Lucas?"

Hallam had to grin. "Shoot, there ain't many Westerns

comin' up that we don't hear about down at the Waterhole. Pays to keep an ear to the ground."

That was true enough. The speakeasy where the Western stuntmen and riding extras gathered was usually rife with rumors about upcoming productions, especially large-scale features like *Sagebrush* that might employ hundreds of extras. The script was still in development, according to what Hallam had heard, but he knew it was going to be centered around the great cattle drives from Texas to Kansas in the 1870s.

He had been born a little too late to take part in the drives himself, but he had paid more than one visit to some Kansas cattle towns that were still wild and woolly. A feller who fancied himself a fast draw had even pulled a gun on him once in a saloon in Abilene. . . .

Hallam gave a little shake of his head. That was another time and place, in days long gone. The only folks slapping leather in Hollywood were doing it on movie sets.

"What do you intend to do about the young feller, Mr. Darby?" he asked.

"We're going to try to honor his father's wishes, whether Eliot wants to cooperate or not. We've already got a great deal of money sunk in *Sagebrush's* production. Peter can be a . . . demanding director. We can't afford to make him too upset."

Hallam had to grin again. He had gotten along well enough with Peter Tremaine, but he understood Darby's comment. Tremaine was plenty strong-willed, all right; a good director had to be. Tremaine sometimes pushed it up a notch further, though—not to the point where he was a dictatorial son-of-a-bitch like DeMille, but almost.

"We're going to try to teach Eliot what he needs to know," Darby went on. "I've already contacted several of our best men who are willing to train him in riding and roping and shooting, all the things you mentioned."

"Not goin' to be easy," Hallam said, "not if he ain't willin' to work hard at it. And with all the distractions a young feller can find in Hollywood, I reckon it'll be that much harder."

"That's why we're not going to keep him here in town," Darby said. "Peter won't be ready to start shooting *Sagebrush* for at least a month. That gives us some time. I'm sending Eliot to the Flying L Ranch in Texas."

Hallam shook his head and looked puzzled. "Don't reckon I've heard of it."

"It's north of Fort Worth. I've been in touch with the owner, and he's agreeable to having Eliot and several of our people stay there for a while, even though it's a working ranch, rather than what they call a dude ranch."

Hallam snorted. "I've heard of them dude ranches. Reckon that's a pretty good name for 'em."

"The man who owns the Flying L, Wayne Lindsey, has some connections in the oil industry out here. That's how I heard of his place. I think it's a perfect solution, Lucas. We send Eliot out of Hollywood, to a place where he'll be surrounded by actual cowboys. There won't be much for him to do there *except* learn what we need to teach him. What do you think?"

Hallam nodded slowly. "Sounds like it might work. I've heard tell of other studios sendin' their Western actors off to ranches to get the feel of the real thing. I still ain't sure how I come into it, though. You said you've already got some of the boys lined up to show him the ropes."

"That's right. What I need now is someone to keep young Mr. Tremaine out of trouble while he's there."

Hallam was not surprised by Darby's answer. He had begun to think that it might be something like that. Darby, along with most of the studio people in town, knew that he had a private detective's license and handled jobs along those lines when he wasn't doing picture work. Some folks called him a private eye; he didn't mind the name, but he was starting to wonder why people naturally seemed to think of him when they had a mess that needed cleaning up. Or, in this case, one they wanted him to stop before it got started.

"I'm not sure, Mr. Darby," Hallam said slowly. "Sounds like you think the boy's goin' to need some nursemaidin'—"

"That's it exactly," Darby replied, leaning forward. "I know I said there wouldn't be anything there on the ranch to occupy Eliot's mind, but you know how young men can be. And I happen to know that Eliot Tremaine has a . . . fondness, shall we say, for old whiskey and young women."

"Pretty potent combination."

"Indeed. His mother has bailed him out of more than one scrape back East, I'm told. And from what I've seen of him, I can believe it. He certainly blew up at me when I told him we were sending him to Texas. He flatly refused to go. He was angry enough that his father wants to put him in a Western; the news about the ranch was the last straw."

"I reckon that was right before I got here. He did look a mite peeved when he left."

Darby laughed, but there was no humor in the sound. "He'll come around. He has no choice. He signed a contract with us. If he doesn't cooperate, he won't be making pictures for anybody else."

"He could always go back to New York, I suppose."

The production chief shook his head. "His mother has cut him off. Evidently he caused one problem too many. Of course, he has some money of his own, but not enough to live in the manner to which he's accustomed. When Peter heard about that, he sent Eliot a telegram immediately, offering him work. You may know about Peter and his wife . . .?"

Hallam knew enough to understand the situation. Peter Tremaine and his wife Georgia had been separated for years, although Hallam didn't think there had ever been a divorce. Georgia had been an actress on the so-called legitimate stage, Tremaine a director. Tremaine had abandoned New York to come west, finding more success in Hollywood than he had ever experienced on Broadway. Georgia had stayed behind, raising their son and becoming a celebrated leading lady in her own right. From what Hallam had heard, the separation had been a bitter one, on both sides.

And now Eliot Tremaine was caught in the middle, with more problems of his own making. Hallam had a feeling that the boy was going to be trouble for anybody who tried to work with him.

"Well, what about it, Lucas?" Darby asked when Hallam hesitated. "Will you take the job? All you have to do is keep Eliot out of any jams he tries to get into until we've gotten him back here to Hollywood."

Hallam rubbed a big hand along his jawline and considered the offer. He hadn't been back to Texas in a long time. He had been born there, not far from Fort Worth, in fact. This would give him a chance to see some of his old stomping grounds.

"If it's a matter of money," Darby went on when Hallam still didn't say anything, "we're prepared to pay you a thousand dollars."

Hallam had to suppress a whistle. That was damn good wages for less than a month's work. All of his instincts told him that riding herd on a proddy young buck like Eliot Tremaine would be quite a chore, but it was hard to turn down that kind of money when he was used to making four or five dollars a day, plus a box lunch, for picture work. Even his private-detective jobs didn't pay a whole hell of a lot more than that, and he had to buy his own lunch besides.

"It's a mighty attractive offer, Mr. Darby . . ." he said.

"Then you'll do it?" Darby's eagerness was obvious in his voice.

An image suddenly appeared in Hallam's mind. A woman with red hair and features that were beautiful to him despite the lines that experience had put there. A woman who had gotten to him like no woman ever had before.

Liz . . .

A woman who was gone.

Hallam stood up and extended a big hand across the desk to J. Frederick Darby. "I'll take the job," he said.

After the last few weeks, it would be damn good to get out of Hollywood for a while.

TWO

Darby gave Hallam a check for two hundred and fifty dollars, pulling a big checkbook out of his desk and writing the draft himself rather than waiting to have a secretary do it later.

"Eliot will be leaving for Texas tomorrow," Darby said as he handed the rectangle of paper across the desk to Hallam. "We have him and the others booked on a train that will be pulling out of Union Station at noon. I took the liberty of making a reservation for you, too, Lucas."

Hallam grinned as he glanced at the check, folded it, and slid it into the pocket of his shirt. "Sounds like you were pretty sure I was goin' to take the job."

"Let's just say I was very hopeful."

Hallam wondered for a moment if Darby knew about his problems with Liz and the way she had taken off for the tall and uncut when things hadn't worked out between them. The little production chief was noted for his ability to keep up with everything that was going on in Hollywood. Hallam doubted that the problems of an old cowboy and a redheaded gal were important enough to come to Darby's attention, though.

He put that out of his mind and went on, "Do you have

anybody keepin' an eye on young Tremaine while he's still here in town?"

Darby nodded. "I had Chief Morton assign some men to Eliot. Unobtrusively, of course."

Hallam knew Seth Morton, knew that the head of the studio police was usually on top of things. "Where's the boy stayin'?" he asked.

"At his father's estate in Beverly Hills. I'm sure he'll be all right till tomorrow, Lucas. It's Texas we're worried about."

Hallam nodded. If that was the way Darby wanted it, that was fine with him. "I'll be on the train when it pulls out," he said.

"Eliot and the others will be getting together here at the studio about eleven in the morning and then going over to the station—if he cools down enough to listen to reason. Why don't you meet us here? You can leave your car in our lot while you're gone."

"Sounds fine," Hallam agreed. "I'll be here."

"Thank you, Lucas," Darby said, shaking hands with him again. "I'm sorry about giving you such short notice—"

Hallam waved a big hand. "Don't worry about that. It don't take me long to pack. All I've got to do is throw a few clothes and a Colt in my warbag."

"Yes. Indeed."

Grinning, Hallam nodded to Darby and turned to leave the office. As he pulled the door shut behind him, he heard Darby muttering. The man's job had to be a hard one, Hallam thought. Darby had to juggle all the different projects going on at the studio, not only handling technical and financial problems, but also dealing with all kinds of people. And Hallam knew from experience that people could be more trouble than anything else . . .

The next morning dawned bright and clear, promising the kind of day that usually made Hallam glad he had wound up in California after a lifetime of wandering all over the West. Today, though, he paid little attention to the weather, not even noticing the warm breeze that swayed the fronds of the palm trees lining the boulevards. As he drove toward the studio, he was thinking instead about the job he had taken and the fact that he was going back to Texas after a lot of years.

Texas held plenty of memories, both good and bad. He had seen his father die violently there, had gone on a vengeance trail that could have wound up putting him on the wrong side of the law. Instead, he had hooked up with the Rangers after a few years, and that had led to other work as a lawman, first as a deputy U.S. marshal and then as peace officer in assorted tough burgs as the last days of the old West were dying away. Eventually he had become a Pinkerton operative, and finally had drifted to Hollywood.

Damn, but the years went by fast.

Some of them were just blurry recollections of gunplay, of blood and death, cold weather and bad food, hard beds under an uncaring sky. But there had been some good times along the way, too, and some good people who had touched his life for a while.

Like Liz Fletcher . . .

Hallam grunted as he put on the brakes and slowed down to make the turn at the studio gate. He had spent a couple of hours the night before thinking about Liz when he should have been sleeping. He had almost decided to polish off half a bottle of Who-Hit-John that he had been keeping for emergencies, just in the hope that it would help him sleep, when he had finally dozed off.

This morning he had told himself sternly that there wasn't going to be any more fretting about Liz. She was a grown woman, capable of making her own decisions, and if she had chosen not to stay with him, that was her own damn business, whether he liked it or not.

From here on out, Hallam vowed, he was worrying about the future, not the past.

The guard at the studio gate consulted a list on his clipboard and then nodded. "Yes, sir, Mr. Hallam, they're expecting you. Just park anywhere over by Building Six. You can leave your car there for as long as you like."

"Thanks, son," Hallam said. "Eliot Tremaine come in yet?"

"Yes, sir. Both Mr. Tremaines are here."

Hallam nodded and eased ahead in the flivver. He had thought that Peter Tremaine might come to the studio to see his son off on the journey to Texas. Obviously, Tremaine had been able to talk some sense into the boy and convince him that the best thing to do was to go along with the studio's wishes.

As Hallam drove around several of the long, massive buildings that housed the stages where all interiors were shot, he passed a couple of tour buses, parked and empty. The pilgrims who had come here on the vehicles were probably in one of the buildings, watching raptly as crews cranked out scenes from the various productions underway at the moment. Tourists were a fact of life in this business, and Hallam had learned that it was best just to put up with them and ignore them as much as possible.

He found a parking space next to the long, featureless wall of Building 6 and left the flivver there. His warbag was the only luggage he had, and he slung it over his shoulder as he walked toward the administration building. He was wearing boots, jeans, a blue cotton shirt, and his Stetson. The Panama was back in his apartment; it had seemed more fitting to wear the Stetson, considering where he was headed. He supposed he didn't look too different from the actors who were making a couple of different Westerns here at the studio, so it came as no surprise to him when the members of the tour group that emerged from one of the buildings began to gape at him.

"Oh, dear me!" one of the women said excitedly. "I think that's William S. Hart!"

Hallam had to grin. On his best day, he had never looked as handsome and distinguished as Bill Hart, not to mention the fact that Hart didn't sport a moustache. Hallam knew from experience that it didn't do any good to argue with the paying customers, though. He just smiled and reached up to touch the brim of his hat, nodding to the woman and saying pleasantly, "Howdy, ma'am."

He strode on quickly, not wanting to give any of the tourists a chance to whip out an autograph book. They would have been disappointed if they had insisted on his signature. His scrawl wasn't easy to read, but it would have been plain enough that he wasn't anybody famous.

The studio was busy this morning, as usual. Actors in costume hurried here and there, along with technicians hauling equipment, script girls with pencils stuck in their hair, and jodhpur-clad directors. The tourist group trailed along behind Hallam, listening to the slightly bored drone of their guide, taking in all the sights with wide eyes.

Hallam looked ahead at the administration building and saw a small group of people emerging from the big double doors of the entrance. He spotted J. Frederick Darby in the lead, and beside the production chief was the burly, red-faced form of Peter Tremaine, looking more like a scrappy middle-weight boxer than a movie director. Just behind Tremaine was the young man Hallam had seen leaving Darby's office the day before. Eliot Tremaine was almost the same height as his father, but he was slender and fair-skinned, with sleek dark hair and a vaguely sullen expression on his handsome face. He wore an expensive suit that looked hot in the bright morning sunshine.

Behind Darby and the two Tremaines were half a dozen men in Western suits. Hallam grinned again as he recognized them. They were even more duded up than he was, sporting their Sunday-go-to-meetin' best for the occasion. He was more accustomed to seeing them in patched and dusty range clothes.

Red Callahan, pure hell on the back of a horse . . . Harv Macklin, who could fall off a cliff better than anybody but Yak Canutt . . . Jeff Grant, a wizard with a rope . . . Stone Riordan, one of the best trick shots in Buffalo Bill's Wild West before coming to Hollywood . . . Max Hilyard, bull-doggin' champ of many a rodeo . . . and Tall Cotton Jones, lean and leathery and one of the best all-around cowboys Hallam had ever known . . . Men who had done it all, some of the best stuntmen and riding extras and character actors in the business. Hallam had worked with all of them, and he couldn't have assembled a better bunch if he had tried.

Hallam lifted a hand in greeting and kept walking toward the group. As he stepped past an alleyway that ran between two of the buildings, a pair of men emerged and almost bumped into him. Their voices were loud and rancorous, and they were glaring at each other and not paying any attention to where they were going.

"You filthy no-good redskin!" one of the men barked at the other. "If you know what's good for you, you'll go back to that reservation you came from!" The speaker was young, with sandy hair and a broad, open face that at the moment was set in angry lines. He wore cowboy clothes and had a Colt revolver holstered on his hip. Obviously, he had just stepped off the set of one of the Western productions.

"You not tell Brave Wolf what to do!" his companion snapped. Roughly the same age, this man was lean-bodied and moved with a lithe grace. He wore fringed buckskins, and his long raven-dark hair was bound in two braids that fell to his shoulders. His red-hued skin, high cheekbones, and piercing eyes were ample evidence of his ancestry.

"I'll tell you what to do if'n I want to, ya damn Injun!" the cowboy said roughly, stopping and thrusting out his jaw belligerently as he stared at the Indian.

Hallam looked over his shoulder as he heard the angry words. He stopped and shook his head, unsure of what to do. The tourists were approaching quickly, all of them regarding the quarreling pair with fascination.

That interest turned to nervousness as the Indian suddenly reached for the big knife that was sheathed on his hip. "Still your tongue, white man," he threatened in a low but carrying voice, "or Brave Wolf will cut it out!"

The cowboy grabbed for the butt of his Colt. "I'll shoot your eyes out first, ya blamed heathen!" he howled.

One of the women in the tour group—the same one who had mistaken Hallam for William S. Hart, he noticed—screamed as the gun and the knife came out of their sheaths. Several of the men hurriedly grasped their wives and children to protect them from the potential violence. Some of the youngsters began to sob.

The cowboy's gun boomed deafeningly, belching smoke and fire, but the Indian had twisted aside, catlike. He launched an attack of his own, lunging forward and slashing at his enemy. The cowboy tried desperately to evade the thrust, throwing up his pistol to block the blow. Gun and knife came together with a clash of metal. Spitting curses, the two men began to wrestle, grappling desperately for the upper hand.

"Here now!" Darby called as the tour group broke ranks and ran for cover to escape any stray bullets. "Stop that, you men!"

The two fighters ignored him, even as Darby ran forward with Peter and Eliot Tremaine following closely behind him. The cowboy and the Indian were in what seemed to be a life-and-death struggle now, and suddenly the cowboy had the advantage as he shoved his buckskin-clad opponent away from him. He brought the barrel of his gun to bear and jerked the trigger again. The Colt blasted, and the Indian staggered back a step, lifting a hand to his chest and clutching at the bright red stain that suddenly appeared there.

"Aaaagh!" he exclaimed. "You have killed me, white man,

but I will not go to the happy hunting ground alone!" He snatched out a tomahawk that was tucked behind his belt and flung it toward the man who had just shot him.

The primitive weapon cracked into the cowboy's pistol, sending it spinning away. The Indian followed with a savage lunge, knocking him to the ground. Grasping his enemy's hair, the red man lifted his knife and said exultantly, "Now, white man, before I die, I take your scalp!"

"No!" Darby shouted as he started to rush past Hallam. On the other side of the battle, one of the female tourists gasped, eyes rolling up, as she fell to the ground in a dead faint.

Hallam muttered, "Oh, hell," and reached out with one long arm to grab the frantic production chief and jerk him to a stop. "Hold on, Mr. Darby," he said. "It ain't what it looks like."

The knife swooped down.

A second later, the Indian was standing over his victim, holding aloft a bloody patch of hair. The cowboy sprawled on the concrete of the path, arms and legs spread. His head lay in a pool of crimson. His booted feet gave a couple of feeble kicks, and then he lay still.

The mortally wounded Indian abruptly collapsed on top of him, the gory trophy slipping from limp fingers.

Some of the tourists had already turned and started running toward their buses. Now, after witnessing the scene of death and mutilation before them, the rest of the group scurried for safety, including the terrified guide. The only one left behind was the woman who had passed out.

Peter Tremaine came pounding up to Hallam and Darby. The director surveyed the carnage, then turned to Hallam and said calmly enough, "Hello, Lucas. I take it Pecos and Teddy are at it again."

"I reckon," Hallam said. He released Darby, who was quivering with rage, and strode over to the two bloody corpses. "Will you two idiots get up and start actin' like grown-ups, 'stead of a couple of little kids?"

The two dead men started to shake with laughter.

Eliot Tremaine came hurrying up and stared at the bloody forms of the cowboy and the Indian. The cowboy's scalp lay on the concrete a few feet away. Eliot frowned in puzzlement as Hallam prodded the Indian with a boot and went on, "I said get up, damn it."

The Indian rolled over onto his back and lay next to the cowboy. Both of them were whooping with laughter now, tears running down their faces. Hallam bent over, grasped their collars, and hauled them roughly to their feet. Not even that stopped their hilarity.

J. Frederick Darby regarded them with a furious stare. "I should have known it was you two!" he snapped. "How dare you pull something like this! I . . . I . . ." His voice trailed off in a sputter as he searched for words to express his anger.

Hallam looked at the two young men and shook his head. "What's the matter with you fellers? You gone plumb crazy? You spooked that lady so bad she up and swooned."

He pointed at the tourist who had fainted, who was now being attended to by the tour guide. The other members of the group, all of whom had fled, were slowly emerging from their hiding places behind the buses, and from the looks on their faces, they were beginning to realize that they had just had a practical joke played on them.

The scalped cowboy looked over his shoulder at the victims of the farce, then reached up and peeled the bloody skin cap off his head. Underneath was a thatch of sandy hair almost identical to the fake scalp. He grinned sheepishly and said, "Aw, hell, Lucas, it was just a joke. Me and Teddy got tired of them gawkers comin' in and starin' at us while we were tryin' to work. It was all in fun."

"That's right," the Indian added. "We were just trying to put on a good show for the tourists." His exaggerated "redskin" accent was gone now.

"A good show?" Darby echoed, his high-pitched voice shaking. "A good show? Don't you realize that you've left the studio wide open for a lawsuit? A good show? Why, I ought to— No, I will! You're fired, both of you! You'll never work in this town again—"

Eliot Tremaine's befuddled look had turned into a broad grin at the revelation that the violent confrontation had been nothing but a joke. Now he put a hand on Darby's shoulder, cutting off the production chief's excited tirade. "Look, Darby, it was just a joke," he said. "No need to get so upset." He glanced over at his father. "Is there, Dad?"

Tremaine shrugged his heavy shoulders. "You don't know these two clowns like the rest of us, Eliot. They've fouled up more than one day's shooting with their little pranks. But I suppose it was all in fun. Why don't you take it easy on them, Fred?"

"Not this time," Darby said coldly. "They've gone too far. I want them off the lot—"

"Fine," Eliot interrupted again. "They seem like amusing chaps. If you're determined to banish me to Texas, I want these two men to accompany us."

The victim of the mock scalping looked at Hallam and asked, "What's he talkin' about, Lucas?"

By now the other cowboys had come up and were taking in the exchange with amused expressions on their faces. Hallam inclined his head toward them and said, "Me and these ol' boys are goin' to Texas with Mr. Eliot Tremaine here. Goin' to spend some time on a real live ranch, 'stead of a movie set."

The two young men who had staged the joke glanced at each other and grinned. "Sounds like fun," the Indian said.

"How about it, Mr. Darby?" his companion in crime asked. "Can we go along with Lucas and these other fellers?"

Darby looked around at the men surrounding him and sighed in exasperation. Eliot Tremaine's face showed the first signs of interest he had displayed since the subject of the trip to Texas had come up. Peter Tremaine was keeping his features impassive, leaving the decision up to Darby. Hallam had a dubious look on his face. He knew that adding the two jokers to the group might make his job even harder. It was up to Darby, though; he and the studio were paying the freight.

Finally, Darby sighed again and said, "All right. The two of you can go—if you can be ready to leave in less than an hour. The train pulls out of Union Station at noon."

"We'll be there," the young cowboy replied. He grabbed his friend's arm. "Come on, Teddy, let's get out of these getups!"

They hurried away toward the wardrobe department, laughing about their escapade again now that it was obvious they were not going to lose their jobs over it. Hallam watched them go and had to smile a little himself. The way those tourists had scattered when the fracas broke out had been pretty funny.

Darby went over to apologize to the tour group, using his most sincere tone on the woman who had fainted. Hallam paid little attention to his peacemaking efforts, turning instead to the Tremaines and the small band of cowboys.

The men were all old friends, and they greeted Hallam warmly. "Hear you're goin' with us, Lucas," Tall Cotton Jones drawled.

"That's right," Hallam confirmed.

Eliot Tremaine stepped up to him. "Didn't I see you outside Darby's office yesterday?"

"Reckon you did." Hallam extended his hand. "I'm Lucas Hallam."

Eliot shook hands with him but still looked slightly suspicious. "I've been told that these other . . . gentlemen will be instructing me in the so-called cowboy arts. What's your speciality, Mr. Hallam?"

Hallam shrugged. "I reckon you could say it's keepin' folks out of trouble."

Eliot cocked an eyebrow. "And are you expecting trouble on this trip?"

"It has a way of poppin' up," Hallam said simply.

THREE

After the angry tourists were somewhat mollified by Darby's apology and his offer to give them passes to a premiere that night at Grauman's Egyptian Theater, the production chief herded his charges into the two limousines taking them to Union Station. Darby, the two Tremaines, and Hallam rode in the first of the big cars, while the six cowboys piled in the other one. Hallam would have enjoyed riding with his friends, but there would be plenty of time for shooting the breeze during the train trip. At the moment, he considered himself on the job, and that meant sticking close to Eliot Tremaine, even though it was unlikely any trouble would develop during the short journey from Hollywood to downtown Los Angeles.

"So, Lucas, how are you doing?" Peter Tremaine asked as he and his son settled into the rear seat and Hallam and Darby took the one facing the back. The director went on, "It's been a while since we've worked together."

"Reckon it has," Hallam agreed. "I've been keepin' busy, Pete. You know me, never did like to sit still for too long."

Tremaine nodded. "I remember. But it was always a pleasure to work with you." He took out a long cigar, stuck it in his mouth, and lit it with a gold lighter engraved with his initials.

Eliot lounged back against the soft cushion of the seat and said, "I'm still not sure I have this straight. Are you an actor, Mr. Hallam?"

Before Hallam could answer, Tremaine said, "Lucas is what we call a riding extra, Eliot. He appears on horseback whenever we need a shot of a posse or a gang of badmen or a cavalry troop. Although he made a fine dog heavy for me in one of my pictures."

Hallam grinned. "Didn't have to do much actin' in that part, Pete, just get plugged when the sheriff rode in."

"Dog heavy?" Eliot echoed. "How colorful. What the hell is a dog heavy?"

Tremaine laughed and nodded at Hallam. "I'll leave that to you to answer, Lucas, since you and your friends have played so many of them."

Hallam looked across at Eliot Tremaine and saw genuine interest in the young man's eyes. "Reckon it's pretty simple," he said. "The heavies are the villains of the picture, and when one of them writer fellers wants to let the audience know right off that a character is a bad 'un, he just has him ride into town, get down off his horse, and kick the nearest dog. Gets the audiences to booin' and hissin' soon as they see that."

Eliot chuckled. "I see. The villain kicks a dog, ergo he's a dog heavy."

Hallam wasn't sure what the hell that meant, but the boy seemed to understand, so he nodded. "Those fellers back there in the other car have done just about everything there is to do in Western pictures. They can show you the ropes better'n anybody else."

Eliot regarded him shrewdly. "You still haven't really explained your presence, though," he said.

Hallam opened his mouth to tell the young actor about his one-man private-detective agency, but before he could say anything, Darby caught his eye and gave a minuscule shake of his head. Given what he had been told about Eliot Tremaine, Hallam realized that the young man might be upset if he knew that the studio had hired a watchdog for him. Hallam shrugged and said, "Reckon I'm just goin' along for the ride. Texas is where I was born, and I haven't been there for a long time."

"I see." Eliot didn't sound convinced. "You said something earlier about trouble . . .?"

"Oh, Lucas was just joking," Darby said quickly. "You know how cowboys like to joke."

"Yes, I saw quite an example of that tendency back at the studio," Eliot commented dryly. "Do those two men pull pranks like that often?"

Darby's voice was grim as he replied, "Too often. They don't seem to realize how dependent our business is on the goodwill of the public."

Peter Tremaine spoke up. "Pecos and Teddy are just high-spirited young men, Fred."

"That didn't stop you from firing them from one of your pictures when they accidentally started a prairie fire with those flaming arrows."

Tremaine shrugged and nodded. "They cost us some precious shooting time. And time is money, Fred, you know that."

"Indeed."

"At any rate, that phony scalping was great fun," Eliot said. "Those tourists were completely taken in. I haven't seen anything so hilarious in a long time. I'm glad those two men are going with us."

"You're welcome to them," Darby replied. "If they show up in time to catch the train, that is. They're notoriously undependable."

Hallam looked out the window of the limousine. They were nearing Union Station. He pulled the turnip watch from his pocket and flipped it open. It was still twenty minutes until noon. He would have been willing to bet that Pecos and

Teddy Spotted Horse would be there in time. It wouldn't be like those two to miss an opportunity for an adventure, and that was just the way they would regard this trip to Texas.

The limousines pulled up to the entrance of the large, impressive depot, their drivers disregarding signs that said no parking was allowed in this area. Hallam and the others climbed out, and the chauffeurs began to unload bags from the trunks of the big black cars. Out of habit, Hallam's gaze darted around the street, looking for any signs of trouble. He saw none and told himself to relax. This wasn't a bodyguard job; no one had threatened Eliot Tremaine. Any disturbances of the peace were likely to come from the young man himself.

They strolled into the station, their footsteps echoing hollowly in the huge, high-ceilinged room. The air was filled with the usual babel of voices from the many people coming and going and the ever-present rumble of locomotive engines. Hallam had been in scores of train stations over the years, and they always gave him a little surge of excitement. You never knew what was going to happen when you got on a train and started for someplace far away.

Hallam talked quietly with his friends, swapping lies and spinning yarns while Darby went to the ticket windows and tended to the details of the upcoming journey. Neatly uniformed porters wheeling handcarts came and took their bags away to be loaded on the train. Hallam hung onto his warbag and noted that the other cowboys did the same. Eliot Tremaine had more than enough baggage to make up for that, however, including several obviously heavy trunks.

Hallam suppressed the urge to ask the boy what the devil he was taking to Texas. Plainly, Eliot didn't believe in traveling light. Men who had spent much of their lives on horseback were in the habit of only carrying what they had to have, Hallam supposed.

Eliot and his father ambled out onto the platform and stood talking. Max Hilyard inclined his head toward them and asked Hallam, "What do you think of that young pup, Lucas?"

"Reckon he's plenty full of himself," Hallam told the stocky, middle-aged Hilyard. "And from what I hear he's been in a heap of scrapes for somebody no older'n he is." Hallam took a deep breath. "I reckon we'll just have to wait and see. His daddy can be pretty ornery, but Pete's a good man when you come right down to it. Maybe the boy got some of that from him."

"Hope so," Tall Cotton Jones said. "Ain't been too friendly so far."

Jeff Grant, looking a little lost without a rope in his hands, said, "What's your part in this, Lucas? Why'd Darby draft you to be one of the boy's teachers?"

Hallam saw the suspicion in Jeff's eyes and knew that the others were asking themselves the same question. He had knocked around the West for a long time, but while he was at home in a saddle, he couldn't ride like Red Callahan, bust broncs like Max Hilyard and Tall Cotton Jones, handle a rope like Jeff Grant, or perform stunts like Harv Macklin. Stone Riordan was pure magic with a six-gun when it came to trick shots; Hallam was fast enough on the draw and accurate enough to have survived for a lot of hard years, but he was no hand with the fancy stuff. No, the others knew as well as he did that his real talent was staying alive.

He shrugged. "Reckon I must be part of the entertainment."

"I've heard you spin yarns, Lucas," Macklin pointed out. "We all have. You ain't that funny."

Hallam frowned. "Hell, to listen to you boys, a man'd think he wasn't welcome. I don't have to go to Texas, you know. Could just leave you on your own . . . with Pecos and Teddy Spotted Horse."

Stone Riordan slapped him on the shoulder. "Don't get your back up, Lucas. Why don't we just say that your job is to ride herd on Pecos and Teddy?" The others nodded their agreement to that proposal.

"Well, thank you most to death," Hallam said dryly. "Happen they cause some sort of ruckus—which is mighty damn likely—what should I do with 'em? Shoot 'em?"

"Now that's a thought," Tall Cotton Jones solemnly intoned.

J. Frederick Darby came bustling over to them, carrying a thick sheaf of tickets. He thrust them toward Hallam and said, "Why don't you take care of these, Lucas?" He looked around. "Where are Peter and Eliot?"

Hallam nodded toward the platform. "They already moseyed out there. We about ready to board, Mr. Darby?" As he spoke, he riffled through the tickets and saw that there were two extras, for Pecos and Teddy Spotted Horse, who had not yet arrived. Hallam didn't know whether to hope that they were too late to catch the train or not.

Darby consulted his watch. "Five minutes to noon. It's time to board, all right."

"What about Pecos and Teddy?"

"I suppose the conductor would hold the train for a few minutes if I asked him . . . but I won't ask him. I warned those two. If they're not here on time, they'll just have to find work somewhere else."

Darby sounded adamant on that point. Hallam shrugged and turned toward the platform, moving out through the big doors with the other cowboys at his side. Darby went straight to Eliot Tremaine and held out his hand. "I'm glad we were able to work out our differences, Eliot," he said. "I'm sure this will be the beginning of a long and productive relationship between you and the studio."

"We'll see," Eliot replied as he shook Darby's hand. He turned to his father. "So long, Dad."

"Goodbye, Eliot. Just remember, you're going to come back from Texas a cowboy," Tremaine said firmly.

"We'll see about that, too." Eliot casually slapped his father on the arm and then turned to stroll toward the steps leading up into the passenger car next to the platform. A conductor stood beside the steps, glancing impatiently at his pocket watch.

Hallam shook hands with Darby. "I'm counting on you, Lucas," the production chief said in a quiet voice. "We've got quite an investment in that boy."

"Not as much as I have," Peter Tremaine grunted as he shook Hallam's hand. He glanced over at the others. "If you men can turn him into a cowboy, I'll be very grateful. It may be too much, though, to ask you to turn him into a man."

"We'll see, Pete," Hallam said, echoing Eliot's earlier statements and sounding just about as convinced.

Hallam and the other cowboys moved to the steps and climbed aboard. Hallam was the last one to climb to the platform of the passenger car, and as he did, Max Hilyard said, "Looks like Pecos and Teddy didn't make it."

"Looks like it," Hallam agreed. Unaccountably, he felt a little disappointed. The two youngsters might have livened things up.

The train's whistle shrilled, and Hallam felt the slight lurch of motion under his feet as the locomotive's drivers took hold. Slowly, the train began to roll. Hallam lifted a hand to wave to Darby and Peter Tremaine.

Movement behind them caught his eye. He grinned as two figures suddenly burst out of the doors from the station's lobby and dashed toward the train. One of them howled over the hubbub, "Hold on there! Hold that train!"

It was too late for that, Hallam knew. Pecos and Teddy were going to have to run for it.

They had changed their movie costumes for Western suits like those the other cowboys were wearing. Teddy's long hair was loose underneath his Stetson. Both young men had to hold their hats on as they ran across the platform. Each of them carried a hastily packed warbag.

Harv Macklin and Jeff Grant called out encouragement to

the two youngsters as the train began to pick up speed. Hallam stayed where he was, next to the railing at the rear of the car. The conductor had picked up the portable steps and replaced them inside the car just before the train pulled out. Already the car was a good thirty feet further down the platform than it had been only moments before.

Pecos and Teddy flew past Darby and Peter Tremaine. Darby glared at their retreating backs for a moment, then waved a hand in disgust and turned away. Tremaine kept watching, a slight smile on his lips.

Eliot reappeared in the doorway of the car and asked the cowboys who were gathered at the railing, "What's going on?"

"Pecos and Teddy are tryin' to catch the train," Stone Riordan answered. "You remember, they were the ones who put on that fake fight at the studio."

"Of course." Eliot moved to the railing as well, taking advantage of the opening Hilyard and Tall Cotton Jones created by moving aside. He leaned forward eagerly, turning his head and looking back down the platform of the station.

Pecos and Teddy could have grabbed the railings on one of the cars further back and swung up there, but it was clear that they were trying to reach the one on which their friends were riding. The high-heeled boots they wore were not made for running, however, and as the train began to pick up speed, it was obvious that they were losing ground.

Hallam suddenly found himself leaning far out from the car's platform, extending a big hand as far as he could, and exhorting the two men to hurry. "I'll give you a hand!" he promised.

Pecos lunged ahead, reaching for Hallam's fingers. He was as red in the face as his Indian companion, and he was puffing for air as he ran. But somewhere he found a little extra speed and reached out to grasp Hallam's hand. Hallam felt the jerk as the train's momentum caught up with Pecos and yanked him ahead at even greater speeds. The boy's feet threatened to go out from under him.

The end of the station platform was coming up quickly. Clamping one hand onto the railing, Hallam leaned out even more and shifted the grip of his other hand onto Pecos's wrist. Pecos let out a yelp as he started to fall, but then Hallam lifted him bodily, swinging him through the air and pulling back. Both men half collapsed onto the platform of the railroad car.

Teddy drew even with the platform for an instant and leaped forward, arms extended. Harv Macklin and Max Hilyard were ready for him, each of them catching an arm and pulling him aboard.

Hallam caught his breath and his balance and straightened. He looked at Pecos and Teddy, who were slapping each other on the back and congratulating themselves for making the train. Hallam said, "I reckon you younkers know that you could've got us killed."

"Hell, Lucas, I've done lots harder stunts than that," Pecos protested laughingly.

"Not with me, you ain't."

"We're here, though," Teddy pointed out, "and nobody got hurt. Now somebody tell me again why it is we're going to Texas?"

"To have a good time, ya forgetful old redskin," Pecos said. He laughed again, and his high spirits were infectious. The other cowboys began to grin, even the normally sober-visaged Stone Riordan.

Hallam just hoped that the trip was as much fun as Pecos and Teddy seemed to think it would be.

Eliot Tremaine pumped Pecos's and Teddy's hands and said, "That was a magnificent entrance, fellows. What say we all go on into the car? I've got some excellent brandy I brought along . . ."

"Lead on, old son, lead on," Pecos told him with a grin.

Hallam started to smile as the others began to file into the car. Maybe he was taking the whole thing too seriously. Could be he was just getting old and crotchety. Spending the next few weeks with some young devils like Pecos and Teddy—and Eliot Tremaine—might be just the thing he needed to make him feel like his old self again.

It was a little early in the day, but some of that brandy Eliot was talking about might just hit the spot.

FOUR

Hallam liked riding trains. There was something about the rhythm of the rails that both comforted him and awoke a sense of anticipation within him.

The car that he and the others had boarded had sleeping compartments. Hallam checked the tickets that he was carrying and told his companions to take their pick of the four compartments reserved for them. Eliot Tremaine chose first, selecting the one closest to the front of the car—and therefore closest to the club car, which was the next in line—and Hallam quickly tossed his warbag into the compartment's upper berth, claiming it before any of the others could. He wanted to stay as close to Eliot as possible, just to make sure that the boy didn't get into any mischief. The other men paired up naturally: Stone Riordan and Tall Cotton Jones, both laconic, would bunk together so that no idle chatter would get on their nerves; Red Callahan and Harv Macklin, who performed more stunts than the others, chose another compartment; and that left Max Hilyard and Jeff Grant, who got along fine, to share the final one.

A frown on his face, Pecos stood in the narrow corridor that ran down one side of the train and asked, "Hey, where the hell're Teddy and I supposed to sleep?"

"There's seats in the club car," Hilyard told him. "Reckon they'd beat the floor."

"You expect us to sit up all the way to Texas?"

Hallam said, "Mr. Darby probably didn't have a chance to reserve a sleeper for you boys, since you got added to this little excursion at the last minute. Maybe we can talk to the conductor, see if he can scare up anything else."

"You can damn well bet we will," Pecos promised.

"Take it easy, pard," Teddy said. "Sitting up might not be so bad. We've slept in worse places."

"I guess you're right. That don't mean I have to like it, though."

Eliot Tremaine emerged from his compartment carrying a bottle he had dug out of the expensive canvas bag he had kept with him. "Here you are, gentlemen," he said, "that elixir I promised you."

Pecos grinned. "Bring on that snake medicine, Eliot," he said familiarly.

"Why don't we go up to the club car and see if we can get some glasses for it?" Eliot suggested.

The others shrugged. Passing around the bottle would have been all right with them, but if Eliot wanted glasses, well, it was his liquor, after all.

Eliot led the way, Hallam bringing up the rear as he followed the group. He could feel the slight swaying of the floor under his boots as the car clicked over the rails. Glancing out the windows alongside the corridor, he saw that they had reached the eastern suburbs of the city. Before long the train would be rolling through open countryside.

Hallam found himself looking forward to that. He had been surrounded by buildings for too long.

The group found the club car doing only a light business at this point. There would be more customers later, after the passengers had settled into their compartments. Eliot headed for the largest booth next to the windows, the rest of the cowboys following him. He still had the bottle of brandy in his hand, and before he sat down, he waved the other hand at a white-jacketed waiter and called, "Bring us some glasses, Doc."

The waiter, a middle-aged man with gray hair and a lined face, came over to them as they sat down. He nodded toward the brandy and said, "I'm sorry, sir. Liquor isn't permitted on the train. Now, if you'd like to take that back to your compartment and put it away before the conductor sees it, I won't say anything."

Eliot frowned. "No liquor? What kind of train is this, anyway?"

"One that obeys the law, sir," the waiter said softly.

Hallam saw the truculent expression beginning to form on Eliot's face. He was going to give the waiter trouble, Hallam was sure, and that wasn't right. The man was just trying to follow the rules, no matter how ill advised they were. Hallam reached across the table in the booth and put his hand on the bottle of brandy.

"I'll take it back for you, son," he said quietly. "No need to trouble yourself."

"But I wanted a drink," Eliot protested.

"Reckon all of us did, but we wouldn't want to cause problems for this gent here."

"That's right," Red Callahan added. "It ain't his fault the railroad don't allow booze."

"Oh, all right," Eliot agreed sullenly, releasing his hold on the bottle.

Hallam was seated on the outside of the booth. He stood up, holding the brandy, and said, "I'll be right back, fellers." Then he turned and headed for the rear door of the club car.

He had only gotten halfway there when the door opened and the blue-suited conductor stepped into the car. The man's sharp eyes immediately spotted the bottle in Hallam's hand and narrowed.

"Where are you going with that?" he asked suspiciously. "Don't you know that liquor is against the law? Or haven't you ever heard of Prohibition, cowboy?"

The conductor's voice was full of scorn, but Hallam kept a tight rein on his temper. He said, "I was just goin' to put it away."

"No, you don't. I'm empowered to confiscate any liquor found on the train, and that's just what I intend to do." The conductor thrust out his hand. "Give that to me, now."

Hallam still didn't care for his tone. He hefted the bottle, feeling the weight of the thick glass. It would make a satisfying thump if he walloped the conductor over the head with it. That would get them thrown off the train for sure, though, and he was supposed to be here to prevent trouble, not start it.

"Wait just a minute!" Eliot Tremaine said angrily from the booth as he stood up. "That happens to be fine old brandy you're talking about, not a bottle of homemade gin. Surely you don't expect to—"

He broke off at the stern warning look that Hallam gave him.

"Don't expect to what, sonny?" the conductor snapped. "What business is it of yours, anyway?"

Hallam shook his head again, cautioning Eliot not to claim ownership of the brandy. If anyone was going to get in dutch for bringing booze on the train, Hallam wanted it to be him.

Evidently, Eliot understood Hallam's warning. He grinned suddenly and said, "I just have an appreciation for fine liquor, friend. But rules are rules, I suppose." He slipped a hand inside his coat, reaching for his wallet. "Still, there are sometimes ways around rules . . ." He let the corner of the wallet show in his hand.

Hallam grimaced. He saw the way the conductor's features stiffened at the blatant suggestion of a bribe. Eliot might not know it, but it had been Hallam's experience that train conductors were some of the most stiff-necked people on earth.

"Put your money away, young man," this one said coldly. "This train runs by the rules and regulations of the Southern Pacific Railroad, not by the whim of some rich boy." He turned back to Hallam. "Now give me that brandy."

Reluctantly, Hallam handed the bottle over.

Tall Cotton Jones and Jeff Grant had hold of Eliot's coat and were gently pulling him back down into his seat. His cocky grin had been replaced by a look of indignation. Eliot was probably used to being able to buy his way out of any problem, Hallam thought.

"Do you have any more of this stuff?" the conductor asked him, holding up the brandy.

"Not a drop," Hallam answered honestly.

"Well, I'm not going to report you to the authorities for violating the law . . . this time. But I've got my eye on you now, cowboy, so don't try anything else while you're on my train."

"Yes, sir," Hallam said meekly. "I'll be on my best behavior."

"See that you are. While I'm here, I want to see your tickets, all of you."

Hallam pulled out the tickets and extended them to the official. "These are for my friends there, too."

The conductor looked them over, then punched holes in them and handed them back to Hallam. "Everything seems to be in order," he said. "Just keep your nose clean between here and Fort Worth."

"Yes, sir. We'll do that."

The conductor moved on, and Hallam went back to the booth. He could tell from the way his friends were looking at him that they were disappointed. As he sat down, Pecos said, "Why'd you let that prune-faced old bastard talk to you like that, Lucas? Hell, I'd've tossed him right off his own train."

Hallam grunted. "Time was, I'd've done the same thing, boy. But we got a long ride in front of us and I wanted to make sure we got there. It'd be a hell of a long walk to Texas."

"He wouldn't have dared to throw us off the train," Eliot scoffed. "Not once we told him who we are."

Hallam shook his head. "Don't reckon that would've made much never mind to a feller like that."

"Well, he still shouldn't have taken my brandy."

Hallam waited for Eliot to apologize for causing the trouble, but that sentiment didn't seem to be forthcoming. With a shrug, Hallam signaled to the waiter, who had withdrawn a few feet during the confrontation with the conductor. "How about coffee all around?" he asked.

The waiter smiled. "That I can do for you, sir."

Eliot shrugged as the white-jacketed man moved back to the counter. "That's better than nothing, I suppose." He looked across the table at Pecos and Teddy, then suddenly stuck out his hand. "We still haven't been formally intro-duced. I'm Eliot Tremaine."

Pecos shook hands with him. "Howdy, Mr. Tremaine. This here long-haired redskin beside me is Theodore Spotted Horse—"

"Call me Teddy." The Indian reached across to shake with Eliot, who took his hand after only the slightest hesitation. Hallam still noticed it, however, and he was willing to bet that the rest of the men around the table did, too, including Teddy.

"And my handle's Pecos," the young cowboy went on. "We're right glad to meet you. And thanks for standin' up for us like you did back there at the studio. Ol' Mr. Darby would've fired us for sure if you hadn't invited us along. 'Course, he'd've hired us back sooner or later, but it might've been a lean few weeks for us until then."

"What in the world made you decide to stage such an elaborate hoax?" Eliot asked.

"You mean that little fracas we put on?" Pecos laughed.

"We figured it was time the tourists saw what it was really like in the Old West, 'stead of all that play-actin' that gets put up on the screen these days."

Hallam grinned. The violent confrontation Pecos and Teddy had staged hadn't been much more realistic than the melodramatic folderol that was filmed on innumerable stages and locations around Hollywood. Most of the bloodletting between white men and red men had been done from ambush, on both sides. There had been plenty of face-to-face battles, but they had been more rare than the book writers and picture makers would have folks believe.

Eliot was enthralled, however, so Hallam kept his mouth shut. The waiter brought cups of strong, steaming coffee a few moments later, and soon the air around the table was full of laughter and lies as the cowboys talked. Eliot took it all in, fascinated despite the sophisticated airs he put on.

Might be hope for the boy yet, Hallam thought.

The afternoon passed quickly. Hallam and the others moved on to the dining car, ordering thick steaks, mounds of potatoes and other vegetables, hot rolls, and thick wedges of apple pie. The food was good for train fare, and expensive, too, but Eliot Tremaine took care of the bill. That would win him some friends, Hallam knew. Nothing made a cowboy happier than to be fed a good meal.

Adjourning to the club car, the group claimed the same large corner booth and spent the rest of the day talking about movie making and some of the experiences they had had on location. Eliot listened to the sometimes ribald, always funny stories with interest.

His attention was drawn away from his companions, though, when the door of the car opened and several newcomers entered. Hallam glanced up, noted that they were a man and a woman, along with two youngsters, and looked back at Eliot, whose gaze was suddenly fixed on one of the people passing by the booth. Hallam followed the look and saw that one of the couple's children was not a child after all, but a young woman. Slender and pretty and probably eighteen or nineteen years old, she had bobbed blond hair, and a shy smile that she directed toward Eliot.

Hallam remembered Darby's comment about Eliot's fondness for the ladies. From the intrigued expression on Eliot's face, Hallam knew that was true.

The family went on to one of the other booths, the girl shepherding her little brother ahead of her. Eliot watched the sway of her hips as she walked, and a speculative smile curved his lips. Hallam knew that he was considering the best way to approach the girl.

He would have to keep an eye on Eliot. There was nothing wrong with a little flirting, but from what Hallam had been told about Eliot, he doubted that the youngster had anything that innocent in mind. The last thing they needed was some angry papa coming after them with a shotgun.

At the moment, though, Eliot contented himself with just smiling at the girl, the smile becoming a confident grin when she returned it. Hallam brought his attention back to their booth by saying, "Ought to be in Texas in a couple of days. Then you'll really see some wild country, Eliot."

"I was under the impression that Fort Worth was fairly civilized . . . for a frontier town."

"Oh, I reckon it is. But we've got to pass through West Texas to get there. That's some mighty desolate territory, but pretty, too, in its way."

"West Texas? Is that a state, like West Virginia?"

Hallam grinned. "More like a state of mind, I'd say."

His memory went back unbidden to the times he had ridden through West Texas, to the beautiful vistas and the hellholes that were sometimes side by side. Too much of the time, there had been folks trying to kill him when he was there; the silver star in a silver circle that was the badge of the Texas Rangers usually attracted attention, mostly of the wrong kind. From what he heard, the days when the Rangers rode alone, bringing law and order with nothing but a horse and a six-gun and a Winchester, were just about over. They were getting more organized now, more like other law enforcement agencies. These days they went after bank robbers and bootleggers and other big-time criminals, rather than the kind of owlhoots Hallam had chased clear to hell and gone across the barren plains.

"I don't know why my father had to send me all the way to Texas," Eliot was complaining as Hallam's mind came back to the present. "If I have to learn all of those cowboy things, surely there are places closer to Hollywood where I could do it."

"Reckon there are," Stone Riordan said. "But I figure your pa has his reasons."

Hallam knew the reasons Peter Tremaine and Darby had selected Texas, but he said nothing. Eliot probably wouldn't like it if he heard that they wanted him as far away from the bright lights of Hollywood as possible.

Eliot shrugged and glanced at the blonde girl again. "Oh, well," he said, "I suppose a long train trip like this could have its advantages."

That was exactly what Hallam was afraid of.

It was dark when the train pulled into Yuma. Hallam had sent more than one man to the prison there during his days as a federal marshal, and he had heard plenty of stories about the place. In its time, it had been probably the most rugged penitentiary in the country, and it was still no bed of roses.

Hallam and the others got off the train to eat in the station dining room, along with the other passengers. The pork chops they were served were not as good as the steaks had been at lunch. Eliot chewed the tough meat and then said, "Hardly dinner at the Ritz, is it?"

"The fare's better'n it used to be," Hallam told him. "Time was you did good to get roast beef that could pass for shoe leather. It was even worse at the stage stations."

Eliot laughed. "Don't tell me you actually rode stage-coaches."

"Many a time, son, many a time."

"You really are a relic, aren't you, Hallam?"

Hallam glanced around the table. He *was* the oldest one here. Stone Riordan was the closest to him in age, and Stone was a good eight or ten years younger. That much of a gap could make a big difference in an era when things changed so quickly.

"Reckon I am, at that." Hallam grinned. "Don't figure I'm quite ready to be put out to pasture yet, though."

"You just let us know when you are, Lucas," Harv Macklin said. "We'll find you a nice peaceful spot in the back forty."

"Well, thanks, Harv," Hallam said dryly.

Pecos spoke up. "Eliot, you ought to get Lucas to tell you about some of the gunfights he's been in. They're hair-raisin' tales, I promise you."

Eliot looked across the long dining-room table at Hallam. "Gunfights? Really?"

Hallam grunted. "The boy don't know what he's talkin' about. I've always been a right peaceable man."

"Sure," Pecos said with a laugh. "Eliot, that old codger sittin' there just happens to be one of the fastest draws and dead-eye shootists that ever come down the pike."

Eliot glanced over at Stone Riordan. "I thought you were the gunman in the group."

"I shoot at targets," Riordan said flatly. "Lucas shot at folks who were shooting at him."

"Well, Hallam, you're just full of surprises," Eliot said. "I'd like to hear about it."

"Some other time, all right?" Hallam didn't want to talk about those days. He had never taken any pride in the men he had been forced to kill, just as he saw no honor in the bullets he himself had taken. The wounds had left him with a game leg and plenty of scars and numerous places that ached when it rained. But that was just the way things had been. No point in dwelling on it now.

For a moment, Eliot looked like he was going to press the issue, but then his attention was distracted. The blonde girl he had seen in the club car was leaving the dining room with her parents and brother, and she was passing close enough to smile at Eliot again.

"Look at that," he said in a low voice as he grinned at her. "Did you ever see such?"

"She's mighty pretty, all right," Pecos agreed.

"A real peach," Teddy added.

"I wouldn't mind getting to know her better," Eliot mused.

"I ain't sure how her daddy would feel about that," Hallam said. "It's usually a good idea not to bother young gals like that who're travelin' with their families."

"Why, Hallam, I'm just talking about a little innocent romance. What could be wrong with that? Anyway, who appointed you my keeper?"

Hallam shrugged. It wouldn't do any good to say "Your daddy and your boss, you damn fool," but that was what he was thinking.

Something else caught his eye as the girl and her family left the depot and went back toward the train. Someone else was watching her. Four men were sitting down at the other end of the long table, and one of them definitely had his eye on the girl. He was burly and redheaded, and like his companions, was dressed like a workingman. They probably had a job lined up somewhere down the tracks, Hallam thought, and had scraped up enough money for the train tickets to take them there.

Well, there was no law against looking at a pretty girl. Eliot and Pecos and Teddy had been doing the same thing.

Hallam's instincts told him to keep an eye on the big redhead, though. And he had learned over the years not to ignore such warnings too often.

FIVE

Nights on the desert could get pretty cold, as Hallam knew quite well. He had spent more than one night shivering in the dark after baking in a blistering sun all day. Eliot and the others wanted to spend the evening in the club car before turning in, so as soon as they were settled in their customary booth, Hallam paid a quick visit to his compartment and picked up his coat.

As he shrugged into it, he saw his warbag lying on the upper bunk. Hesitating, he thought about the warning that his brain had been trying to give him, then reached out for the battered old bag. He opened it and reached inside.

His fingers touched the smooth walnut butt of the Colt. He pulled the gun out and hefted it. It was an old Single Action Army revolver with a four-and-three-quarter inch barrel, the so-called Peacemaker. Hallam had been carrying the .45 for over thirty years, and it shot as true today as when it had been brand-new.

The shell belt and holster that went with it were still coiled in the warbag. Hallam knew that wearing them would attract more attention than he wanted. Hell, he wasn't even sure why he was considering carrying the gun now. But whatever the reason, he felt better once he had slid the Colt behind his belt on the left side and then draped the tail of his coat over it. He buttoned the coat, then checked the gun; if he was careful, it wouldn't show.

When Hallam got back to the club car, Pecos was in the middle of a story about a prank he and some other cowboys had pulled on a director. Hallam happened to know that the director in question had been DeMille, but he didn't say anything. No need for Eliot to know all of their secrets. Hallam slid into the booth, next to Red Callahan.

A few minutes later, the four men he had seen in the dining room back in Yuma entered the club car, taking seats several booths away. To Hallam's keen eye, all of them seemed to be weaving just a bit, and he would have been willing to bet that they had some whiskey stashed somewhere on the train. Even a by-the-book man like the flinty-eyed conductor couldn't be expected to find all the booze that people brought aboard the train.

Pecos had finished his story and Jeff Grant had started another one when the girl showed up. She opened the door of the club car and stepped somewhat tentatively inside, then went to the counter and sat down on one of the stools there. Hallam noticed her as soon as she came in, and he wasn't the only one. Most of the men in the place were watching her, including Eliot Tremaine and the big redheaded laborer.

She was alone now, and she had changed into a shorter dress that revealed more of her calves. It was cut lower in the bodice, too. She had a neat little hat perched on her wavy blond hair.

"Oho," Eliot said, grinning. "Look at the little flapper now. Quite a change from the demure young lady we saw earlier, don't you think, gentlemen?"

"Must've slipped off from her folks' compartment," Hallam muttered. He frowned. "Reckon them and her little brother have turned in already."

"And now she's out looking for a little excitement," Eliot

went on. "It's a shame I can't go over there and buy her a drink. Damn Prohibition, anyway." His voice was lazy, mocking.

"Maybe you could buy her a lemonade instead," Pecos suggested.

A grimace pulled at Hallam's mouth. He wished Pecos had kept his ideas to himself. He had seen girls like this blonde before, innocent and virginal as long as their families were around but looking for thrills when they were alone. Hallam didn't much care what the girl did, as long as Eliot Tremaine didn't get involved.

That wasn't the way it was going to be, though. Eliot was getting to his feet, that cocky grin back on his face. "Lemonade. A good idea, indeed," he said. "I'll see you fellows later. Don't wait up."

All of them smiled at the young man's confidence—except Hallam. Pecos said, "Normally I'd figure to give you a run for your money, Eliot, but I reckon you did see her first."

"That's right." Eliot gave them a jaunty little wave and turned toward the counter.

Someone else had had the same idea, Hallam saw.

The redheaded man he had seen watching the girl back in Yuma was on his feet, too, and he was heading for the counter at the same time as Eliot Tremaine. They arrived at practically the same instant, one on each side of the blonde girl.

"Hello," Eliot said smoothly. "I was wondering if I might buy you a lemonade, my dear."

At the same moment, the redhead was saying, "Hi. You by yourself, darlin'?"

The blonde glanced back and forth, her eyes shining with excitement. Hallam could see her expression in the mirror behind the counter and knew that this sort of attention was exactly what she had wanted.

The redhead leaned forward, glaring past the girl at Eliot. "Buzz off, pretty boy," he snapped. "I was talking to the gal first."

Eliot's features tightened in anger. "I beg your pardon," he said stiffly. "I believe I offered to buy the young lady a lemonade, and that's none of your business, my good man."

"I ain't your good man. Now shove off, bozo."

Hallam saw the redhead's callused hands clench into fists. He saw the way the blonde was breathing heavily. The prospect of two men fighting over her was obviously thrilling. That was about the stupidest notion Hallam could think of—there was nothing romantic about two fools beating on each other—but then he wasn't a young girl, either. And the blonde was plainly not going to do anything to stop this, despite her feeble protest of "Please, there's no need to argue . . ."

Eliot took a step back from the counter and turned slightly. The other man did the same, so that they were facing each other squarely. The girl revolved on her stool so that she would have a good view if a fight broke out. Everyone in the club car was watching the confrontation now, in fact.

"Look, why don't you just go back to your seat and stop bothering us?" Eliot asked. "The young lady and I don't need your company." His back was ramrod straight.

"Why don't you go to hell?" the redhead barked. He reached out and clamped a hand on the blonde's arm. "Come on with me, babe. We'll have some fun."

Eliot's arm shot out, and his fingers closed tightly on the man's wrist. "Let her go, goddamn you!" he ordered.

The girl let out a squeal.

The redhead's friends abruptly stood up in their booth and moved away from it, coming across the car to stand behind their companion.

"Lucas . . ." Pecos said in a low, warning voice.

"We can't let them get away with that," Teddy put in.

Hallam sighed. "Nope. I don't reckon we can."

He stood up.

The others close behind him, he ambled across the club car, not getting in any hurry. Eliot and the redhead were still glaring at each other, frozen in their angry poses. Hallam reached the counter and leaned an elbow on it, looking around until he caught the eye of the nervous counterman a few feet away. "Could use a cup of coffee," he said quietly.

"Yes, sir," the counterman replied, bobbing his head. He reached for a cup and saucer, the two pieces of crockery rattling slightly as he picked them up.

Hallam turned his attention to the redhead and his friends. He saw that the other three were watching him and the large group of men clustered around him. The odds had changed dramatically, and even in their drunken state they were starting to feel cautious.

Hallam looked the redhead in the eye and said levelly, "Nobody wants any trouble, mister. Why don't we all just back off?"

"Dammit, stay out of this, Hallam," Eliot grated. "It's none of your business."

"Yeah, old man, butt out," the redhead said. "You're liable to get hurt if you don't." He was too angry to pay much attention to the fact that he and his friends were outnumbered.

Hallam ignored the redhead for a moment and looked at Eliot. "Reckon it is our business, son," he said. "Like it or not, you're our pard. You ain't goin' to go off and get in a fight by yourself. That just ain't the way it's done."

The redhead laughed harshly. "What kind of shit is that? You sound like you've been watching too many of those sappy cowboy movies, Gramps."

Hallam's eyes narrowed. Slowly, he reached up and unbuttoned his coat, letting it fall open just enough so that the man could see the butt of the Colt peeking out. "Maybe that's exactly what I've been doin', mister," he said coldly.

For the first time, a look of alarm appeared in the redhead's eyes. He was beginning to realize that he might have gotten in over his head, Hallam knew.

At that moment, the counterman said, "H-here's your coffee, sir."

Hallam reached across his body with his left hand and picked up the steaming cup. "Thanks, son," he said quietly. His right hand moved even closer to the Colt.

"Ah, hell!" the redhead exploded. He let go of the girl's arm, then jerked his own arm out of Eliot's grip. "You ain't worth this much trouble, babe," he said scornfully as he started to turn away.

"I think you ought to apologize to the lady," Eliot said quickly.

The redhead looked past him at Hallam, still leaning negligently against the counter—or so it seemed. The man grimaced, then bit off a curt "Sorry." He and his friends stalked off, not going back to the booth they had previously occupied but leaving the car entirely instead.

Eliot turned and gave Hallam an angry look. "You didn't have to do that," he said sharply. "I could have handled that oaf. I was on the boxing team at Harvard before I was expelled."

Hallam shrugged, said nothing, sipped his coffee. The others started drifting back toward the booth, now that the potential brawl had been averted.

Eliot gave a shake of his head, then turned toward the girl again. "I believe we were discussing the possibility of me buying a lemonade for you," he began.

Before she could reply, a man's furious voice called from the rear of the car, "Julie!"

"Oh, no!" the girl squeaked.

Her father hurried forward, pushing past Hallam and Eliot and grasping her arm. He was wearing a robe over his pajamas, and he snapped, "What have I told you about sneaking out like this, young lady? Now you come with me, and I'm going to keep my eye on you for the rest of this trip!"

"Hold on there, sir—" Eliot started to say.

The girl's father swung toward him. "You stay out of this. I saw you lurking around my daughter, you . . . you lounge lizard! Why don't you stick to your own kind, instead of playing up to innocent young girls like this?"

"I assure you, sir, I had only the best intentions—"

"Ha! I'm sure. Come on, Julie."

The girl threw a look over her shoulder as her father pulled her toward the door. She lifted her eyebrows as if to ask what she could do, then pursed her lips and blew a kiss toward Eliot. The fingers of her free hand fluttered in a wave as her father tugged her out of the car.

Eliot sighed. "What a waste . . ."

"I reckon that gal's daddy's got his hands full, all right," Hallam said.

Eliot glared at him. "What happened to that business about being partners and sticking up for each other? I notice none of you said anything while that man was berating me. Why, he called me a lounge lizard, for God's sake! Me!"

"Fellers lookin' for a fight is one thing," Hallam told him solemnly. "Mad papas is another."

Eliot rolled his eyes and shook his head. "I'll never figure out you cowboys and that bizarre code of conduct you seem to have."

"Sure you will," Hallam said, slapping him on the back. "Just give it time. Now come on back and sit down."

"All right." Eliot looked down significantly at Hallam's middle. "You'd better button that coat again, though, before somebody else notices that gun you're carrying."

"Reckon you're right," Hallam said with a sheepish smile, surprised that Eliot had been observant enough to see the Colt. "That conductor would probably get his dander up about somebody totin' a hogleg on his train, too."

Later, Hallam stood on the rear platform of the sleeping car. He leaned on the rail and looked at the darkness passing by, broken only occasionally by the faraway light of a ranch house. This part of southern Arizona was sparsely settled. Hallam had ridden across it a few times on horseback, and he knew just how few and far between the settlements were out here.

The night was chilly, just as he had expected it to be. The others were in their compartments, either already asleep or getting ready to turn in for the night. Hallam had felt the need for a little fresh air before crawling into his bunk, though, so he had stepped out here.

Eliot Tremaine had not asked him where he was going. The young man had already gotten into dark blue silk pajamas, and when Hallam left, he was lying in the bottom bunk smoking a cigarette and flipping through a script. Hallam had glanced at the cover page long enough to see that it was a preliminary draft of the scenario for *Sagebrush,* the picture that Peter Tremaine would be starting in a few weeks.

Hallam had wondered briefly what part Tremaine had in mind for his son to play. Then he had put that question out of his mind, along with all the other concerns about this job.

It was time to feel the wind in his face and look up at the stars in the Western sky.

Despite the coolness, there was a warm feeling inside him as he studied the passing landscape. In the distance, he could see an occasional mesa in the moonlight. Closer to the tracks were long stretches of arid sand, broken up now and then by clumps of tall cactus with their vicious thorns.

Like most of the West, this was hard country, Hallam thought. But it was good country, too.

The door opened behind him.

Hallam glanced over his shoulder, expecting to see Pecos or one of the other cowboys. Instead, with the dim light from the corridor making him look even bulkier, the big redhead who had argued with Eliot stood there and frowned at Hallam.

"I thought I saw you out here when we were coming down the corridor, old man," the redhead said harshly. "We were looking for that pretty-boy friend of yours, but I guess we can even up the score with you first."

Hallam turned and put his back against the railing. Looking past the redhead, he could see the man's three companions waiting in the corridor, outside the door to the compartment where Eliot was probably asleep by now.

"Ain't no score needs evenin' up," Hallam said. "No harm was done to anybody."

"That's not the way I see it," the redhead snapped. "The two of you made me look like a fool in front of that girl. Somebody's got to pay for that."

"You were the one who made yourself look foolish, son," Hallam told him quietly. "No call to make things worse now."

"Shut your yap, old man. Are all you old coots so talkative?"

Hallam ignored the question and asked one of his own. "How'd you know where to find us?"

"I had to slip one of the porters a fiver to tell us which compartment you and the pretty boy have." The redhead grinned. "Pretty expensive, but it's going to be worth it."

"Let it go, mister," Hallam warned one last time.

The redhead shook his head. "No. You don't have that gun anymore, or you'd be waving it by now. No, Gramps, I'm going to take you apart, right here and now. And I'm going to enjoy it."

"Either that or talk me to damn death," Hallam grunted, his patience gone.

The redhead spat a curse and swung a knobby fist at Hallam's head.

Hallam saw it coming, but the redhead was fast. Barely getting his left arm up in time, Hallam blocked the punch and threw one of his own. His right thudded into the man's middle, jarring him back a step. Hallam's feet were planted, and he had been able to get all of his weight into the blow.

He had to give the redhead credit, though. A left came at Hallam's head. He moved nimbly aside to let it pass and

• 50 •

stepped directly into the redhead's right. Hallam grunted as it crashed into his jaw and knocked him back against the railing.

The redhead lunged forward, hands reaching for Hallam's throat.

Hallam grabbed the man's right arm, but the left got through. Long fingers closed on Hallam's throat, bearing down savagely and cutting off his air. Hallam gasped as he looped his right around, banging the fist off the redhead's left ear, once, twice. The man's grip loosened with the second punch.

Hallam tore away from him and staggered against the railing, off balance for a moment. The redhead attacked again as Hallam righted himself, peppering his chest and stomach with hard blows. Hallam used his longer reach and brought his right across, catching the redhead on the chin and snapping his head to the side.

The door burst open as the man's three cronies came hurrying to join the fight. Suddenly the platform at the rear of the car was a melee of fists and grunts and pain. Hallam blocked as many of the punches as he could, but some of them got through, rocking him. His back hit the railing again, and he abruptly realized that unless he did something to turn the tide of this battle, they were going to force him up and over the rail—and right off the train.

At the speed the train was going, that could easily prove fatal. This wasn't a grudge match any longer. Now it was life and death.

Hallam drove the toe of his boot into the groin of one of the men as hard as he could.

The man screamed and fell back, and Hallam moved forward in the opening that created, lashing out to the sides with both hands. He knocked two more of the men away and found himself facing the redhead again. The man had his fists cocked and ready, but Hallam didn't give him a chance to use them.

Hallam lowered his head and drove into the man, ignoring

the blows that rained down on his neck and back. His arms went around the redhead's waist. Bellowing with anger and effort, Hallam picked him up bodily and slammed him into the rear wall of the railroad car.

His chest was heaving as he let go of the redhead and stepped back. The man seemed to hang against the wall for a moment; then he abruptly pitched forward onto his face. Hallam whirled, his craggy face taut with rage, and faced the two men who were still on their feet.

"You want more?" he rasped, lifting his fists. "Come on, damn it!"

They were backing away from him in a hurry now. "F-forget it, mister!" one of them said as he bent to help up the man Hallam had kicked. "We just want to get out of here!"

Hallam nodded at the unconscious redhead. "Take that with you," he ordered. "And if any of you bother me or my friends again, I'll kill you." At that moment, he meant the threat, and everyone on the crowded platform knew it.

He stood there, fists still clenched, as the three men picked up the redhead and hauled him back into the corridor, half dragging him away toward the front of the train. Hallam watched them go, and he didn't turn away or relax until they had disappeared through the door on the opposite end of the car.

Then he turned toward the railing and reached out to catch it before he fell.

His heart was pounding, his muscles were aching, and his bad knee was hurting like the very devil. Through clenched teeth, he said aloud, "Reckon I'm gettin' too damned old to be waltzin' around like that."

He stayed where he was, waiting for the pain to subside, and when the door opened again he didn't even look around. If the redhead and his friends had come back, they'd have to just go ahead and toss him off the train.

"Trouble, Lucas?" Stone Riordan asked.

Hallam shook his head without looking around. "Nothin' I couldn't handle."

"I thought I heard that roar of yours a few minutes ago. Those men from the club car came back, didn't they?"

Hallam shrugged, then winced. "They were lookin' for Eliot, but I got lucky. They found me first."

"And you took on the lot of them, rather than let them get to the boy."

Hallam said nothing.

"How much are Darby and Peter Tremaine paying you to look after him?" Riordan asked. "No, wait, that's none of my business. But that is why you're along on this trip, isn't it?"

"Could be," Hallam admitted. There was no point in trying to fool Riordan. The pistolero was too sharp for that.

"Don't worry, I won't say anything. I'm sure the others won't, either. We haven't made up our minds yet about young Mister Tremaine. I think his time in Texas may prove quite interesting."

"And that's more words than I've heard you say in a dozen years," Hallam replied.

"Maybe I'm getting more talkative in my old age."

"And I'm gettin' more tired in mine," Hallam said. He pushed away from the railing and bent to pick up his hat from the platform. It had gotten knocked off in the fighting, and someone had stepped right in the middle of it in the confusion. Hallam pushed it back into shape disgustedly.

"I don't have any fine old brandy like Eliot," Stone Riordan said. "But I do have some cheap rotgut whiskey that was cooked up by a lady of dubious virtue, if you'd care for a taste."

Hallam grinned as he went back into the car with Stone Riordan. That sounded more like it.

SIX

The train left Arizona during the night and cut through the barren southern reaches of New Mexico, roughly retracing the old Butterfield stage route. Around noon the next day, it reached El Paso.

The redhead and his friends had been giving Hallam a wide berth since the fight on the platform. They left the train in El Paso. Hallam spotted them carrying their bags out of the station and disappearing into a crowd on the street, and he breathed a sigh of relief. He figured they had learned their lesson and wouldn't try to bother him or Eliot Tremaine again; but as long as they were on the train there was still a chance of trouble.

The train stopped there long enough for Hallam to take the others to a small café he remembered that was only a couple of blocks away from the depot. The chili there was fiery enough to make even old-timers gasp and turn red in the face; after Eliot took his first bite of the stuff, he grabbed desperately for the big mug of bootleg beer sitting next to his plate. Hallam stopped him and handed him one of the tamales he had been shucking.

"Try this instead," Hallam suggested. "It'll cut that pepper faster'n beer."

Eliot looked dubious, but he took a big bite of the tamale, then slowly nodded. His eyes returned to a more normal size. "What's in that stuff?" he asked a moment later, glaring at the bowl of chili.

"Just a little jalapeño," Max Hilyard told him. "Hell, it ain't a proper bowl o' red less'n it makes your eyes water."

Eliot shook his head, pushed the chili aside, and reached for more tamales.

Hallam just looked at the other cowboys and shrugged.

Later, from the window of the train Hallam watched the small Spanish settlement of Ysleta roll past on the outskirts of El Paso. To the south, he could see the majestic, blue-gray bulk of mountains, and knew that they rose in Mexico.

The train angled northeastward through Pecos, Monahans, Odessa and Midland. The country was flat and dotted with sagebrush and oil wells. This was the first time Hallam had been through the area since oil had been discovered in the Permian Basin a few years earlier, and the sight of all the derricks was a little disconcerting to him. He was used to seeing pumping stations, with the endless up-and-down motion of their dickie-bird apparatus, in southern California, but not here in the middle of cattle country, for God's sake. He couldn't do anything but shake his head in wonderment.

Signs of the burgeoning oil industry were less evident but still there as the train rolled on into the evening, through Sweetwater and Big Spring, Colorado City and Abilene, all names which held memories for Hallam. Some of those memories invaded his dreams, making him a bit restless as he slept.

By morning the train had reached Weatherford, and Fort Worth was only twenty-some-odd miles farther on.

Hallam almost wished that the train hadn't stopped for breakfast in Weatherford. Now that they were this close, he was ready to reach their destination. He could tell that the others felt the same way. As they settled down to eat in the dining room of the big sand-colored stone depot just north of downtown, Pecos asked Eliot Tremaine, "Well, what do you think of Texas so far?"

Eliot sipped at his coffee and then replied, "It's rather rural, isn't it?"

"A lot of this land's not good for anything except ranching," Hallam admitted. "The farther east you go, the better the farming is. I guess you could say the whole place is a heap different than Hollywood or New York, though."

"A whole heap, as you might say," Eliot commented dryly.

Hallam grinned. Eliot could be a pain in the rear end, but Hallam couldn't help but like him at times. The youngster had kept himself in line since the incident in the club car with the blonde; there hadn't been any more woman trouble, and Eliot had stayed away from the booze. Maybe this was going to be an easier job than he had first thought, Hallam mused.

The train moved on a little later, heading toward Fort Worth. Hallam paused in the corridor outside their compartments, looking out the window toward the north. The terrain here was rolling hills, and he knew that just ten or fifteen miles away, over the horizon, was the place he had been born. Flat Rock . . . the name was accurate enough. The big plateau that overlooked the Trinity River valley had been formed by an upthrust of rock, and a man couldn't dig more than a foot or so anywhere on it without hitting stone. There was enough grass for horses, though, so that was what Hallam's father and mother had raised. Horses, and five kids.

His parents, his brothers and sisters, all of them gone now except him. A grimace pulled at Hallam's mouth as he stared in the direction of the place that had once been his home. After his father's death, he had seen all too little of his family. First there had been the matter of avenging John Hallam's murder, and after that, word had gotten around about him in a hurry. He had always figured that his family wouldn't want anything to do with him once folks started calling him a gunslinger.

Hallam shook his head. There wasn't a damn thing anybody could do about the past except live with it.

The train reached Fort Worth in mid-morning. Hallam stepped out on the platform at the front of the car as they approached the station. He could see the tall, impressive tower that topped the Texas and Pacific terminal building. To the north stretched downtown Fort Worth. At the far end of Main Street, perched on a bluff above the Trinity, sat the massive Tarrant County Courthouse. Farther north, Hallam remembered, on the other side of the river, were the stockyards and the area that had once been known as Niles City. Closer to the railroad tracks was Hell's Half Acre, only a shadow now of what it had been a few decades earlier, when dozens of saloons and whorehouses had been packed into an area only a few blocks square.

Hallam felt a wide grin stretching his face as the train rolled to a stop, and there wasn't anything he could do to stop it, even if he had wanted to.

Eliot Tremaine appeared in the doorway behind him, along with Pecos and Teddy Spotted Horse. The three young men had become almost constant companions. Eliot seemed to have gotten over the prejudice that had shown up momentarily when he was introduced to Teddy a few days earlier. That much was encouraging, Hallam thought. One of the first signs of growing up was the ability to accept a man for what he was, not what you thought he might be.

With his hands thrust in the pockets of his expensive suit coat, Eliot regarded the town and said, "So this is the booming metropolis of Fort Worth, eh?"

"Queen City of the Prairies," Hallam replied. "At least that's what folks around here used to call it."

Fort Worth was a good-sized place, at least compared to

what it had been back in the days when Hallam was a young man. There were quite a few buildings of several stories lining Main and Houston and Throckmorton streets. As the train slowly ground to a halt, Hallam glanced toward the area a few blocks away where the Spring Palace had been built. Constructed entirely of native Texas products, it had been the fanciest thing the Southwest had ever seen back in the nineties. Of course, it had burned down almost right after it had opened. Hallam had been there that night; he recalled vividly the smoke and the flames and the screams. It had been quite a tragedy, but Fort Worth had bounced back.

Stone Riordan and Tall Cotton Jones emerged from the car, followed moments later by the other four cowboys. Hallam didn't wait for the conductor to appear and put down the portable steps, but just hopped down from the car to the station platform. The others did the same. The platform was crowded with passengers coming and going. Hallam turned to the others and said, "Why don't you fellers go on into the depot? I'll see about getting our bags unloaded."

Stone Riordan nodded and said, "All right, Lucas." He started toward the arched entrance that led into the lobby of the station.

Pecos lagged behind the others as they followed Riordan. "Need any help, Lucas?" he asked.

"No, you run along with them others," Hallam told him.

Pecos grinned. "Yes, Pa."

Hallam had to grin, too. He supposed that sometimes he did seem to be acting like everybody's father. Being old was what did that to a man, he thought.

Hallam found a porter and slipped him a dollar to see to it that all of their luggage, especially Eliot Tremaine's, was unloaded and brought into the station. Then he ambled into the lobby, looking around at the station with a mixture of recognition and surprise. Not everything was exactly as he recalled it, but it was close enough to make the differences that much more noticeable. For one thing, most of the men he saw were wearing plain business suits and hats. There wasn't a Stetson to be seen except those worn by his companions.

As he joined them, Eliot asked, "Now what do we do?"

"Someone from the ranch is supposed to meet us," Stone Riordan said. "I'm sure they'll be along any minute. Until then, I reckon we wait."

Max Hilyard went over to a newsstand in a corner of the lobby and bought a copy of that day's Fort Worth *Star-Telegram*. He split it with Red Callahan and Harv Macklin, and they sat down on benches to read and wait with the patience of men used to the lengthy delays of the movie industry. Jeff Grant, Tall Cotton, and Riordan were content to sit down and watch the world going past. Hallam looked at Eliot and Pecos and Teddy and saw that they were not going to be so easily amused, however. They had just gotten here, and already they were starting to look fiddle-footed.

"Say, Lucas, why don't we take Eliot here up to look at Hell's Half Acre?" Pecos suddenly suggested. "Might make good historical background for him."

Hallam had started to shake his head when Eliot said, "Hell's Half Acre? Another of those colorful names that sounds intriguing. A rather disreputable section of the city, I'd venture to guess."

"You'd be right," Hallam growled, glaring at Pecos. "It ain't any place you'd want to go, Eliot."

"From what I've heard, it's calmed down a lot since your time, Lucas," Pecos said.

"Not enough," Hallam said flatly.

Eliot studied him through narrowed eyes. "It seems to me that you're taking on quite a bit of responsibility, Hallam. If anyone didn't know better, they might say you're acting like you're in charge of this little expedition."

"Just don't want to see you young fellers gettin' in over

your heads." Hallam shrugged. "But I reckon if you're dead set on seein' a bunch of run-down dives, I ain't goin' to stop you."

Eliot grinned and turned to Pecos and Teddy. "Well, men, what do you say? Are you game?"

Teddy's attention had been drawn by something else. Without turning around, he said, "You boys go on if you want to. I think I'll just stay here and take in the sights."

The others followed the direction of his gaze, and Pecos let out a low whistle of admiration. "Reckon I'll stay around for a while, too," he said.

"I concur wholeheartedly," Eliot murmured.

Striding across the lobby was as pretty a girl as Hallam had seen in quite a while . . . and in Hollywood, pretty girls were all over the place. This one didn't have the movie-star beauty you found in California, though. She wore boots and pants and a man's shirt, but only a blind man wouldn't have been able to tell she was a girl. Thick reddish-gold hair fell in waves to her shoulders, and she filled out the shirt just fine despite being slim. As she drew nearer, Hallam saw that her eyes were a deep green that reminded him of the ocean.

She was coming right toward them.

The girl stopped about ten feet from them and regarded them with her hands on her hips. Her striking features were set in a solemn expression. She said, "I suppose you gents are the people from Hollywood?"

Eliot stepped forward, sweeping the soft felt hat off his carefully combed hair. "That's right, my dear," he replied before any of the others could say a word. "I'm Eliot Tremaine."

The girl didn't seem impressed. "I'm looking for a Lucas Hallam."

Hallam took his own hat off as he came forward to stand beside Eliot. "That'd be me, ma'am," he told her softly. "Are you the one the Flyin' L Ranch sent to meet us?"

She nodded and extended a hand to Hallam. "That's right. I'm Rae Lindsey."

Hallam shook her hand. He could tell from the calluses on it that Rae Lindsey did her share of work on the spread.

"Dad told me to pick you up here at the station and bring you out to the ranch," Rae went on. She still hadn't smiled, and Hallam couldn't tell from her tone of voice whether she resented being given this chore or not. She looked around at the cowboys, who had now stood up respectfully, and said, "I was told there would only be eight of you. I count ten."

Pecos and Teddy both had grins on their faces as they tugged their hats off. Pecos said, "Hope it don't put you out any, ma'am, but me and Teddy here got added to this little fandango at the last minute." He held out his hand. "They call me Pecos."

He got about as much response as Eliot Tremaine had, a cool stare. "Is that so?" was all Rae said. She turned back to Hallam. "I suppose it's all right, but Dad's going to have to talk to that producer out in Hollywood if we're going to be feeding two extra mouths."

"Shucks, ma'am, we don't eat a whole lot," Teddy said. He didn't try to shake hands with Rae, having learned from Pecos's failure.

The girl lifted an eyebrow. "I've lived around cowboys all my life, son," she said. "I *know* how they eat." She turned and spoke over her shoulder. "The pickup's parked outside."

Clearly, she expected them to follow her. Hallam glanced around, looking for the porters with their luggage. Luckily, they were just wheeling the handcarts bearing the trunks out of the baggage car and onto the platform. Hallam caught the eye of the man in the lead and waved for them to follow him.

As they walked out of the terminal building and into the parking lot that fronted it, Eliot said in a low voice, "Not particularly friendly, is she?"

Rae was walking several yards ahead of them, but Hallam

wasn't sure she was so far in front that she could not hear. He didn't say anything, but Pecos commented, "Mighty pretty, though."

"A lot prettier than that gal on the train," Teddy added.

"Indeed," Eliot agreed.

Hallam still kept his mouth shut. If the girl had really grown up around cowboys, as she had said, she was probably used to their talk. Most of them would be unfailingly polite to her face, but there were going to be things said behind her back that she was bound to overhear. She had probably learned to ignore them and not be offended by them.

There was a Ford pickup sitting in the lot. Rae stopped beside it and pulled the driver's door open. "Grab a place to sit where you can in the back," she told them. "It's going to be a little crowded with those big trunks in there, but there's nothing I can do about that."

They did make quite an entourage, Hallam supposed. Nine cowboys, a Broadway actor in a fancy suit, and a couple of handcarts loaded down with luggage and being pulled by red-jacketed porters. Fitting everything into one pickup was going to be tricky.

Eliot started toward the passenger door of the truck's cab, but Hallam, acting on an impulse, took one long stride and beat him to it. He grasped the door handle firmly and said with a grin, "Time you learned to respect your elders, son. Let an old man ride up front."

For a moment, Eliot looked like he wanted to argue the point, but then he shrugged and said, "All right." He went to the back of the pickup and began to climb awkwardly into its bed.

Hallam swung the cab door open and lifted himself inside while the other men settled down around the outer edges of the truck bed. The bags were stacked in the center. As Rae had warned, the quarters were close, with the men riding in back having to draw their legs up to make room for the bags.

Hallam felt a spring poking him through the upholstery of the seat as he settled down. He shifted slightly to avoid it, then closed the door. Rae slid behind the wheel and slammed her door. Her left foot found the starter and set the truck's engine to grinding and grumbling while her right pressed down on the clutch. Her long-fingered right hand grasped the ball at the top of the gearshift lever angling up from the floorboard.

The engine caught with a pop and a sputter. Hallam said over the noise, "Sounds like this buggy could use a little work."

"What couldn't?" Rae shot back sharply. She caught her breath and gave a little shake of her head. "I'm sorry, Mr. Hallam. I didn't mean to snap at you. I've just got a lot of things on my mind these days."

"That's all right, ma'am. I reckon I understand."

For the first time, something resembling a smile touched Rae Lindsey's lips. She inclined her head toward the truck bed behind them and said, "I've heard about you, Mr. Hallam. How did a man like you get mixed up in something like this?"

Hallam shrugged, surprised that the girl knew who he was. "Just tryin' to make a livin', like everybody else," he said.

"There must be an easier way than playing nursemaid to some spoiled Easterner and trying to teach him how to play cowboys and Indians." Her voice was crisp.

"Reckon you're right, ma'am. Seemed like a good idea at the time, though."

A genuine laugh came from her. "Isn't that the way it always is? And call me Rae."

"Yes, ma'am."

Still smiling, she put the truck in gear and backed up, turning to pull out of the parking lot onto Vickery Boulevard. A couple of blocks later, she turned north onto Main Street and followed it through downtown, looping around the courthouse and heading into the stockyard district. Hallam's window was down a couple of inches, and the smell was unmistakable.

Eliot Tremaine was getting an introduction to something that was a vital part of range life, Hallam thought, and he would do well to get used to it. He glanced back through the grimy window in the rear of the cab and saw Eliot's face wrinkled in distaste.

As the pickup continued to roll north, Hallam asked Rae Lindsey, "How'd your daddy come to set up this deal with the studio? The way I heard it, you folks have got a regular workin' ranch."

"That's right, Mr. Hallam. At least we used to. Before—" She broke off with a shake of her head. That made her hair do pretty things, but it didn't answer Hallam's question.

He settled back against the truck seat and looked out the window as the girl drove through the northern fringes of Fort Worth. Several things were nagging at him. Something was obviously bothering Rae Lindsey; she hadn't seemed particularly glad to see them, and she certainly hadn't been impressed by Eliot Tremaine. Also, this pickup, while functional enough, wasn't fancy by any stretch of the imagination. It was hardly the kind of vehicle that most people would use to pick up important visitors.

The girl had started to say something, then stopped abruptly. That didn't have to mean a damn thing, and neither did the other things Hallam had noticed.

But he was curious now, curious about just what they would find when they reached the Flying L Ranch.

SEVEN

The highway leading north out of Fort Worth was a narrow macadam strip, and the truck's suspension let Hallam feel every bump between sections of the road. He imagined the men riding in the back were experiencing even more of a jolting. Eliot Tremaine was getting a pretty rude introduction to Texas.

The girl said little else, concentrating instead on her driving. Fort Worth was left behind, and they began a steady climb into the rolling hills north of the city. This was pretty country, Hallam thought, equally useful for farming or ranching. And not an oil well in sight; the only things poking up out of the ground were oak trees and windmills, and Hallam didn't mind either of those.

Rae Lindsey worked the truck's speed up to thirty miles an hour, but that seemed to be its limit. About half an hour after leaving town, she turned left on an even smaller road, this one paved with concrete. She followed it for a couple of miles, then headed northwest, veering the pickup onto a sandy gravel road that was wider than the previous routes but even rougher.

Hallam grimaced as the truck bounced over the washboardlike surface. He could feel the jolting in his bones, and he hoped that nobody in the back got their teeth rattled out.

"We must be gettin' close," Hallam said to the girl, looking at the cattle in the fields on either side of the road. "Those some of your daddy's stock?"

"That's right." Rae nodded. "We'll be at the house in just a few minutes."

True to her word, less than five minutes later she made one last turn, this one to the left onto a dirt road that was a little smoother than the gravel one. It wound around a couple of hills, then topped a slight rise and dipped down into a small valley. There was a stream running through the valley, lined with oaks and cottonwood trees, and a hundred yards or so on the near side of the creek was another large grove of oaks. The Flying L ranch house was located there, a three-story frame structure surrounded by trees. There were barns and corrals behind it, and to one side, between the house and the stream, was a long bunkhouse with a cookshack beside it. The main house and most of the outbuildings were old, Hallam saw right away, estimating that they more than likely dated back to the 1890s. A garage had been added onto the side of the house later, and that was where the road they were on led. Rae followed the single lane past the front of the house and then swung the pickup toward the garage, bringing it to a halt next to the well-kept yard in front of the house.

"Welcome to the Flying L," she said to Hallam as she cut off the truck's engine. The abrupt silence sounded a little strange to his ears.

Hallam got out, stretching his legs. The ride from Fort Worth had taken a little less than an hour, but there had not been a great deal of room in the cab of the pickup. His bad leg stiffened up in a hurry these days.

Pecos and Teddy were the first ones out of the back of the truck, followed by Riordan, Hilyard, and the other cowboys. That left Eliot Tremaine, sitting in a corner of the truck bed and hanging onto its sides. His face was pale under the coating of dust it had received during the ride. Pecos turned to look back at him and wave. "Come on, Eliot. We're here."

"Have we really arrived?" Eliot asked in a weak voice. "Or must I be put through more torture?"

"Shucks, that wasn't such a bad ride," Jeff Grant told him with a grin. "Back in New Mexico, where I come from, we've got some *really* bad roads."

Eliot pulled himself to his feet and came shakily to the rear of the truck. He stepped down carefully, hanging on so that he wouldn't lose his balance. "These are quite bad enough, thank you," he said. "Darby and my father must have been insane!"

Hallam heard the front door of the house slam and turned to look in that direction. A man in denims, a cotton work shirt, and a battered straw Stetson with the brim tightly rolled was coming toward them. He smiled and held out his hand. "Howdy," he said. "I'm Wayne Lindsey."

"Lucas Hallam," the big man replied as he shook hands, studying Lindsey. He liked what he saw. The rancher had a ruddy, weathered face and piercing blue eyes.

"I've heard of you, Mr. Hallam. You were a Ranger a while back, weren't you?"

"A good long while," Hallam said. "I'm a mite surprised anybody around here remembers me."

"Old-timers like me haven't forgotten what Texas was like in those days, Mr. Hallam. We know how much of a debt we owe the Rangers."

"We were just doin' our jobs. And call me Lucas."

Lindsey nodded his head. "Be glad to. Now, who're these other fellers?"

Hallam performed the introductions quickly. Lindsey shook hands with Riordan, Hilyard, Grant, Macklin, Callahan, and Tall Cotton Jones, obviously glad to make the acquaintance of all of them. Then Hallam nodded to Pecos and Teddy and said, "These two youngsters'rs a couple of mavericks we had to bring with us. That's Teddy Spotted Horse, and the ugly one there goes by Pecos."

"Ugly one!" Pecos exclaimed. "Why, you old goat! I'll have you know—"

"Glad to meet you, son," Lindsey interrupted, shaking hands with Pecos and then turning to Teddy. "You, too, mister."

"We're glad to be here," Teddy told him honestly. "This looks like a real nice place you've got here, Mr. Lindsey."

"It ought to be, as hard as we've all worked on it. Isn't that right, Rae?"

The girl nodded and said nothing. Hallam noticed how quiet she had gotten again.

Lindsey turned toward Eliot, who was busy trying to brush some of the dust off his suit. He had mopped most of it off his face with his handkerchief, but the expensive linen of his coat and trousers was still covered with the stuff. Lindsey said, "You must be the boy Fred Darby told me about. We're mighty pleased to have you with us, Mr. Tremaine."

Eliot seemed not to notice Lindsey's outthrust hand for a moment; then he took it with ill grace and shook as briefly as possible. As he went back to knocking grit out of his clothes, he asked, "Is it always so dusty out here?"

"Not always," Rae answered before her father could say anything. "Sometimes it rains, and then it's muddy."

Eliot grimaced. He said, "I'd really like to freshen up. Could someone show me to my room, please, and have my bags brought inside?"

"Sure," Lindsey said. "We've got rooms for all of you. This old house has way too much space in it for just Rae and me. It'll be good to fill it up again for a while." He turned and motioned toward one of the barns.

Hallam had been taking a look around the place while the introductions were going on. He saw a couple of cars, one parked in the garage, the other beside the bunkhouse, and there were several horses in one of the corrals. Men were moving around in the corrals and the barns; they wore hats and range clothes, and Hallam figured them for some of the Flying L hands. Two of them ambled toward the house in reply to Lindsey's summons, and the rancher told them to unload the bags and carry them into the house. "Rae'll show you where to put them," he said.

The cowhands nodded, not seeming to mind the chore. Rae stayed next to the pickup to supervise the unloading, while Lindsey said, "Why don't I show you boys around the place? That'd be a good way to start things off, seems to me."

"Not me," Eliot said. "I've had enough of ranch life for the moment. I'm going inside."

Hallam wasn't sure that was a good idea. He had intended on keeping Eliot where he could be watched most of the time. But Hallam was also anxious to get a better look at the ranch headquarters himself. From the way Rae had been acting on the way up here and the things she had almost but not quite said, he had begun to get the idea that the Flying L was having problems of some sort.

"I'll show Mr. Tremaine to his room," Rae said, easing Hallam's mind somewhat. Even though she was a very attractive young woman, he knew that her no-nonsense attitude would keep Eliot from starting anything. At least Hallam hoped that would be the case. Under the circumstances, he thought he could chance leaving Eliot in her charge for a few minutes.

"Reckon the rest of us would enjoy seein' your spread, Mr. Lindsey," he told the rancher.

If the Flying L *was* having trouble, it was not readily visible around this part of the ranch. Hallam took in as many details as he could while Lindsey led the group around the house and outbuildings. The main house itself looked to have a fresh coat of whitewash on it, and it was obviously kept up well. The barns and the corrals were in good repair, the barns as clean as most and cleaner than a lot Hallam had seen. The saddles and harnesses in the tack room located in the largest barn were oiled and polished.

The horses in the corrals were equally fine, and Hallam remembered that the cattle they had passed on the way to the ranch had looked well fed. All in all, the Flying L seemed to be a spread that was doing quite well for itself.

"Well, why don't we head on back to the house?" Lindsey suggested when the impromptu tour was complete. "My boys will have all of your stuff unloaded by now, and Rae can show you where your rooms are."

The cowboys nodded. The train trip had been a long one, and Hallam supposed that all of them would like to wash up. He knew he would.

Rae Lindsey was waiting in the living room when they got back to the house. She was sitting at a big, paper-cluttered desk in one corner of the room, gnawing on a pencil stub while she studied the open ledger in front of her. She looked up as the men trooped into the room, led by her father.

Hallam glanced around the room. The furniture, dominated by a long sofa and several armchairs, was heavy and overstuffed. There were hooked rugs on the floor and paintings of Western landscapes on the walls, along with a set of longhorns. One wall was mostly taken up by a massive fireplace and mantel, and above the beams of the mantel were hung a pair of Winchesters. Another wall was covered with bookshelves that were stuffed with leather-bound volumes which looked much-read. The place reminded Hallam of plenty of other living rooms he had seen in ranch houses— solid and comfortable. It was a masculine room; if Rae had had a feminine influence on the house, it must have been in some of the other rooms.

She closed the ledger and stood up. "If you men are ready to go upstairs, I'll show you to your rooms," she said. "Dad, I've been going over the expenses. You're going to have to call that man out in Hollywood and get him to come through with some more money, since there's two extra in this bunch."

Wayne Lindsey looked slightly uncomfortable. "We can talk about that later, Rae," he said sharply. "Right now let's just get our guests settled in."

She nodded, but Hallam saw the slight tightening around her mouth. There was some friction between father and daughter, and Hallam had a pretty good idea what was causing it. Lindsey was an old-timer; hospitality came first with him. Rae, on the other hand, was a modern girl, and practicality dictated that the ranch get everything that was coming to it.

Hallam was sure that Darby wouldn't mind kicking in a little more money to cover the cost of putting up Pecos and Teddy. A smile tugged at Hallam's mouth as that thought crossed his mind. Well, under the circumstances, Darby might threaten to take the expense out of the two men's pay, and Hallam supposed that would be fair enough. The youngsters wouldn't even be here if they had been able to keep their sense of humor under control.

Rae led them upstairs to a long hall with a carpet runner down its center. Bedrooms opened off both sides of the corridor. As the group started down the hall, the first door on the left opened and Eliot Tremaine emerged. He had changed clothes and looked natty in brown corduroy pants, a cream-colored linen shirt, and a tan jacket. He smiled broadly when he saw them and said, "Well, I feel positively human again. Thank you for your assistance, my dear."

"All I did was show you your room and have one of the boys fetch some water, Mr. Tremaine," Rae replied coolly. She moved past him and spoke over her shoulder to the others. "The rooms are all pretty much alike, so you can claim whichever one you want."

Hallam stopped at the door of the room next to Eliot's. "Reckon this one will do for me," he said. The others selected their quarters quickly. There was only one room left over for Pecos and Teddy, so they were forced to double up again, but neither of them seemed to mind.

"I'll send up basins of water," Rae told the cowboys. "You can get washed up." She pulled a watch from her pocket and glanced at it. "Lunch will be in a half hour or so. You'll know when to come down. When Smitty rings the dinner bell, you can hear it all over the ranch."

Rae started down the hall toward the stairs. Eliot stopped her by asking, "Excuse me, Miss Lindsey, but where are the . . . ah . . . facilities?"

Hallam saw that the girl was trying not to grin as she said, "Why don't you step right over here, Mr. Tremaine, and I'll show you."

The landing at the top of the stairs had a window looking out toward the rear of the house, and Hallam knew what was coming. Rae drew Eliot over to the window, pushed back the curtains, and said, "You see that building right back there, Mr. Tremaine?"

Eliot nodded, clearly puzzled. "Yes."

"Well, that's them."

He stared at her, his forehead drawing down into a frown. "An outhouse?" he asked in disbelief. "You have an outhouse, in this day and age?"

"Consider yourself lucky you didn't come to visit last year, Mr. Tremaine," Rae said solemnly. "We patched the roof on it since then."

Then she turned and left Eliot staring out the window while Hallam and the others tried not to laugh. Hallam saw the look of dismay on the face of the young actor from New York and knew that Eliot was thinking about everything that had happened today—the dust, the rough ride, the lack of running water in the upper floors of the house, and now the prospect of having to use an outhouse.

Eliot Tremaine had to be wondering just what the hell he had gotten himself into, all right.

As for Hallam, though, he felt almost like he had come home. And it was a good feeling, a damn good feeling. . . .

EIGHT

Rae Lindsey was right about the dinner bell. Hallam had no trouble hearing its pealing tones. He imagined the ranch hands in the barns and corrals could hear it just as plainly as anyone in the house.

He had washed up and changed into denim pants and a plain workshirt. As he came out of his room and joined the other cowboys in the hall, he saw that they were wearing similar outfits. Pecos and Teddy had on garb that was a little gaudier, their bright shirts sporting rhinestone snaps, but that was to be expected from them.

Rae was waiting at the foot of the stairs. "Right this way, gentlemen," she said, gesturing for them to turn toward a dining room that opened to the right. A long, heavy table covered with a checked cloth took up most of the room, and it was already covered with platters of food. At the far end of the room was another door, this one leading outside. The screen door was closed, but the wooden one was open, allowing Hallam to see the bunkhouse and the cookshack. A man wearing a cook's apron was hurrying toward the house, carrying a big pan of something. As the man pulled the screen door open and stepped in, Hallam caught the scent of fresh-baked biscuits.

"Get it while it's hot," the man in the apron called as he placed the biscuits on the table. "Else I'll have to th'ow it to the hogs."

"We don't have any hogs, Smitty," Rae told him. Hallam sensed that they had had this exchange before.

"Well, I'll feed it to them cowhands then," the cook replied tartly. "Way they eat, a man'd mistake 'em for hogs sometimes."

"I heard that, you old coot," a man said, pushing in the door behind the cook. "You ain't careful, we'll send you packin', old-timer."

"Be fine with me," the man in the apron said. "I'm almighty tired o' cookin' for a bunch of ungrateful wretches who ain't got no more good taste than a horned toad!"

Another cowboy appeared in the doorway in time to hear the cook's acerbic comment. He laughed and said, "Horned toad might taste better'n some of the things you fix, Smitty."

The cook flushed. He was a middle-aged man, short and broad, with a prominent belly underneath his greasy apron. He was bald except for two tufts of white hair that stuck out around his ears, and his face seemed permanently set in a belligerent expression.

Wayne Lindsey entered the dining room from the house just as Smitty was about to say something else. "That'll be enough," the rancher spoke up quietly, putting an end to the barbs. "In case you men hadn't noticed, we've got company."

"We've noticed, all right, Mr. Lindsey," the cowboy who had come in first said. "Hard not to see a bunch of tenderfeet like that."

"Hollywood cowpokes," the other ranch hand put in. Neither man seemed fond of the idea of playing host. More of the hands were coming into the dining room now, and while the looks they gave the visitors were not outright hostile, neither were they very friendly.

The first cowboy turned and hung his dusty black Stetson on a hook just inside the door. He was a big man, topping six feet by a couple of inches and weighing in at well over two hundred pounds, Hallam estimated. Some of the weight was fat, but not much. The man's shoulders were broad, his arms long and heavy. He had a thatch of curly brown hair and a jaw that jutted out like a shelf of rock. Not a handsome man by any means, but an impressive one. Hallam wondered who he was.

Wayne Lindsey answered that question. "Sit down, Dan," he told the cowboy. "You other fellas sit down and eat." He turned to Hallam and the men from Hollywood. "Gents, this is my foreman, Dan Armstrong, and some of my other hands."

Hallam nodded to Armstrong. "Howdy. Pleased to meet you."

Armstrong just grunted as he pulled out a chair at the other end of the table and settled his bulk on it. A few of the ranch hands muttered greetings, but most followed Armstrong's example and just sat down with sullen expressions on their faces.

Hallam exchanged a glance with Stone Riordan. It looked like newcomers were none too welcome here on the Flying L, despite Lindsey's efforts to be courteous.

Rae spoke up. "Please sit down," she said to Hallam and the others. She took a seat at the end of the table, opposite her father. Eliot Tremaine, who had not seemed to notice the tension in the room, moved quickly and claimed the seat immediately to Rae's right. Hallam sat across from him, on her left. The others pulled out chairs and sat down, the ranch hands staying up at the other end of the long table, grouping around Lindsey and leaving a gap of several chairs between themselves and the visitors.

That arrangement was going to make passing the food pretty interesting, Hallam thought wryly.

The meal looked good. There were platters of steak and ham and fried chicken, bowls of corn and green beans and black-eyed peas. Two plates were heaped high with bread, and there was the pan of biscuits that Smitty had brought in as well. Pitchers of tea and a pot of coffee sat in the middle of the table. On a side table were a pair of deep-dish pies, apple from the smell of them. It was simple enough fare, but Hallam suspected it was going to be delicious.

He was right.

The Flying L hands were barely polite as they passed the platters of food down to the visitors from Hollywood. The tension in the air didn't appear to bother Pecos and Teddy. They dug in with enthusiasm, piling their plates high and all but attacking the food. Hallam and the other cowboys were a little more restrained, but not much—not after they had tasted the fixings and realized that the cook called Smitty was a master of his art. Eliot Tremaine filled his plate, but he seemed to be too busy talking to Rae to fully appreciate the meal.

The ranch hands kept their talk to themselves, pitching their voices low and occasionally shooting a glance at the newcomers. Hallam had been around enough cowboys to understand what was going on. In the rest of the world, it might be a modern, progressive era, but to these cowboys, it might as well have been forty or fifty years earlier. Like the men who had come before them, they rode for the brand; they were fiercely loyal to their home ranch and unsympathetic toward anything from outside—including what they would consider make-believe cowboys from Hollywood.

There was nothing that could be done about such an attitude, Hallam knew. He and the others would just have to go about their business. Eventually, the ranch hands would either come to accept them or not.

In the meantime, he wasn't going to let that stop him from indulging his curiosity. He lifted his voice so that it could be heard at the other end of the table and said, "Mr. Lindsey, if you don't mind my askin', how'd you happen to come to know folks in Hollywood?"

Lindsey chewed a mouthful of steak and then grinned. "Just lucky, I guess," he replied. "Naw, really, what happened is that I used to have some money in an oil field down in East Texas. One of my partners was a fella from California who helped open up the Long Beach field. Fred Darby—I expect you know him—"

Hallam nodded.

"Well, Darby was an investor in the Long Beach operation with this other fella. I ran into Darby when I was out there on the coast settlin' some details of a deal one time. We hit it off pretty well and stayed in touch."

Hallam nodded again. If he knew Darby, the shrewd little production chief had had something like this in mind as soon as he met Lindsey. Most of the other studios had connections with ranches where filming sometimes took place, in addition to the kind of training for actors that had brought Eliot to the Flying L. Such ranches were usually in California, closer to the headquarters of the picture business, but it wasn't unheard of for them to be farther away. One studio had such a place in Montana, Hallam knew, although he had never been there.

Once again, Hallam wondered briefly if the Flying L had been having some sort of problems. If that was the case, a deal with a Hollywood studio might be just what the ranch needed to keep it going. After he got to know Lindsey better, he might sound the man out about that. It was none of his business, of course, but being a private eye just naturally made a man a mite curious about things that were none of his business.

"Anyway," Lindsey was continuing, "when Fred wired me about letting some of his folks come down here for a while, I thought it was a pretty good idea. Rae agreed, so I told him to let you boys come ahead."

Eliot had been listening to the conversation, and now he turned to Rae and asked, "Does your father always consult you on business matters like that, Miss Lindsey? That's certainly an enlightened attitude."

Before his daughter could answer, Lindsey said, "Why shouldn't I ask her? It's her spread, after all."

Hallam glanced at Lindsey in surprise, then looked over at Rae. That tightness was back around her mouth again.

Eliot frowned. "You own this ranch, my dear?" he asked Rae.

"My mother left it to me," she answered shortly. "Dad knows he runs the place, though."

"I should hope so," Teddy spoke up.

Dan Armstrong, the ranch foreman, put down his fork with a rattle against his plate. "What the hell does that mean, mister?" he demanded.

Teddy shrugged. "Doesn't mean anything, I suppose. I was just a little surprised to hear that a girl actually owns a place like this."

"It's all right, Mr. Spotted Horse . . ." Rae began softly, but Armstrong cut her off.

"No, it ain't," he snapped. "Just keep your opinions to yourself, redskin."

Hallam grimaced, remembering the exchange between Pecos and Teddy that had led to the phony scalping back in Hollywood. Unlike that argument, the insulting tone in Armstrong's voice was real, even though the words sounded almost like dialogue from a title card in one of the pictures Hallam had worked on. Breath hissed between Teddy's teeth, and he put his hands flat on the table to push himself up.

Hallam reached over and closed his fingers around Teddy's arm, holding him tightly enough to keep him in his seat. "No need for that," Hallam said quietly.

"Let him go, mister," Armstrong said. "I ain't scared of some Indian." The foreman's chair scraped back. "All the Indians I've ever seen were nothing but a bunch of drunks, anyway."

"Dan!" Lindsey said, standing up as well. "Either sit down and eat or get out of here. We're not going to have a fight at the dinner table."

Smitty the cook sniffed contemptuously from his seat. "Wouldn't be the first time," he put in. "Folks don't 'preciate good food when they see it. Spend their time fussin' when they ought to be eatin'."

A few of the ranch hands grinned at Smitty's comment, and so did Max Hilyard and Red Callahan. Tall Cotton Jones said to Teddy, "Anybody who goes to thrashin' around and knocks over my food's goin' to regret it."

Teddy grunted, then suddenly smiled sheepishly. "Reckon you're right." He turned to Rae. "I'm mighty sorry if I offended you, ma'am. I didn't mean to."

"That's all right," she said, returning his smile even though her eyes were still worried. "No harm done. Let's all go back to eating, shall we? Dan?"

Armstrong nodded and sank back into his seat, not saying anything else. But Hallam saw the look Armstrong sent toward Teddy, saw the resentment and anger there.

Armstrong seemed more opposed than the other hands to the presence of the Hollywood people on the ranch, and it looked as though he had picked Teddy as the target of that opposition. The youngster's red skin made him even more of an outsider, although Hallam and his friends regarded Teddy simply as one of their own. Hallam decided he was going to have to take pains to keep Teddy and Armstrong apart as much as possible, in addition to keeping an eye on Eliot Tremaine.

The rest of the meal was peaceful enough. When they were through, the ranch hands went back outside to return to their work. Eliot was still talking to Rae Lindsey, and while it seemed to Hallam that the young man had not been able to draw her out as much as he would have liked, Rae was warming up a little to the attention.

She put her napkin next to her empty plate and said, "Well, Mr. Tremaine, I suppose the first thing you'll want to do now is head out to the corrals and pick out a horse for yourself."

Eliot didn't look like that was the first thing he had in mind, but he shrugged. "All right, I guess we can do that."

"I'll give you a hand, Eliot," Red Callahan said. "Reckon I'm the best judge of horseflesh around here."

"Some folks might argue that," Tall Cotton Jones drawled.

"We'll all go," Stone Riordan said. He pushed back his chair. "Come on."

The group stood, Rae taking the lead and heading for the screen door that led outside. Hallam lagged behind a bit, pausing as he saw that the cook was starting to clean off the few remains of the meal.

"Mighty good cookin'," Hallam said to the man. It never hurt to get on the right side of the man in charge of chow, he had found over the years.

"Thanks." The cook wiped a hand on his apron and then extended it toward Hallam. "Name's Smitty Wardell."

Hallam returned the grip and found that Smitty's hand was as strong and callused as any cowboy's, which came as no surprise. Cooks worked about as hard as anybody else on a spread like this. "I'm Lucas Hallam. Pleased to meet you, Mr. Wardell."

"Smitty. Call me Mr. Wardell and I ain't likely to answer."

Hallam grinned. "Sure, Smitty."

The cook jerked a blunt thumb toward the door. "Ain't you goin' to watch the tenderfoot try to pick out a hoss? Should be right funny, if he don't break his neck."

"I'll head on out there in a minute. I just wanted to make the acquaintance of a man who can cook pies like those we had just now."

Smitty's pleasantly ugly face beamed. "I noticed you takin' seconds, Lucas. Does a man's heart good to have folks 'preciate his work, not like them heathen cowboys."

Hallam slapped him on the shoulder. "You keep puttin' on

feeds like this one, Smitty, and I know one feller who's not goin' to want to go back to Hollywood." He waved and then ambled on out, turning toward the corrals.

The sound of laughter told him which way to go. He found the group gathered around the rail fence of a corral on the other side of one of the barns. There were several horses inside the enclosure, along with Eliot Tremaine, Wayne Lindsey, Rae, and Red Callahan. Pecos and Teddy were perched on the top rail of the fence, their boot heels hooked over the next board, while the others leaned on the fence and watched. All of the observers had grins on their faces.

Eliot was staring dubiously at a roan mare that stood a few feet away from him. Lindsey had hold of the mare's halter, while Rae was stroking its nose and talking gently to it. Callahan patted the animal's flank and said to Eliot, "See, this horse appears to be just about the gentlest soul you'll ever find. She's not going to give you any trouble, Eliot."

"I don't know," Eliot said skeptically. "She gave me a mean look when you put the saddle on her."

From the looks of the mare, Hallam didn't figure there was a mean bone in her body. A three-year-old could probably ride her, he thought. But Eliot was definitely leery of the animal.

"I thought you said you'd ridden horses before," Callahan said.

Eliot nodded. "Yes, I certainly have. I've ridden in Central Park several times. But those were trained mounts that were accustomed to riders. How do I know this horse won't try to throw me off?"

"Trust me, Mr. Tremaine," Lindsey said. "This old mare's not the least bit interested in buckin' you or anybody else off."

Eliot still held back. Rae gave a disgusted sigh and said, "Here. Let me show him." She took the reins from her father and swung up lithely into the saddle. The mare stood there stoically, not budging until Rae heeled it into motion. Then it walked around the corral, not plodding but not showing any signs of fight, either. Rae looked at Eliot and said, "You see? She's harmless, even for somebody like you."

Eliot's face stiffened. "You think I'm a . . . a tenderfoot, is that it? That I'm scared? All right, let me up there."

Pecos chuckled from his spot on top of the fence. "Didn't figure Eliot would want a girl showin' him up," he said, not worrying about keeping his voice low enough so that Eliot couldn't hear the comment.

Hallam noticed that several of the ranch hands had drifted up to the fence on the other side of the corral and were watching with interest to see how the actor would do once he finally got onto the horse. Rae dismounted, then held the reins out to Eliot. He took them in his left hand. Rae said, "All right, hang onto the reins like that, and use that same hand to grab the saddle horn here. Put your right hand on the pommel of the saddle . . . there. Left foot in the stirrup—"

"I know how to get onto a horse," Eliot interrupted.

She cocked an eyebrow and stepped back, waving for him to proceed without saying anything else.

Eliot put his foot in the stirrup, then took a deep breath. He stepped up, swinging his right leg over the back of the mare and settling down into the saddle. The mare didn't make a move as Eliot got his other foot into the right stirrup and then lifted the reins. He bumped the horse with his heels, rocking back slightly as the mare started forward.

After a few minutes of walking the horse around the corral, Eliot visibly relaxed. There was even a slight smile on his face as he rode past the fence where Hallam and the others were watching. He turned the horse, heeled her into a faster pace. By the time he had made another circuit of the corral, the mare was moving in an easy canter.

Hallam wanted to sigh in relief. Now that Eliot had overcome his initial nervousness, it was obvious that he had at least ridden a little bit in the past. That was a starting point for the lessons he would have to learn during his time here on the ranch.

Eliot was riding past the opposite side of the corral when a long arm suddenly reached through one of the broad gaps in the fence. A big hand—Hallam saw that it belonged to Dan Armstrong, which came as no surprise—slapped the rump of the mare with a resounding crack. The horse suddenly leaped forward, as any horse would under the circumstances, no matter how gentle its nature.

With a startled yell, Eliot grabbed desperately for the reins, which had been abruptly jerked out of his hand. He was too late, and before he could stop himself he was sliding out of the saddle. Hallam grimaced, knowing that Eliot should have reached for the saddle horn first. Now the damage was already done, and Eliot landed hard on his butt in the dust of the corral.

Howls of laughter went up from the ranch hands, led by their foreman.

Pecos and Teddy pushed off the top of the fence, their boots hitting the ground almost before Eliot's rear end. Pecos ran over to Eliot, who was sitting and shaking his head, while Teddy headed for the fence on the other side of the corral. The Indian's face was set in angry lines as he stopped and said, "That was a damned lousy thing to do, Armstrong!" His sharp voice cut through the laughter from the Flying L hands.

Under his breath, Hallam muttered, "Damn it!" He started climbing the corral fence, wincing as his bad leg twinged from the effort.

Armstrong wasn't laughing now. He glared through the fence at Teddy, his hands tightly grasping one of the planks of the corral. "You talkin' to me, Indian?" he snapped.

"You know damn well I'm talking to you."

Hallam swung over the top of the fence and dropped to the ground on the other side. Out of the corner of his eye, he saw

• 83 •

Riordan and the others start to move around the corral toward the opposite side. Hallam strode over to Eliot, who was still sitting. Pecos, Lindsey, and Rae knelt beside him.

"You all right, Eliot?" Hallam asked as he paused.

Eliot was pale, but he nodded. "I don't think I've broken anything, although my, ah, rear end is quite painful at the moment."

"That'll go away," Pecos assured him. "Every cowboy busts his butt ever' now and then. Pardon my French, ma'am."

Rae smiled slightly. "That's all right, cowboy. I've busted my butt from time to time, too."

Hallam moved on as Pecos and Lindsey started to lift Eliot to his feet. Teddy and Armstrong were still glaring at each other, and as Hallam approached, the burly foreman started to climb the fence.

Armstrong was agile for a man of his size and bulk. He swung over the top of the fence and dropped into the corral, landing lightly. His hands knotted into fists as he faced Teddy. "I'm already mighty tired of you, mister," he growled. "I was just havin' a little fun with your fancy actor friend."

"You could have hurt him," Teddy accused. "You knew that horse might throw him."

Armstrong sneered. "Hell, if he can't stay on the back of a plug like that, he ought to go back to Hollywood where he belongs. Anyway, how come he's got to have a stinkin' Indian stand up for him? Can't he fight his own battles?"

Eliot started to push forward, even as he rubbed at his sore backside, but Hallam half turned and blocked his way. "Stay out of it, Eliot," he warned. "You don't really know what this is about."

"But that lout made me fall off the horse!" Eliot protested. "Not only that, but he's being quite rude and insulting to Teddy as well as me."

"Don't worry about it, Eliot," Teddy said without taking his eyes off Armstrong. "It's me this gent wants now."

Eliot took a deep breath and looked at Hallam. "You said

we were all partners, didn't you? I'm a part of this fight, too, damn it."

Slowly, Hallam nodded. He was a little surprised by Eliot's combative attitude. Maybe some of what they had been telling him in the days since leaving Hollywood had started to soak in.

"There's not goin' to be any fight," Wayne Lindsey said sharply, moving in between Teddy and Armstrong. "I told you, Dan, these folks are our guests, and they're goin' to be treated right. You understand that?"

Armstrong glanced over at Rae. "What do you say about that, Miss Lindsey?" he asked.

She sighed wearily. "You were wrong to do what you did, Dan. Now let it go before things just get worse."

For a long moment, Armstrong did not reply. He stood there, fists still clenched, muscles poised. Hallam glanced around the corral, saw that the other ranch hands and the visitors were standing in two knots about ten feet apart, both groups ready to plunge into the fracas as soon as somebody threw the first punch. Here inside the corral, Teddy and Armstrong were still facing each other, although Lindsey was between them. Rae stood off to one side, while Hallam, Eliot, and Pecos were close behind Teddy. This had all the makings of a first-class brawl, and what happened next depended on the temper of Dan Armstrong.

A shotgun blast made everybody jump.

Hallam wheeled around, instinct making him reach for a Colt that wasn't there. Smitty Wardell stood about twenty feet from the corral, the old double-barreled greener in his hands angled toward the blue sky. The cook shook his head and said disgustedly, "If this ain't the proddiest bunch I ever did see! Dan, you ain't got no business fightin' with these folks, and you know it. Shoot, havin' them here's goin' to help all of us. Now just go on about your business!"

Smitty was mighty bossy for a cook, Hallam thought, but that was nothing unusual. The foreman might be the boss out on the range, but a ranch cook generally called the shots around headquarters. For a moment, Armstrong still looked like he wanted to fight, but then he abruptly unclenched a fist and waved the hand. "Hell, it ain't worth it to get that old banty rooster mad at me," he said. He pointed a finger at Teddy. "You just stay out of my way, mister," he warned.

"And you stay out of mine," Teddy shot back.

Armstrong snorted, then turned away and climbed back over the fence. He and the ranch hands went toward the bunkhouse, casting a few surly glances back over their shoulders.

Eliot brushed the rest of the dust off his pants. "They certainly aren't the friendliest group I've ever encountered," he said.

"I'm sorry, Mr. Tremaine," Rae said. "They're just not used to strangers."

"That's no excuse for actin' like that," her father added. "I'm goin' to have me a long talk with Armstrong and try to set things right."

Hallam didn't say anything, but he thought it was too late for that. They had gotten off on the wrong foot here at the Flying L. Now all he could do was try to head off any more trouble.

With a bunch of hotheaded cowboys on both sides of the conflict, though, that wasn't going to be easy.

NINE

The rest of the afternoon was spent working around the corrals, picking out horses for the other men and coming up with saddles and gear for everyone. Hallam had to give Eliot Tremaine credit; the actor got back on the mare and by mid-afternoon was trotting the horse around the corral again. Eliot winced occasionally as his sore rump bounced off the saddle, but he didn't complain.

Late in the afternoon, Lindsey and Rae led the whole group on horseback on a short tour of the area around the ranch headquarters. The Flying L itself covered over two hundred acres, but the riders didn't venture more than a few hundred yards from the ranch house. Still, that was far enough to reach a knoll north of the house that gave a commanding view of most of the ranch.

Probably three-quarters of the spread consisted of the rolling pastureland that made such good grazing for the cattle, Hallam estimated, but the northwest corner of the ranch appeared to be rougher terrain. From the top of the knoll, Hallam could see several gullies cutting through the hills. The slopes were rockier, too, and the vegetation more sparse. There were probably some cattle up there, but they would be harder to round up and it would take more acreage per head to support them, Hallam knew.

Still, the Flying L was a good spread, he thought. Sitting up here like this on horseback reminded him of other times he had reined in to study the country around him. This time, though, he wasn't tracking down owlhoots or checking his back trail for signs of pursuit. The only signs of civilization visible from up here were the narrow concrete ribbon of a road several miles away and the poles that carried telephone wires to the neighboring ranches. But still, Hallam knew, this land was civilized now, no matter how much it looked like it had fifty years earlier. The Comanches who had once roamed here were long gone, and all the outlaws had moved to the big city and now wore suits and drove roadsters and blasted away at each other with tommy guns.

Progress, Hallam thought dryly, was a wonderful thing.

Supper was just as good as lunch had been. Smitty Wardell must have spent the whole afternoon in the cookshack, Hallam decided. Once again the ranch hands sat at one end of the table, the visitors at the other. The gap between the two groups was narrower this time, however, because several hands who had been out on the range during the earlier meal had come in for the day. But everyone ate quietly, and except for a few hard looks from Armstrong and a couple of the other cowboys, there was no continuation of the trouble.

After the meal was finished and the hands had returned to the bunkhouse, Eliot Tremaine strolled into the living room with the others and languidly lit a cigarette. "What does a person do for entertainment in the evenings around here?" he asked.

"I saw a couple of sets of dominoes over there on the desk," Max Hilyard said. "How 'bout we get up a couple games of Forty-two?"

"Rather play Moon, if it's up to me," Tall Cotton Jones replied. "Never have cared much for straight Forty-two."

Eliot looked at them and frowned, obviously not having any idea what they were talking about. "What about cards?" he said. "I thought you cowboys were supposed to be demon poker players."

Jeff Grant went over to the desk and picked up one of the boxes of dominoes. "Poker's serious business," he said. "Dominoes aren't quite as cutthroat."

"You ain't seen some of the games I have," Hilyard laughed.

Eliot shook his head. "I believe I'll take a walk instead. After eating so much, I seem to feel the need of a spot of exercise."

"Reckon I could use a spot myself," Hallam agreed. He headed for the front door along with Eliot while the others began setting up their domino games.

Hallam was a little surprised that Eliot hadn't had some comment to make about him tagging along on this walk. Eliot smoked quietly, however, as they strolled around the corner of the house. Night had settled down over the ranch, and the stars were shining brightly in the black sky overhead.

Eliot glanced up at them and muttered, "I never knew the stars could be so brilliant."

"That's because you've never seen them except when you were in a town somewhere," Hallam told him. "Electric light washes 'em out faster'n anything. Moon'll be up in a little bit. You'll figure it's near bright as day out here when it comes up."

"Perhaps." Eliot took one last drag on the cigarette, then dropped the butt and ground it out. He said bluntly, "Listen, Hallam, I know why you're here."

Hallam stopped. "Told you back in Hollywood, I'm just along for the ride."

"Bullshit," Eliot replied. "My father and that Darby fellow hired you to come along and keep me out of trouble, didn't they? They don't trust me to keep my nose clean."

Hallam shrugged. He didn't feel much like lying to Eliot

anymore. "Reckon maybe you gave 'em cause to worry in the past?" he asked.

Eliot laughed humorlessly. "They don't understand. My mother never understood. If you can't have any fun in life, what's the damned point of living?"

"Some folks think their work means something," Hallam pointed out. "Doin' a good job's important to them."

"I take my work seriously," Eliot said, anger tinging his voice in the darkness. "I try to be the best actor I can be. That's why it's so blasted frustrating to be told that I'm going to have to play some sort of . . . *cowboy.*"

Hallam shrugged again. "Cowboys got their stories, too. Folks who go to the picture shows seem to like 'em."

"But what about art?" Eliot protested.

Hallam had to grin. "Only Art I know is named Acord, and he's a ring-tailed wonder."

Eliot shook his head. "Never mind," he said. "I didn't really expect you to understand, Hallam. I just wanted to tell you to stay out of my way. I don't appreciate the way you leap in every time it looks like there's going to be trouble. I can handle myself all right, you know."

"I've been paid to do a job," Hallam told him flatly. "I intend to do it."

Eliot raised a hand and poked a finger into Hallam's chest. "And I'm telling you to leave me alone—"

Hallam's hand closed over Eliot's wrist. "Don't do that," he said softly.

"Or what?" Eliot asked, his voice tense. "You'll pull out some hogleg and pistol-whip me? You can't do that, Hallam, and you know it. You're supposed to take care of me, remember?"

Hallam bit back a curse. Eliot had shown signs of shaping up, but this conversation proved he had a long way to go. On the other hand, the boy had to resent having his daddy and his boss sic a watchdog on him. That was only natural, and Hallam knew he wouldn't like it if the situation was reversed.

It wasn't, though, and until it was, Hallam intended to do his job, just like he had told Eliot.

He let go of Eliot's wrist and said, "Maybe we'd both better cool off a little. We're here; reckon we should just try to make the best of it."

"I suppose," Eliot agreed grudgingly. He looked around as a screen door shut somewhere nearby. The light from the stars was bright enough to reveal Rae Lindsey walking out of the house. She was heading for one of the barns, and Hallam recalled hearing her say something earlier about mending some harness in the tack room.

Eliot evidently remembered, too. He looked back at Hallam and grinned. "Do you think I'll be in any danger if I go talk to Miss Lindsey?" he asked sarcastically.

"Reckon not. But you behave yourself. That gal may wear pants and work like any other hand around here, but she's a lady."

"Of course. I just want to . . . get a better feel for the place, shall we say? I'm sure she can tell me a great deal about ranch life."

"I reckon," Hallam agreed. He squinted into the shadows as Eliot turned and hurried after Rae. He wondered if it would do any good to clout the youngster on the head a few times, maybe knock some sense into his noggin. Probably not, he thought gloomily.

"Feisty young pup, ain't he?" a new voice said from the darkness.

Hallam turned quickly to see Smitty Wardell emerging from the deeper shadows next to the house, the cook's apron a white blur in the darkness. Hallam shook his head. He should have heard Smitty approaching. Getting taken by surprise like that would have probably gotten him killed in the old days.

"He is that," Hallam agreed. "I must be gettin' old, lettin' you sneak up on us like that."

"Shoot, you was just busy tryin' to talk some sense into that boy. That's why you didn't hear me." Smitty grinned. "And I *am* a sly ol' codger, at that."

"I'll just bet you are," Hallam chuckled.

Smitty lifted his apron, flour from the day's baking sifting down from it, and stuck his hands in the pockets of his jeans. He cocked his head and asked, "You reckon Miss Rae will be safe with that feller?"

"I imagine. Eliot talks a lot, but I figure he's never run up against a gal like that who can think for herself. You know her better'n I do, Smitty. Is she the kind who'd let herself be taken in by a smooth talker?"

Smitty snorted. "Not damn likely. She's a hardheaded one, all right. She's had to be, here lately, to keep this place goin'."

That was one too many references to trouble for Hallam. He asked the question straight out. "Havin' problems, are you?"

The cook's beefy shoulders rose and fell in a shrug. "Most of the ranches around here are, these days. All the spreads've been losin' stock."

Hallam frowned. "Rustlin'? In this day and age?"

"Reckon there's always money to be made in stealin'," Smitty said. "You seem mighty interested in the matter, Hallam."

"I've run into my share of rustlers," Hallam told him, "but it's been a long time ago. Now I'm just an old cowboy who makes movin' pictures."

"Old cowboy, my foot. The name Lucas Hallam rung a bell, so I been rackin' my brain tryin' to recollect what I know about you, mister. It all come back to me a while ago. You packed a mighty big reputation as a fast gun."

"Like I said, that was a long time ago," Hallam insisted.

"Gunslinger, Ranger, marshal . . . I kind of lost track of you after that. How the hell'd you wind up out there in Hollywood?"

"Everybody's got to be somewhere," Hallam said, chuckling again. He was relieved that Smitty hadn't heard about his days as a Pinkerton, or about his current detective work. He had a feeling the cook was a talker, and Hallam wanted to keep his real job as quiet as possible. Of course, Eliot had already guessed why he was really along on this trip, and Pecos and Teddy and the others no doubt knew, too. But there was no point in everybody else on the ranch finding out. Hallam suddenly wondered just how much of the conversation between him and Eliot had been overheard by Smitty.

"I reckon that's true enough," Smitty mused. "Anyway, I'm sure you did track down a few rustlers in your time, Hallam. Things are different now, though."

Hallam thought about the criminals he had encountered in the last few years. The methods might change, but that was all. Underneath, an outlaw was still an outlaw.

"Maybe you're right," he said to Smitty, not wanting to argue with the cook.

"I know I'm right," Smitty insisted. "Used to be, a wide-looper didn't need nothin' except a good hoss and a runnin' iron. Now they got trucks and air-eo-planes and all kinds of newfangled gadgets. I wouldn't want to be a lawman today, let me tell you."

"The local authorities haven't been able to find out who's doin' the rustlin' around here?"

"I reckon Mart Bascomb tries. He's the sheriff in this county. Them blamed rustlers just move too fast for him, though. He ain't been able to scare up hide nor hair of 'em."

Hallam nodded thoughtfully. "It seemed to me like something was botherin' Miss Lindsey. How much stock has the Flyin' L lost?"

"'Bout like ever'body else in these parts. Few dozen head here, few dozen head there. Probably don't add up to more'n a couple hundred. That's enough to be mighty annoyin', though. The bad part is, it looks like it's goin' to keep on until every spread around here is bled dry."

"I reckon us comin' here is goin' to help out then, financially, I mean."

"Sure," Smitty nodded. "Mr. Lindsey and Miss Rae don't tell me all their dealin's, of course, but I suppose that movie studio is payin' 'em enough for the use of the ranch to make it worthwhile. And the money'll come in handy, that's for sure." The cook slapped Hallam on the shoulder. "But, hell, none of this is your problem. Seems to me like you and your pards should just enjoy your stay here and teach that Tremaine feller all you can 'bout bein' a cowboy. He's goin' to need a lot of teachin' if he's goin' to fool anybody."

"He'll be all right," Hallam said, hoping that was true.

"Well, I got to go mix up the dough for tomorrow mornin's biscuits," Smitty said. "A cook's work starts 'fore anybody else's on a ranch."

"That's right," Hallam agreed. "And you do a mighty fine job of it, Smitty."

"Thank you kindly, sir." Smitty grinned again, revealing the gaps in his teeth. He waved a hand and started toward the cookshack.

Hallam watched him go. The moon had started to rise during their conversation. It was still fairly low in the sky, a big round orange ball that would turn silvery as it climbed into the heavens. As he had told Eliot Tremaine, it would soon be almost as bright as day out here.

Hallam glanced toward the barn where Eliot had disappeared, following Rae Lindsey. There hadn't been any ruckus from in there, so he assumed that Eliot was behaving himself. If he didn't, Hallam thought with a smile, Rae would probably take a whip to him.

His face became more serious. So there was rustling going on around here. His instincts had been right all along; there was trouble on the Flying L Ranch. But Smitty Wardell had been right, too.

Rustling or not, it was none of Hallam's business.

TEN

It was amazing how many things there were to cowboying that Hallam never thought about anymore. He simply got up on a horse and rode, the way he had been doing for the last fifty years or so. But Eliot Tremaine, for all of his experience at riding in Central Park, had a lot to learn.

They started the first full day of his training with a simple objective: being able to stay on the back of the horse while it was galloping. The mare Eliot was riding wasn't capable of a great deal of speed, but it was able to work up to a fair run. As Eliot put the animal through its paces in a large open field near the ranch house, Hallam and the others sat on their own horses and watched. Hallam had to wince as he saw Eliot bounce wildly in the saddle and hang on for dear life. Next to him, Red Callahan shook his head in disgust.

"We maybe took on too big a job, Lucas," Callahan said.

"Give the boy time, Red," Hallam replied. "Could be he's not totally hopeless."

By the end of the first day, however, Eliot was totally sore. Every muscle in his body ached, and he made no secret of that fact. His complaints at dinner drew contemptuous grins from the ranch's cowboys, but they all kept their mouths shut, even Dan Armstrong.

The next morning, when Hallam knocked on Eliot's door, the only response was a groan. Hallam went in and found the young man burrowed deeply under the covers of his bed. "I'm not coming out," Eliot insisted. "You'll just torture me some more."

Hallam shook his head and went downstairs to find the others already gathered around the table in the dining room, enjoying the breakfast Smitty had prepared. Hallam didn't see how anybody could stay in bed like Eliot was doing when the smells of coffee and bacon and flapjacks filled the air in the house.

"Where's Eliot?" Pecos wanted to know.

Hallam jerked his head toward the stairs. "Says he doesn't want to get out of bed today. Something about being tired and sore, I expect . . ."

Pecos and Teddy exchanged grins. There was a pitcher of water on the table, and Pecos reached out to pick it up. "We'll just see about that," he said as he and Teddy pushed back their chairs and stood.

"I'm not sure that's a good idea," Hallam said as they started past him.

"Always works on Pecos when he's feeling lazy," Teddy chuckled.

"Yeah, and you take great pleasure in it, don't you, you heathen?" Pecos demanded.

"You do tend to jump around and yell a mite, I'll allow."

Hallam shook his head and waved them on. They disappeared up the stairs with a clatter of boots, and a moment later, a bloodcurdling shriek echoed down from the second floor, followed an instant later by heartfelt cursing. Hallam was glad that Rae Lindsey was nowhere around as the air started to turn blue with profanity. He headed for the table before all the flapjacks were gone.

A few minutes later, Eliot Tremaine came down the stairs, fully dressed now and with Pecos and Teddy on either side of him, holding his arms. Eliot's hair was damp and his features were flushed, but he looked none the worse for the rude awakening.

He paused beside the table as Pecos and Teddy released him and glared back and forth at them. "I'm going to get even with you two for this," he promised in a bleak voice.

Pecos slapped him on the back. "We'll be lookin' forward to it, old son!"

Eliot displayed a surprisingly hearty appetite as he sat down to breakfast, polishing off quite a bit of bacon and several biscuits, along with two cups of the strong black coffee. When he was finished, he pushed his plate back and sighed. "Well, if we must continue this session in purgatory, let's get started, shall we?"

"You sound downright eager," Harv Macklin told him with a grin.

"The sooner we get on with it, the sooner I go ahead and die and get it over with," Eliot replied coolly, putting a cigarette in his mouth and lighting it.

Despite his protests, Eliot seemed easier in the saddle today. By midday, he was handling the horse quite well on the straightaways, even at a gallop. During the afternoon, under the watchful eye of Red Callahan, he worked on pulling the mare in tight turns around rocks and trees. Eliot took one spill, but it was a minor one and he was right back up, climbing into the saddle again and surprising Hallam and the others. When Hallam glanced behind him and saw that Rae Lindsey had come up to watch the practicing, he was less surprised that Eliot was putting up a brave front.

Several days passed, one beginning to blend into the next as the other cowboys took turns demonstrating their skills to Eliot. He spent an hour in the mornings working with Jeff Grant, learning how to throw a loop into a rope and then spinning that loop until his arm felt like it was going to fall off. Now that he was more comfortable on horseback, Max Hilyard and Tall Cotton Jones began showing him how to work cattle, using stock that the Flying L hands had driven into one of the corrals. Hallam watched from the top of a fence rail as Eliot and Hilyard and Tall Cotton drove those steers around and around the ranch house, like a miniature cattle drive going nowhere. The sight was more than a little ludicrous, and Hallam couldn't help but grin. Eliot was getting a valuable education, though. At the very least, he was learning how to eat dust.

Armstrong and the other hands didn't seem to be around much now, Hallam noticed. They ate breakfast early, before the others, and were already out and about their chores by the time Eliot's training got under way each morning. Hallam wondered if that was by design, if Lindsey and Rae had come up with more work for the cowboys to keep them out of the way. If that was the case, it might keep things more peaceful for the moment, but it was bound to cause resentment among the hands. Sooner or later, that would boil over, and then there might be real trouble. Hallam hoped he and the others were gone before that had time to happen.

Eliot was starting to look leaner now, even though he was eating more and more at meals. He had sunburned during the first couple of days, but that had peeled to leave a healthy tan. He was much more at home in the saddle now, although Red Callahan started one morning by berating him about how tightly he had fastened one of the cinches around the mare's belly.

"Now, see here!" Eliot cut in. "I've saddled horses before, I'll have you know."

"Back in New York?" Callahan asked.

"Of course. And that's exactly the way I did it in New York."

Callahan shook his head in exasperation. "That may be the New York way, mister, but it sure as hell ain't the cowboy way. Now do it like *this* . . ."

Hallam was standing near one of the corrals with Stone Riordan after lunch when Eliot came striding up to them, a determined expression on his face. "Mr. Riordan," he said firmly, "I believe I'm ready to start using a gun."

"You do, do you?" Stone said, his features set in their usual solemn cast.

"Yes, I do. Callahan says I'm starting to handle a horse fairly well, although I think it pains him to admit that, and Grant had me roping a tree stump for over an hour this morning. I only missed twice." There was pride in Eliot's voice. "I think I'm ready to move on to something else."

Riordan nodded slowly. "Maybe you're right." He looked over at Hallam. "What do you think, Lucas?"

Hallam shrugged. "Boy's got to put a gun on sometime, Stone. Might as well get it over with."

Eliot snorted derisively and said, "Thank you for the vote of confidence, Hallam. You don't have to stay around and watch if you don't want to."

"Oh, I want to," Hallam said, trying not to grin. "I want to."

Stone Riordan went into the house and emerged a few minutes later carrying a holster and a coiled shell belt. Riding in the holster was a Colt .45 much like the one Hallam usually carried. This revolver had ivory grips instead of walnut, and the metal of the cylinder and barrel had been silvered instead of blued. It was a show pistol, Hallam knew, but that didn't mean that it wouldn't shoot just as true as any other gun.

"All right, put this on," Riordan said, holding out the rig to Eliot. "Show me how you think a fast gun would wear it."

Eliot took the Colt, his fingers fumbling slightly in their eagerness as he fastened the belt around his hips. He put his hand on the butt of the pistol and pushed it far down on his thigh, then bent to fasten the holster's tie-down around his leg. When he straightened, the butt of the Colt was a couple of inches below his dangling fingertips.

Riordan looked at him and said, "Well, that's just mighty near the most foolish thing I've ever seen."

Eliot frowned. "What do you mean? I thought all gunfighters wore their weapons down low like this."

"You want to have to bend over every time you reach for your gun?" Riordan asked. "Take that off."

Glaring, Eliot removed the holster and belt. Riordan thrust it toward Hallam. "Show him how, Lucas."

Hallam put the belt around his waist, just below his regular belt. The weight of the Colt pulled the holster down just enough on the right side to put the shell belt at a slight angle. The middle of Hallam's forearm brushed the ivory grips as he let his arm hang naturally at his side.

"But that gun's too high now," Eliot protested.

Riordan shook his head. "That position allows for a nice, smooth, natural draw. Speed's important, but so is accuracy. That position lets you keep your balance. Your shoulders stay squared up that way. Show him, Lucas."

Hallam was aware that several of the others had wandered up. He shook his head. "The fast-draw stuff is your line, Stone, not mine," he said.

Riordan shrugged. "Whatever you say, Lucas." He held out his hand for the rig.

Eliot moved closer to Hallam, shaking his head. "No, Hallam, I want to see what you can do with that," he said sharply. "I've heard Pecos and Teddy talking about what a holy terror you used to be. Why don't you show me?"

A grimace pulled at Hallam's mouth. Eliot could still be a pain in the butt sometimes. "I didn't come out here to shoot the place up," Hallam said.

Eliot grinned cockily. "Maybe you're just afraid you've lost your touch."

Hallam regarded him for a long moment, then said, "Son, I've been prodded by the best and walked away."

"That's right, old man. I'll just bet you have."

The voice came from behind Hallam. He looked around and saw Dan Armstrong standing there. Armstrong and a couple of the ranch hands had obviously just come out of one of the barns nearby. Hallam hadn't known they were there, but it looked like they had seen and heard the whole exchange.

"I didn't know you were supposed to be a gunfighter, old man," Armstrong went on. "You old-timers really like to stretch the truth, don't you?"

Hallam glanced around. Wayne Lindsey was nowhere in sight, and neither were Rae or Smitty. Armstrong and the other two cowboys were the only Flying L hands in the vicinity. Luckily, Pecos and Teddy weren't around, either, or the two young hotheads would be clamoring for Hallam to show Armstrong a thing or two. Eliot and Riordan stood a few feet from him, and a little further away, lounging under the shade of a big oak tree, were Max Hilyard and Jeff Grant.

Stone Riordan spoke up, addressing Armstrong. "Mister, you really don't know who you're talking to, do you?"

"Just looks like some broke-down old bastard to me, but I don't really give a damn," Armstrong replied. He slipped a flask out of his back pocket, uncapped it one-handed, and lifted it to his lips. After taking a long swallow, he lowered it and then wiped the back of his other hand across his mouth. "No, sir, I just don't give a damn."

Hallam sighed. From the flushed look of his features, Armstrong had been stoking up on bootleg whiskey, and was ready for trouble again after keeping the peace for a few days. Maybe the best thing to do would be to sober him up in a hurry.

Hallam faced Riordan and reached back to the loops on the shell belt. "Got any live cartridges, Stone?" he asked.

"First six to the left."

Hallam nodded, pulled the shells from the loops, slid the Colt from the holster and began to thumb them into the cylinder. His back was to the cookshack, but he knew that it was about thirty feet away. Earlier, after lunch, he had seen Smitty carrying some empty cans out of the shack toward the garbage dump behind the outhouse. Hallam remembered that one of the cans had fallen out of Smitty's arms and that the cook hadn't bothered to pick it up at the moment.

"That empty peach can still sitting over by the cookshack?" he asked Riordan as he replaced the gun in its sheath. The trick-shot artist nodded without saying anything.

Hallam took a deep breath. He had been right; this was a lot more in Riordan's line than his, but *he* was the one that Armstrong had called a broke-down old bastard.

Hallam turned sharply, palming out the Colt, firing from the hip.

The pistol blasted, the shots rolling like thunder as Hallam squeezed the trigger. The tin can suddenly leaped into the air and started bouncing—once, twice, again, and yet again. Hallam emptied the Colt in a matter of seconds, and when the empty can thudded back to the ground an instant later, it was shot to pieces.

Hallam glanced back at Armstrong. The man had sobered up, all right. In fact, he was downright pale.

Smitty burst out of the cookshack, eyes wide. "What in the blue blazes!" he yelled. "What the hell's goin' on out here, a war?"

Hallam slid the Colt back into its holster and didn't reply. Stone Riordan, a faint smile on his austere features, answered, "No war, Smitty. Just a little demonstration."

Smitty pointed through the door of the cookshack. "Well, if that cake I got in the oven falls, I'm goin' to do some demonstratin' on somebody's skull!" He stomped back into the shack, adding to the cake's danger.

When Hallam looked around, Armstrong and the other two cowboys were gone. Hilyard and Grant were grinning broadly underneath the tree, and Hilyard called out, "Looked like those boys remembered some work they needed to do, Lucas. Remembered it right sudden-like, they did."

Eliot Tremaine was regarding Hallam with an unreadable expression. After a moment, he said, "It looks like Pecos and

Teddy were telling the truth, after all. Very impressive, Hallam."

Hallam took the gun off and handed the belt and holster back to Stone Riordan. "I never gave a damn about impressing people," he told Eliot. "But I've stayed alive this long."

Over the next couple of days, Stone Riordan taught Eliot how to wear the gun, how to draw it, and how to fire it. Eliot was surprised by how heavy the Colt was, and his wrist was sore after several hours of practicing. Hallam stayed in the background, watching but not taking an active part in the boy's training. He could remember, but just barely, when his own wrist had been sore from the weight of a gun and the recoil of its shots.

Eliot was a long way from being a fast draw, but he could get the revolver out relatively quickly. He looked all right as he fired from the hip; he would never hit anything, the way he was going, but that didn't matter. The move would look good on camera.

He was still working with the other cowboys, too, and they were moving into a more strenuous area of instruction. "You won't be doin' your own stunts," Harv Macklin told Eliot one morning, "but you do need to know how to fall off a horse without killin' yourself."

Eliot nodded a little reluctantly. "I suppose so."

The rest of the morning was occupied with simple horse falls, Macklin instructing Eliot in the art of landing and rolling so that the impact was minimized. There were plenty of other things that Macklin could have taught him, such as the dead-man fall, the running W, and the stationary W, but considering the studio's investment in Eliot Tremaine, it was highly unlikely that he would ever be called on to do any of them. He probably wouldn't even have to do any horse falls, but accidents had been known to happen. This part of the routine was simply precautionary.

Eliot probably would have been satisfied with that, Hallam knew, if he hadn't seen Pecos and Teddy helling around one of the pastures the next afternoon. Each of them was riding one horse and leading another close beside the animal he was mounted on. Eliot was lounging under a tree, taking a break and watching the two young cowboys, when Hallam strolled up and saw what was about to happen.

"What the blazes are they going to do?" Eliot asked. "Why do they each have two horses, Hallam?"

"Keep watchin'," Hallam told him. "I reckon they'll start any second now."

True to that prediction, Pecos and Teddy both urged their horses into a run. Suddenly, they kicked their feet out of the stirrups and lifted their legs, bending almost double as they raised their booted feet to the seats of the saddles. "My God!" Eliot exclaimed as the two youngsters abruptly stood up on the backs of the galloping horses in an amazing demonstration of strength and agility.

Pecos was in the lead. He caught his balance, then extended his right foot over to the saddle of the horse he was leading. Its reins were still tightly gripped in his hands. As the animals raced side by side, keeping even and never breaking stride, Pecos rode them standing up, one foot on each saddle. A few yards behind him, Teddy was performing the same maneuver.

"It's called Roman ridin'," Hallam told Eliot. "The way the story goes, soldiers back in ancient Rome used to do that when they put on shows."

"Incredible," Eliot muttered.

"Well, I reckon it's more civilized than them gladiators hackin' each other to death with swords," Hallam said. "Although I bet more'n a few of those riders wound up fallin' and gettin' stomped."

Pecos and Teddy were racing in a broad circle around the pasture, and Eliot was watching raptly. After a few minutes, he turned to Hallam and said eagerly, "Do you think Callahan could teach me how to do that?"

Hallam frowned. "Stunts like that take a heap of experience and a good-sized dose of foolishness. Stunt riders are laid up half the time, and they usually wind up with broke bones and busted-up insides. You don't want that, Eliot, and neither does the studio."

Eliot's handsome features tightened. "Are you telling me I can't learn any stunts? I thought cowboy actors were expected to do some of their own stunts. What about Tom Mix?"

"Mix is a good rider," Hallam admitted. "But don't believe all of his publicity. He uses doubles just like any other star."

Out in the field, Pecos and Teddy were still riding Roman style, but they had turned around so that they were facing backward now. As Eliot and Hallam watched, each of the young cowboys whirled around again, then released the reins of the second horses and stood on their original mounts again. They slid back down into their saddles, but instead of stopping with that, they kept sliding, moving down on the right sides of the horses, hanging on with one hand tangled in the mane and one foot hooked over the saddle. As the horses turned, both riders suddenly became invisible, hidden from view by the bodies of the galloping animals.

"What about that?" Eliot asked.

"Indian style," Hallam said. "The Comanches used to ride that way so they could use their horses for cover while they were shootin' underneath their necks."

Eliot nodded. "I suppose Teddy taught Pecos how to do that."

Hallam shook his head and said, "Nope. Other way around. Teddy wasn't much of a rider until he came to Hollywood and became pards with Pecos."

"You see," Eliot said triumphantly. "Teddy learned. So can I."

"Teddy's daddy ain't the studio's leadin' director," Hallam

pointed out. "And Teddy ain't a famous Broadway actor. No, you'd best take care of yourself and not go bustin' anything up."

There was still a stubborn expression on Eliot's face as Hallam walked off. Once Eliot got an idea in his head, it was hard to get it out, Hallam knew.

They had survived a week here on the Flying L. Maybe with any luck, Hallam thought, they could make it a while longer.

ELEVEN

Sure enough, the next day Eliot had Red Callahan and Harv Macklin showing him how to ride Indian-style. They had flatly refused to even let him attempt the Roman riding, and Hallam was thankful for that much, at least.

Eliot never complained about being sore anymore. He had thrown himself into the training with an enthusiasm that surprised Hallam. Evidently he had decided that he enjoyed "playing cowboy." Watching Eliot riding and roping and shooting, Hallam was reminded of a little boy who had himself a brand-new toy. By the time they all returned to Hollywood in another week or so, Eliot would probably be competent enough in all the skills he needed to impersonate the real thing in *Sagebrush*.

Dan Armstrong hadn't made any more trouble since Hallam had shot up the empty peach can. He still had a sullen look on his face whenever the visitors were around, and Hallam had seen the outline of the flask in his pants pocket more than once, but at least there hadn't been any more confrontations.

Maybe they were going to slide on through without any more problems, Hallam was thinking as he sat down to another one of Smitty Wardell's delicious suppers.

Eliot was seated across from him, next to Rae Lindsey, as usual. The young actor was talking earnestly to her, also as usual. Eliot spent most of his evenings with Rae now, sitting in the living room with her or helping her with some last-minute chores. As far as Hallam knew, Eliot hadn't tried anything funny with her, which was a little surprising given his reputation as a ladies' man. Maybe Eliot had realized that an approach like that wouldn't work with a girl like Rae.

Armstrong had not come in yet. In fact, several of the ranch hands weren't there. Hallam took note of that fact but didn't find it anything to worry about. Sometimes when a man was working out on the range, he couldn't turn loose of what he was doing and come in just because it was suppertime. You had to stay with the job until it was finished.

The food was as good as ever. Hallam would miss Smitty's cooking when it came time to go back to Hollywood. He loaded his plate with ham and beans and corn bread so hot it was still steaming. You couldn't get food like that at the Brown Derby or Musso & Frank's Grill, Hallam thought.

Eliot was talking about New York, and Rae laughed several times during the conversation. The drawn look that had seemed always to be on her face back when they had arrived had softened somewhat during their stay. Hallam thought Eliot Tremaine had been as responsible for that as the money that their visit would bring in for the ranch.

Armstrong and the handful of cowboys who were probably with him never showed up.

After supper, Eliot and Rae moved to the long sofa in the living room, sitting fairly close together. Hallam wandered into the room after them and found himself standing in front of the big fireplace, looking at the Winchesters that were hung over the mantel. Wayne Lindsey came up beside him and said quietly, "Those were my daddy's rifles. Fought off Indians and rustlers with 'em more than once, he always said, and they never let him down."

"They're good weapons," Hallam agreed. "I've used ones just like them."

"Would you like to take 'em down and try 'em out sometime?" Lindsey asked. "I don't like to just let a gun set up and not ever get used."

Hallam nodded. "Good idea. I'd enjoy firin' a few rounds, Mr. Lindsey."

The rancher slapped him on the shoulder. "Good. Maybe tomorrow—"

The sound of hoofbeats from outside made Lindsey pause. The windows of the house were closed against the cool night air, but the thudding noise of running horses was clear enough for everyone in the house to hear it. A moment later, the hoofbeats stopped abruptly just outside, and booted feet pounded across the planks of the front porch.

The door burst open. Dan Armstrong pushed through the entrance into the living room, looking around until he spotted Lindsey standing by the fireplace with Hallam. He came toward the rancher, his face flushed, and said, "We got trouble, Mr. Lindsey." He glanced over at the sofa and went on, "Sorry, Miss Rae. You need to hear about this, too."

Rae stood up quickly and came over to stand beside her father. Eliot came along, hanging back slightly. Lindsey fixed his level gaze on Armstrong and said, "What is it, Dan?"

"Those damned rustlers hit again." Armstrong grimaced. "Me and a few of the boys went up to the north pasture to check on the stock there, and they're gone, every one of them."

Rae's breath came more quickly as the news soaked in. "There were a hundred head up there," she said.

Armstrong nodded. "Yes, ma'am, I know. But they're gone now."

"Could you tell how long it had been since they were driven off?" Lindsey asked. "Were there any tracks?"

"Plenty of tracks," Armstrong said. "You can't move that

many cattle and not leave sign, boss. I figure it was sometime late this afternoon, not more'n a couple of hours ago."

Hallam spoke up without even thinking about the fact that this was none of his business. His lawman's instincts were operating as he said, "They can't move too fast if they're pushing that many head. We ought to be able to catch up to them."

Lindsey glanced in his direction. "Don't you reckon we ought to call the sheriff?"

"Bascomb?" Dan Armstrong snorted. "He can't even find his own ass! I'll take some of the boys and go after those crooks. We'll find them, sure enough. I would've followed them right away once we found out what had happened, but I figured the two of you ought to know."

"Thank you, Dan," Rae said, "but Dad's right. We need to call the law."

Lindsey looked like he was changing his mind about that. He regarded Hallam for a long moment, then said, "We've got a lawman right here already, Rae. Mr. Hallam was a Ranger for a long time. He's probably chased down more than one bunch of rustlers." Lindsey faced Hallam squarely now. "What about it? You willin' to give it a try?"

Hallam looked at the men crowding around him, saw the eagerness on the faces of Pecos and Teddy. He knew what their answer would be to Lindsey's question. And that same enthusiasm was visible on Eliot Tremaine's face, Hallam suddenly realized.

Armstrong's heavy features were set in disapproving lines. Obviously, he didn't want Hallam horning in on this. A smile tugged at Hallam's mouth. What was the use of being old if you couldn't be contrary every once in a while?

"Be glad to," he told Lindsey. He jerked his head toward the Winchesters hanging on the wall. "Can you spare the loan of one of those rifles and some shells?"

"Damn right!" Lindsey exclaimed.

Pecos lifted a clenched fist, grinning from ear to ear. "Hot damn! We're goin' to chase rustlers!" Teddy matched his expression.

"I'm ready," Eliot said excitedly. "If someone will just let me borrow a gun . . ."

"Now hold on," Hallam said. "Nobody said any of you fellers could go along."

"That's right," Armstrong snapped. He glared at Hallam. "Bad enough we're saddled with some old has-been. We sure as hell don't need no fancy play-actors along!"

Lindsey took one of the rifles down from its pegs and handed it to Hallam, along with a box of cartridges that the rancher took from one of the drawers in the desk. He said, "I can't ask you men to go along. You're guests here. Our men can handle it, can't they, Rae?"

"Why are you asking me?" she replied tautly. "I wanted to call the sheriff. I don't like the idea of sending out a posse of vigilantes."

"We can't do any worse than Mart Bascomb has been," Armstrong pointed out. He looked at Hallam. "We're goin'. If you're comin' along, mister, you'd better be ready to keep up, 'cause we ain't slowin' down for you."

Hallam hefted the Winchester, liking the way the smooth metal of the breech felt in his hand. "You watch out for your own hide, Armstrong," he said, "and I'll tend to mine."

The foreman grunted his agreement, then turned to leave the room. Hallam started to follow him.

"Hey, what about us?" Eliot called after them.

"Stay here," Hallam said flatly. He snagged his hat from one of the hooks beside the door, then walked out of the living room, letting the screen door bang shut behind him.

He hoped they would do what he told them. The last thing he wanted to have to explain to Peter Tremaine and J. Frederick Darby was how Eliot had gotten himself hurt chasing rustlers. For one thing, they probably wouldn't think that such a thing was possible in this day and age.

Hallam strode toward the corrals behind Dan Armstrong.

Armstrong glanced over his shoulder and said, "Get saddled up in a hurry, if you're comin'. My men are already changin' our saddles over to fresh horses."

"I'll be ready to ride, don't worry," Hallam told him.

Smitty Wardell must have heard the commotion, because he came out of the cookshack, where he had as usual retreated after supper. "What's goin' on here?" the cook demanded.

"Somebody drove off a hundred head of cattle," Armstrong told him.

"Damn it! Wide-loopers again!" Smitty noticed Hallam then. "You goin' along after 'em, Hallam?"

"Thought I would," Hallam replied. "Mr. Lindsey thought it'd be a good idea."

"Well, I ain't so sure," Armstrong snapped as he paused and turned toward Hallam. "Let's get one thing straight. I don't care if you used to be a Ranger, mister. I'm the foreman around here, and I'm in charge. You understand?"

Hallam nodded curtly. "Reckon that's your right."

"See that you remember it." Armstrong wheeled around again and went on toward the barns and the corrals.

Smitty reached out and caught Hallam's arm. "Dan's a mite touchy," he said, "but he ain't a bad man."

"I'll try to stay out of his way," Hallam promised.

As Armstrong had said, the other cowboys had fresh mounts saddled up by the time Hallam reached the corral. In short order, he cut out the horse he had been using, a big bay stallion sturdy enough to carry his weight. It took only a moment to bring his saddle out of the barn and throw it on the horse's back, but the delay was enough to grate on Armstrong.

"We're ridin'," he announced as Hallam cinched up. "You can catch up to us if you can." He turned his horse and put the spurs to it, galloping away from the ranch headquarters with the other cowboys following behind him.

Hallam bit back a curse, made sure the saddle was secure,

then swung up onto the horse. He rode out of the corral, pulling the gate shut behind him, then headed in the direction Armstrong and the others had gone. He could still see them up ahead, a moving patch of deeper darkness in the shadows. The moon was not up yet, but it would be soon. It would only be three-quarters, not full, but that ought to provide enough light to track such a big bunch of cattle, Hallam thought.

He pushed the horse a little harder than he should have, considering the circumstances, but within a few minutes he had caught up to the Flying L hands. Armstrong glanced over at him but said nothing.

It took a little over half an hour to reach the pasture where the cattle were supposed to have been grazing. As Armstrong had said, the beasts were gone, the big pasture empty. Armstrong led the way across it, then reined in as he reached a narrow line of trees on the far side.

"You can see this is where they went," he said, pointing to the jumbled mass of tracks that led through the trees. The moon was up now, throwing silver-white illumination across the scene. The shadows were deep underneath the trees, but as the group of riders moved slowly through them, the tracks reappeared on the other side.

The trail led northwest, into the roughest part of the ranch.

"Can they make it through those gullies and breaks up in that direction?" Hallam asked.

"Sure," Armstrong grunted. "The terrain's not as rugged as it looks. It's rough enough, but not so much that stock can't be driven through it. The trail's goin' to be harder to follow, though, and I reckon that's what they had in mind."

"Is there any way of circlin' around the worst part?"

"If we do that, we might have to spend hours pickin' up their trail again," Armstrong said. He laughed harshly. "That's about the kind of advice I'd expect from some has-been movie cowboy."

"That's twice you've called me a has-been, mister," Hallam said quietly. "I don't much care for it."

"Tough. Come on, let's go." He lifted his voice as he spoke, turning in his saddle and waving the other cowboys on. With Armstrong at their head, they rode on, deeper into the rugged landscape. Hallam rode after them.

Armstrong was wrong, he knew. Circling around might cost a little time in locating the trail again, but it could save even more. Once they hit the gullies, the going would be mighty slow, slower still because they would be trying to follow the tracks over ground that was getting more and more rocky. It was doubtful that the rustlers would be able to gain a bigger lead on them, but at the same time, the pursuers probably wouldn't be able to cut the gap any, either.

Hallam didn't know the country well enough to take off on his own, though. He would have to stick with Armstrong and the other cowboys, at least for the time being.

The moonlight strengthened as the glowing, gibbous orb in the sky rose higher. It was light enough for Hallam to see the three riders closing in behind him when the sound of their hoofbeats came to his ears. He swiveled in the saddle, bringing up the now-loaded Winchester in case this was some sort of ambush.

No such luck, he saw, cursing bitterly.

Eliot Tremaine, Pecos, and Teddy Spotted Horse were galloping after him as hard as they could, pushing their horses for all they were worth.

"Hold on!" Hallam called up to Dan Armstrong. He reined in and waited for the three young men to catch up with him.

Dust rose around their horses as they pulled the animals to a halt. When the cloud had settled a little, Pecos grinned in the moonlight and said, "You didn't think we were goin' to let you have all the fun, did you, Lucas?"

"We never got to chase rustlers for real before," Teddy added. "Just in the movies."

"It's my fault, Hallam," Eliot put in. "I insisted I was going, and Pecos and Teddy accompanied me to make certain that no accidents befell me."

Hallam would have befelled him right about then, and done it gladly, as he looked at the smug grins on the faces of the three youngsters. They should have stayed back at the ranch like he had told them to, but there was nothing he could do about it now short of ordering them to go back. And he had already seen a good example of how well they took orders.

"Come on," he said wearily. "But if there's any trouble, you boys keep your heads down, hear?"

"Sure, Lucas," Pecos replied. The other two nodded.

Hallam didn't believe them for a second.

Armstrong was cursing under his breath, and the other cowboys didn't look happy about the situation, either. "I said we didn't need no play-actors along," Armstrong grated. "This is the real thing, not some nickelodeon show."

"I'll watch out for 'em," Hallam said.

"See that you do." Armstrong started riding again.

Eliot urged his horse up alongside Hallam's as the group started moving again. He reached into the saddlebags draped over the animal's back and said, "I thought you might want this, Hallam, if you were going to be chasing outlaws."

He held out Hallam's Colt, resting snugly in its holster with the shell belt coiled around it.

Hallam looked at the gun for a moment, then reached out and took it. "Thanks," he said softly. He slid the Colt out of the holster, pulled the hammer back to half-cock, thumbed open the loading gate, and spun the cylinder. Five fresh cartridges, and the hammer had been resting on an empty.

The boy had actually been paying attention along the way, Hallam thought.

TWELVE

It took most of the night for them to make their way through the northwestern section of the ranch, just as Hallam had expected. They had lost the trail of the stolen cattle more than once and had to cast back and forth along the banks of the gullies until they found it again. Armstrong wasn't much of a tracker, Hallam realized; in fact, if he hadn't found the trail himself a few times, they might have lost the rustlers entirely.

But Hallam was always able to cut the sign, even after the moon finally sank below the horizon. Its glow was still faintly visible in the western sky, and there was a corresponding lightness in the east as dawn approached. The group of riders reached a barbed-wire fence, Armstrong calling a halt.

Hallam sat in his saddle and studied the way the fence had been cut, a large section bent back so that the rustled stock could be driven through it. He looked over at Armstrong and asked, "This the boundary of the Flyin' L?"

"That's right," Armstrong confirmed. "I'm not sure we should go on or not. I really thought we'd catch up to them before we got this far."

Hallam refrained from pointing out that they might have if only the foreman had followed his suggestion earlier in the night. Armstrong wouldn't want to hear that, and anyway, it was too late to be worrying about such things. Hallam said, "I reckon you're goin' on anyway."

Armstrong rubbed his prominent jaw. "I ain't sure we should. I wasn't too worried about not callin' the law as long as we were on the Lindseys' range, but now . . ."

"Excuse me"—Eliot spoke up—"but I believe that you do have a legal right to continue this pursuit, since there's ample evidence that this is the way the thieves went. And as the foreman of the ranch, I would think that you certainly have a right to make a citizen's arrest once we catch up to them."

"It ain't that simple," Armstrong said scornfully. "We can't just ride up to a bunch of rustlers and tell 'em that we're arrestin' 'em. There's liable to be shootin'."

"You knew that when we left the ranch," Hallam said. After a night of trailing owlhoots, all of his old instincts were in command again. The private eye and riding extra were just about gone right now, and the Texas Ranger was back. He heeled his horse into motion again. "I'm goin' after them."

"Count us in," Pecos said. Eliot and Teddy echoed his enthusiasm.

Armstrong watched them ride by, then muttered, "I ain't lettin' no damn redskin show me up, by God!" He spurred his horse ahead.

Hallam saw Teddy glance over at Armstrong, saw in the dim light of dawn the hostile glare on the foreman's heavy features. If there was any shooting, Hallam told himself, he would do well to keep an eye on Armstrong, just to make sure that Teddy didn't accidentally get himself shot in the back.

The terrain became even more rugged, the slopes steeper, the gullies more choked with brush. Hallam found himself in the lead most of the time. As the sun rose, the tracks became easier to follow.

Hunger gnawed at Hallam's belly. They hadn't prepared for a chase lasting as long as this one. None of the cowboys had brought anything to eat. There were plenty of creeks to provide water for horses and men alike, but they wouldn't be able to continue much longer without food. They crossed several dirt roads and saw quite a few farmhouses. Hallam knew they might be able to get something to eat at one of those places, but he hated to let the rustlers get that much farther ahead of them. He had a feeling that the men pushing the stolen cattle weren't letting them rest much.

There were more fences now, and that let Hallam know they were still on the right trail. Every time the tracks reached a fence, there was a large gap cut into the wire. He wondered where the devil the rustlers were headed.

"We're in Wise County now," Armstrong said about mid-morning. "This is the farthest anybody's been able to track those rustlers. The trails have always petered out before this."

"You just never had Lucas Hallam cuttin' sign for you before," Pecos said proudly.

"You make that old man sound like Buffalo Bill or Kit Carson," Armstrong snapped.

"Why, you don't know the half of it, mister!" Pecos said. "I could tell you stories—"

"Not now, Pecos," Hallam snapped, waving the youngster to silence. He nodded toward the trail. "Those tracks are gettin' fresher. I think we'll be comin' up on those rustlers before too much longer."

"Really?" Eliot asked. "Lord, this is exciting."

Somehow, though, Hallam thought that Eliot was starting to sound a little nervous. Maybe he was realizing that if there was trouble, there would be real bullets flying through the air, not blanks.

Another half hour went by, and suddenly Hallam held up his hand, calling a halt and warning the others to be quiet. He listened intently for a moment. The sound of cattle bawling came to his ears.

He turned to the other men and said, "They're up ahead."

He had strapped on the Colt the night before after checking it. Now he worked the lever of the Winchester, throwing a shell into the chamber. Looping the reins around the saddle horn and then using his knees to guide the horse, he sent the animal forward at a slow walk.

Hallam studied the surrounding landscape as he rode. They were going down a gentle slope into a small valley with wooded hills on both sides. He could see another dirt road snaking through the valley. The sound of the cattle was louder now, and Hallam suddenly heard another noise to his right. Peering in that direction, he saw movement through the trees and realized that there was a road there, too. It was more heavily traveled, however. The new sound he had heard was automobile engines.

Angling his head toward the main road, Hallam asked Armstrong in a quiet voice, "What's that over there?"

"Must be the highway between Denton and Decatur," Armstrong replied after a moment. "I can hear trucks on it."

"So can I." And that had to be the answer, Hallam thought. The stolen cattle were driven over here into the next county, loaded on trucks, and hauled away. He was going to keep that theory to himself for the moment, however.

Suddenly he saw the cattle up ahead, being hazed through a pasture at the bottom of the rise by about half a dozen men on horseback. One of the riders must have felt Hallam's eyes on him, because he turned in his saddle, stared up the slope, and then let out a frantic yell. The other men looked around and immediately started trying to push the stolen cattle faster.

No point in being quiet now, Hallam thought. "Come on!" he shouted, banging his heels into the sides of his horse and kicking it into a run.

There was a crack and a puff of smoke from the direction of one of the rustlers, and Hallam heard a high-pitched whine. He knew that sound, knew it all too well. A bullet had just passed overhead.

Well, they had fired the first shot. Hallam lifted the

Winchester to his shoulder, still guiding his horse with his knees, and squeezed the trigger. The rifle blasted and bucked against him.

He worked the Winchester's action, fired again, then again. He was aiming high on purpose, not wanting to kill anybody. They had the rustlers outnumbered more than two to one, and there was a good chance the men would give up when they saw the superior force charging toward them.

A moment later, he saw that they had no intention of giving up. The air was filled with the crackle of gunfire as all of the rustlers turned away from the cattle and started shooting.

Hallam glanced over at Eliot Tremaine and saw that the actor was pale-faced as he leaned out over the neck of his racing horse. Eliot didn't even have a gun, Hallam suddenly realized. There was a rifle in a saddle boot slung on the horse, but Eliot was making no move to pull it.

"Get back!" Hallam yelled to him, trying to wave him off. Eliot did not respond. He kept charging straight ahead.

Pecos and Teddy both had rifles in their hands and were firing high, following Hallam's example. Armstrong and several of the other cowboys were shooting, too, but most of them couldn't fire for fear of hitting some of their own men who were in the lead.

The rustlers were less than a hundred yards away now. The sounds that filled the air were a nightmarish blend of gunshots, shouts, the thunder of hoofbeats, the bawling of spooked cattle. The rustlers had been driving the stolen stock in a compact bunch, but now as the battle broke out behind them, the cows started to scatter, running blindly across the pasture. If what Hallam had watched back at the ranch a few days earlier had been a cattle drive in miniature, then this was a small-scale stampede. There was no way the rustlers would be able to get the animals under control again.

They did the sensible thing. They cut and ran.

Hallam saw the rustlers peeling away, all of them heading in different directions. He snapped, "Damn it!", knowing that they would be lucky to catch up to one or two of the thieves. The others would be able to slip away.

"Get those cows!" Armstrong bellowed to his men, waving for them to start rounding up the stampeding cattle.

Hallam had started to rein in when he saw someone flash past him. It was Eliot Tremaine, he saw, and the actor was coaxing every bit of speed possible out of his mount. Eliot was heading straight after one of the fleeing rustlers.

Hallam jabbed his boot heels into the flanks of his horse. He rode as hard as he could after Eliot, realizing that the young man intended to try to make a capture of his own. Eliot still didn't have a gun in his hands, so that left only one course of action that Hallam could see.

When he was close enough, Eliot intended to throw himself out of his saddle and tackle the rustler.

That was the most damn-fool idea Hallam could think of, which meant it was probably exactly what Eliot had in mind. Hallam had seen Harv Macklin and Red Callahan and Yakima Canutt do stunts like that hundreds of times; it was an easy enough gag if you knew what you were doing and had practiced it. Eliot didn't and hadn't. He would break his blasted neck—if the rustler didn't turn in the saddle and shoot him first.

Eliot was about twenty yards in front of Hallam, but even closer to the man he was chasing. That gap was steadily shrinking. Eliot leaned over, urging his horse on to greater speed, and suddenly he was drawing alongside the rustler. Hallam was close enough now to see that the man was wearing work clothes and a billed cap, rather than cowboy garb. He rode a horse well enough, though. As the man's head swiveled, Hallam caught a glimpse of his face, saw lean features and a dark stubble of beard. The rustler had an automatic in his hand, a 1911A1 army .45 from the looks of it. The slide was locked back, meaning that it was empty and that the rustler either hadn't had a chance to change magazines or didn't have any spares. Either way, that was all that had saved Eliot Tremaine's life for this long.

With a dramatic shout, Eliot leaped out of his saddle, kicking his feet free perfectly and throwing himself toward the rustler, arms outstretched to grab him and knock him off his horse.

The man jerked his reins, veering to the right.

Eliot missed him cleanly, slamming to the ground instead and rolling over and over.

Hallam snapped a shot at the rustler but knew as soon as he squeezed the Winchester's trigger that he had missed. With his left hand, he grabbed the reins that he had wrapped around the saddle horn earlier and hauled back on them, bringing his horse to a stop. He dropped out of the saddle, landing next to the still, prone figure of Eliot Tremaine. Hallam levered the rifle and aimed for the rustler's horse, still not wanting to kill the man if he could avoid it.

The hammer clicked as it fell. Empty. Hallam reached down for the Colt, then stopped and grimaced. The range was already too great. Instead, he knelt beside Eliot and reached out to turn the youngster over gently.

Eliot let out a groan, and his eyes flickered open. There was a huge smudge of dirt down the side of his face, and his jaw was already swelling with what would be a honey of a bruise. He blinked a couple of times, swallowed, and then asked hoarsely, "Did I get him?"

Hallam shook his head. "Sorry, son. Not even close."

"Damn." Eliot lifted himself on his elbows, wincing as he did so. "Help me up."

"You all right?"

"Of course I'm all right. But I should have had that bastard."

Hallam stood up and hauled Eliot to his feet as Pecos and Teddy rode up. "You two okay?" Pecos called anxiously.

"Reckon I'm fine," Hallam replied, supporting Eliot with

an arm around his shoulders. "Eliot here's a little bunged up, but I think he's goin' to make it."

"I'm all right, I'm all right," Eliot insisted, but when he tried to take a step, he sagged in Hallam's grip. Hallam kept holding him up as he looked around the pasture.

He couldn't see any of the rustlers anymore. They had all escaped, just as he had feared they would. But at least he and the others had recovered the stolen cattle. Armstrong and the Flying L hands seemed to have the would-be stampede under control, and they were bunching the cows up again so that they could be driven.

"Sorry, Hallam," Eliot muttered. "I really thought I could capture that bounder."

Hallam squeezed the young actor's shoulder. "You gave it a try, I'll say that for you," he told Eliot. "That was a mighty fine leap you did. The other feller just didn't do his part."

Teddy rode over and caught up the reins of Eliot's horse, then led it back to where Hallam and Eliot were waiting. "Here you go," Teddy said to Eliot as he handed him the reins.

Armstrong loped up on his horse. He looked at Hallam, Eliot, Pecos, and Teddy, and said, "Anybody hurt? Lindsey and Miss Rae won't like it if I let any of you get hurt too bad."

"We're all right," Hallam told him. "And the Lindseys ought to be happy. We got their stock back, even if we didn't latch onto the men who stole them."

"Yeah," Armstrong grunted. "Shame about that."

The foreman didn't sound too disappointed, though. Hallam supposed he could understand that. Once the initial excitement of the chase had worn off, Armstrong and, for that matter, all the other cowboys had to have been asking themselves if they wanted to get killed over some stolen beeves. He had a feeling that if it had been up to Armstrong, all of them would have turned back when they reached the boundary line of the Flying L. It was his own stubbornness and tracking ability that had allowed them to catch up to the thieves, Hallam knew.

He wondered what Darby and Peter Tremaine would say if they knew that he had gotten Eliot into a running gunfight just because old habits died hard. They were bound to hear about it, once the group returned to Hollywood. For one thing, Hallam had a feeling that Eliot was so proud of his own part in the adventure, he would tell his father and the studio production chief himself.

He would deal with that when it happened, Hallam supposed. For now, they had some cattle to drive home.

That drive took the rest of the day. The cattle were tired from being pushed all night, and Hallam knew that they should have rested the animals before starting them back to the ranch. He was sure that Lindsey and Rae were worried about them, though, and Armstrong agreed. By the time they reached the Flying L in the early evening, cattle, horses, and men were all bone-weary.

Wayne Lindsey and his daughter heard them coming and were waiting on the porch of the ranch house. Rae ran out to meet them as the riders turned their mounts in at the open corral. "What happened?" she called out. "Is everyone all right?"

"We're fine, Miss Rae," Armstrong replied. "We got the cattle back, but the men who took 'em got away. Sorry."

"Sorry?" Rae echoed incredulously. "You recovered a hundred head of stock, Dan. You don't have anything to be sorry about. But Dad and I were so worried about . . . all of you."

Hallam saw her eyes searching among them in the gathering dusk and had a good idea who she was looking for. Eliot Tremaine was riding on the other side of him. Hallam said to him, "I'll take care of your horse, Eliot. You get on inside and take it easy. Maybe Miss Lindsey will have some salve or something she can put on that bruise of yours. There's some cuts and scratches on your hands that need cleanin', too."

"Thanks, Hallam," Eliot said tiredly as he slid down from the saddle. Hallam dismounted and took the reins from him.

"Eliot!" Rae cried, spotting him then. Someone lit a lamp inside the barn, and the yellow glow that spilled out showed Eliot's battered appearance plainly. Rae hurried toward him.

Eliot started toward her, then paused and looked back at Hallam. "Tell me the truth," he said to the big man. "Did I do all right?"

Hallam didn't hesitate. He nodded and said, "You did fine."

Tired and bunged up or not, a grin stretched across Eliot Tremaine's face as he went to meet Rae. She came into his arms and lifted a hand to his face. "My God," she breathed, "are you all right?"

Eliot glanced back at Hallam. "I'm fine," he said, his voice stronger now. "I'm just fine."

THIRTEEN

It was mid-morning of the next day when the big Ford sedan with stars painted on the front doors pulled in the Flying L's driveway. Hallam was standing beside the corral at the time, and he could see the words COUNTY and SHERIFF emblazoned at the top and bottom of the stars. The Ford came to a stop, and two men got out. Both of them wore khaki uniforms, Stetsons, and .38 revolvers. The one who had been driving was big and young; the other man was a head shorter, with a pinched, middle-aged face and white hair.

Wayne Lindsey came out of the house and walked quickly toward them, extending a hand to the smaller man. "Howdy, Mart," he said. "Thanks for comin' out."

The white-haired man shook hands briefly with Lindsey. "That's my job," he said. "Now, what can you tell me about this rustling?"

"Come on in the house. I imagine Smitty's still got some coffee heated up." Lindsey led the two uniformed men into the ranch house.

Jeff Grant and Max Hilyard wandered over from the other side of the corral. "Who were those gents?" Hilyard asked Hallam.

"The sheriff and one of his deputies, from the looks of it," Hallam replied, angling his head toward the official Ford. "Lindsey said he was going to call the sheriff and tell him about what happened."

"That lawman may not be too happy with you, Lucas, takin' off after those rustlers on your own like that," Grant said.

Hallam shrugged. "It was Armstrong's idea. I just went along to help out."

Eliot Tremaine came out of the barn then, along with Stone Riordan, Pecos, and Teddy. The actor spotted the sheriff's car and came hurrying toward Hallam.

"I see the law's here," he said. "Do you think the sheriff will want to question me, Hallam?"

"Don't know. He might. You were there during the shootin', after all."

Eliot shook his head. "I don't think my father and Darby would be very happy if it got out that I was here trying to learn how to be a cowboy. They're probably working with the publicity department at the studio right now, coming up with some fake biography for me that makes me sound like Young Wild West himself."

"More'n likely," Hallam grunted, knowing how publicity departments worked. "Tell you what, Eliot, I'll keep your name out of it if I can."

"Thanks, Hallam. Normally I don't mind a little publicity, you understand, but under circumstances like these . . ."

"Sure," Hallam nodded.

Eliot gestured toward his swollen, discolored jaw. "And I certainly don't want my picture in any of the newspapers while I look like *this*. My fans—and my potential fans—just wouldn't understand."

"That is quite a bruise you got there, Eliot," Pecos said. "Looks a little like you ran into the wrong end of a mule."

The bruise was spectacular, ranging in color from a deep blue to a sickly yellow on the edges. Eliot was damned lucky he hadn't broken his jaw when he landed on it, Hallam thought.

Other than the bruise, though, and a few other cuts and scrapes, Eliot was in remarkably good shape this morning. Hallam supposed Rae Lindsey's tender loving care was responsible for Eliot bouncing back so quickly. The girl had certainly been fussing over him when she led him into the house the night before to tend to his injuries.

None of the other members of the impromptu posse had been hurt in the fracas with the rustlers. When the recovered stock had been tallied, it was discovered that there were a hundred and four head in the stolen herd. There was no way of knowing exactly how many cows had been in the bunch driven off from the north pasture, but Dan Armstrong seemed confident that only a few head had been lost, if any. Except for the fact that the rustlers got away, it had been a successful pursuit.

Wayne Lindsey appeared in the doorway of the ranch house and called, "Mr. Hallam! Could you come in here for a minute, please?"

Hallam waved and nodded, said, "Be right there." In a lower voice, he went on to Eliot, "Why don't you and Pecos and Teddy make yourselves scarce for a while? I'll handle this."

"Of course," Eliot replied. He and the other two youngsters started drifting back toward the barn, while Hallam headed toward the house.

Lindsey led Hallam into the living room. The white-haired man was sitting in one of the big armchairs with his legs crossed and his hat balanced on one knee, while his companion stood near the fireplace, hands clasped behind his back. Lindsey nodded toward the white-haired man and said, "Mr. Hallam, this is Mart Bascomb, our local sheriff. Mart, Lucas Hallam."

Bascomb didn't offer to get up and shake hands, so Hallam just nodded and said, "Howdy, Sheriff."

"Hallam." The lawman's voice was as cold as his blue eyes, which regarded Hallam with something mighty like suspicion. "Seems like I've heard that name before."

"Used to be a lawman myself," Hallam told Bascomb. "Rode with the Rangers back in the Nineties."

Bascomb nodded slowly. "Yep, I remember hearing about you. Didn't know you was the same Hallam. Hell, I didn't know you was still alive."

"Alive and kickin', every now and then," Hallam grinned.

"So I hear. Lindsey tells me you led a bunch of vigilantes after those rustlers that hit his spread."

Lindsey spoke up quickly. "Now, that's not exactly the way I put it, Mart—"

"But that's the way it was, wasn't it, Hallam?" Bascomb asked crisply.

"Well, not so's you'd notice," Hallam replied. "Mr. Lindsey's foreman, Dan Armstrong, was in charge. I just went along to help out, since I'd had a little experience chasin' rustlers."

"You still had no authority. None of you did."

"Nobody's denyin' that, Mart," Lindsey said. "Rae said we ought to call you. I was the one who sent Armstrong and Mr. Hallam and some of the other boys out after those cow thieves. If anybody's to blame, it's me." The rancher shrugged. "But they *did* get the stolen cattle back, and that's more than—" He broke off abruptly.

The sheriff's mouth, already a thin line, got thinner. "Go ahead," he said stiffly. "Go ahead and finish what you were going to say, Lindsey. You were going to say that that's more than I would have done."

"Damn it, Mart." Lindsey sounded exasperated. "You and I have known each other for a long time. You know I didn't mean any offense. But it's true you ain't had much luck runnin' down these rustlers in the past."

"We're working on leads all the time," Bascomb said. "I just don't go around telling the public about it. Criminal investigations are the business of the sheriff's office, nobody else's."

Lindsey said, "I reckon you're right about that, Mart."

"Just like chasing rustlers is the sheriff's business." Bascomb took out a thin cigar, peeled off the wrapper, stuck the stogie in his mouth and lit it with a kitchen match that he scraped into life on his boot heel. He went on talking around the cigar. "I haven't had any complaints about that little set-to from the authorities over in Wise County, not yet anyway. But if I do hear any squawks, I'm going to tell the law over there to come see you, Lindsey. Understand?"

Lindsey nodded. "Reckon I do."

Hallam could see the anger in the rancher's eyes and in the taut lines of his weathered face. A man like Wayne Lindsey wasn't used to being talked to like Sheriff Mart Bascomb was talking. But Lindsey respected the law, Hallam knew, and he wasn't going to say anything—not unless Bascomb pushed him too far. Lindsey had to live here, after all.

Hallam didn't.

"Seems to me like you ought to be thankin' us, Sheriff," Hallam said sharply.

Bascomb took the cigar out of his mouth. "What the hell for?" he growled.

"Tryin' to do your job for you."

The deputy stepped away from the fireplace, taking his hands from behind his back and letting them hang at his sides. "What do you mean by that, mister?" he asked.

"Just what I said," Hallam told him. "When the law can't handle a problem, I don't see any reason why the people bein' hurt shouldn't give it a try."

"The sheriff can handle a bunch of damn rustlers," the deputy said hotly.

"Then why the hell hasn't he?"

The deputy's hands formed fists as he took another step forward. Without looking at him, Bascomb rapped, "Let it go, Roy. This old man's just talking to hear himself talk." The sheriff pushed himself up out of the armchair and turned to Lindsey. "We'll be going now. I'd send somebody down to look at the scene of the crime, but it wouldn't do any good now, not after everybody and his dog's gone trampling over it. Just remember what I told you about taking the law into your own hands in the future, Lindsey."

"Sure," the rancher nodded, still keeping a tight rein on his own temper.

The deputy gave Hallam a hard look as he followed Bascomb out of the room. Hallam and Lindsey stood there, not saying anything until they heard the sound of the sheriff's Ford pulling away. Then Lindsey sighed and shook his head and said, "Reckon now maybe you understand why nobody's caught those rustlers yet, Mr. Hallam."

"Make it Lucas. I understand, all right. That feller don't strike me as much of a lawman."

"There was a time when he was a mighty good one. Reckon most things change over the years, though, includin' people. I suppose Mart tries, but . . ."

Hallam nodded. "Maybe he'll track 'em down yet. Stranger things have happened."

"That's right." Lindsey clapped Hallam on the shoulder. "Anyway, you've got my gratitude for gettin' those cows back, and I know Rae feels the same way. That young fella Pecos told me that Dan would've lost the trail several times if you hadn't been along to find it again."

"I don't know about that," Hallam said. "Armstrong and I might not get along too well, but I figure he was doin' the best he could."

That was giving the foreman the benefit of the doubt, Hallam knew, but he didn't see any point in bad-mouthing the man to his boss.

"Well, whatever, I appreciate what you did." Lindsey's expression became thoughtful, and he went on, "You know, another idea just occurred to me. Pecos said you did a little detective work every now and then out in Hollywood."

Hallam grimaced. "Boy needs to learn to keep that jaw of his from flappin'."

Lindsey laughed and said, "He does seem to think you hung the moon, all right. Anyway, I'm wonderin' if I could hire you to track down those rustlers, Lucas. It'd do this whole part of the country a world of good if somebody put them out of business."

As soon as Lindsey had brought up his status as a private detective, Hallam had been afraid that the rancher was going to ask him that exact question. He reached up and rubbed his jaw as he considered how to answer it.

"It's true I sometimes do a little pokin' around in things," he finally said. "But my license ain't any good except in California. I'm just a citizen like everybody else while I'm in Texas."

"That wouldn't stop you from doin' some . . . pokin' around, unofficial-like," Lindsey pointed out.

"Well, I'm already workin' . . . ." Hallam hesitated, unsure how much of his real purpose here to reveal to Lindsey. He had known enough men of the veteran rancher's stripe to be certain that Lindsey was trustworthy, though. As he reached his decision, he went on, "I'm here to keep an eye on that Tremaine feller and make sure he don't get into any trouble."

Quickly, he went on to explain about being hired by Darby to bird-dog Eliot. Lindsey nodded, then said, "From what I've heard about what happened over there in Wise County, it sounds like the boy could've got hurt."

Hallam winced. "That's right enough. Reckon I forgot my job for a while, once we got wind of those rustlers. I intend to keep anything like that from happenin' again, though."

"Tremaine's been spendin' a lot of time with Rae. Some of those scrapes you said he'd been in . . . I reckon they had to do with women?"

"That's what I figure," Hallam told him. "I don't know that for certain sure, though."

Lindsey nodded solemnly. "I've raised Rae to be a smart girl. Reckon I'll just have to trust her not to get taken in by some slick city boy."

"Don't think you've got to worry about that, from what I've seen of the gal." Hallam chuckled. "She's sharp as she can be, Mr. Lindsey. Anyway, I think Eliot's done a little growin' up when nobody was lookin'. Leastways I hope so."

"So do I." Lindsey met Hallam's level gaze. "So I can't talk you into hirin' on to catch those thieves?"

"Not for wages. I don't take more than one payin' job at a time. Just never got in the habit of it." Hallam grinned. "That don't mean I can't keep my eyes open. I'll be glad to do that, considerin' the way Smitty's been feedin' us."

"He is quite a hand in the cookshack, isn't he?"

"The best I've run across in a long time," Hallam said. "He been with you long?"

Lindsey shook his head. "Just a year or so. To hear him tell it, he's cooked at every big spread in Texas, though, from the King ranch to the Four Sixes."

"Well, those other places were fools to let him get away," Hallam said. He started toward the door. "I'd best get back to work. Don't like to leave Eliot on his own for too long. No tellin' what fool stunt him and Pecos and Teddy'll cook up if I do."

"I wouldn't have let them go after you the other night if I'd known what they were doing," Lindsey said, following Hallam to the door. "They were gone before any of us knew what was happenin', though."

"I can imagine." Hallam settled his hat on his head. "Be seein' you." He started toward the barn where Eliot, Pecos, and Teddy had gone.

As he walked, he thought about his decision to do some unofficial investigating for Wayne Lindsey. Somebody needed to look into the area's rustling problem, all right, considering Sheriff Bascomb's failure in stopping it. In the old days, it wouldn't have been unusual to send a Ranger into a situation like this. Hallam had no idea how the Rangers operated now, though.

He should have told Bascomb about his theory concerning the cattle thefts, he knew. He would have if the sheriff hadn't rubbed him the wrong way. It certainly made sense that the rustlers were trucking the stolen stock away. The state's biggest stockyards were in Fort Worth, but that was probably too close to risk disposing of the cattle there. But there were plenty of other places where stock sales were held. The thieves could go northwest to Wichita Falls or west to Abilene or south to Waco. Changing the brands wouldn't be much trouble, and neither would faking ownership papers. The profits from such a scheme wouldn't be spectacular, but they would be steady.

Maybe he *would* do some nosing around, Hallam thought. For the sake of Wayne Lindsey and his daughter Rae, and for old times' sake, too. It might be nice to break up a rustling ring again, even a modern-day one.

Smitty Wardell's chicken 'n' dumplings was as good as everything else he had prepared during the visit, and Hallam thoroughly enjoyed it at supper that night. He had polished off several helpings and was finishing a big bowl of peach cobbler when Wayne Lindsey stood up at the head of the table and said, "Folks, I've got an announcement to make."

Hallam glanced quickly at Eliot Tremaine, the thought flashing through his mind that maybe Eliot had gone and done something crazy like asking Rae to marry him. Well, Hallam supposed, that wouldn't be crazy, considering the fact that Rae was smart as a whip and pretty as a cactus rose, but Darby and Peter Tremaine might not see it that way. However, he could tell that Eliot was as puzzled about what Lindsey was going to say as any of the rest of them.

Rae had a smile on her face, though, as if she was in on the secret.

"Rae and I have been talkin'," Lindsey went on, "and we've decided that in appreciation for everything that our guests have done for us, we want to have a little get-together for them."

"A party?" Eliot asked, glancing at Rae with an eager smile on his face.

"A real fandango," Lindsey said. "We'll invite all the folks from around here, so that you can get to know them. Smitty's goin' to barbecue a steer for us, and we'll really put on the feedbag!"

"That sounds utterly fantastic!" Eliot said. He stood up. "I'm speaking for all of us, I know, but I feel confident in saying, Thank you, Mr. Lindsey . . ." He looked down at Rae, and his smile grew even broader. "And thank *you.*"

The girl was almost blushing, Hallam saw. Pecos and Teddy were enthusiastic in their thanks, too, and the other cowboys from Hollywood were also nodding and laughing. Even the Flying L hands looked happy at the idea of a celebration. Everyone around the table seemed pleased—except Hallam and Dan Armstrong.

Armstrong was glowering down at them from his usual spot at the other end of the table. Obviously, he resented the fuss Lindsey was making. Abruptly, he said, "What have they done except make trouble?"

Lindsey frowned. "I don't want any arguin', Dan," he said. "They helped us get those stolen cows back, just in case your memory's got short on you."

"I was in charge of that," Armstrong snapped. "You said so yourself, boss."

"I know that, but Hallam and those youngsters went along to help."

Silence had fallen around the table at Armstrong's objection. The foreman glared at Hallam and said, "Helped get in the way, that's what he did."

"That's not true!" Teddy protested. "We wouldn't even have found those rustlers if it hadn't been for Lucas."

Armstrong pushed his chair back and stood up. "You callin' me a liar, boy?" he grated.

"Dan, sit down and shut up," Lindsey ordered before Teddy could say anything else.

"No, sir." Armstrong pulled out the napkin he had stuck in his shirt and threw it down on the table. "You go ahead and have your party. But I won't be there."

He turned and stalked out of the dining room, letting the screen door slam behind him.

Lindsey shook his head and turned back toward the others after watching Armstrong go. "Sorry about the interruption, folks," he said. "Dan'll cool down later." The rancher grinned again. "I never knew anybody who could resist a big plate of barbecue and beans, and that includes Dan Armstrong!"

Everyone finished up the last few bites of the meal, then headed into the living room to continue discussing the upcoming party. Hallam caught Eliot Tremaine's arm and drew him back, waiting until the others had left the room.

"What is it, Hallam?" Eliot asked impatiently. "I want to go talk to Rae."

"Plenty of time for that. I just wanted to remind you that you didn't want a bunch of publicity about you bein' here, remember?"

"Oh, that." Eliot waved a hand negligently. "I thought that over earlier, and I've hit on a practical solution. We'll simply lie."

"Lie?" Hallam asked.

"Of course. If anyone asks, we'll just tell them that I've always been a cowboy and that by visiting here I'm returning to my roots, so to speak. That should fit in with whatever bunch of claptrap the studio comes up with for me. Besides, it'll make great press for that picture of my dad's if anything gets out about me helping to chase down a gang of rustlers."

"Maybe so, but I ain't sure . . ."

"Don't worry so much." Eliot punched Hallam on the

shoulder. "Don't tell me you've been in Hollywood for as long as you have and haven't yet grasped the principle on which the whole town is founded." He laughed. "It's all make-believe, Hallam, all of it. If the facts don't fit, make some up. Simple, isn't it?"

And then he turned, grinning, and went to look for Rae Lindsey.

FOURTEEN

The preparations for the party took a couple of days, during which time things on the ranch settled back into almost the same routine they had been in before the raid by the rustlers. There were a few subtle differences, though. For one thing, Hallam noticed, most of the Flying L hands seemed to have changed their attitude about the visitors from Hollywood. They were friendlier now, more inclined to hang around during Eliot Tremaine's training and practicing. Several of them offered tips to the young actor, concerning ways he could look more authentic for the camera.

Quite a few of the hands had seen the way Hallam, Eliot, Pecos, and Teddy had pitched right in to try to help capture the rustlers. They had seen the way Eliot had chased one of the thieves and tried to bring him down. Even though the effort had failed, it had taken courage. The cowboys who hadn't witnessed the scene had heard about it.

As far as they were concerned, Eliot and the others had risked their necks for the Flying L. That made the cowboys look at all the guests in a new light.

Dan Armstrong's attitude had not changed, however. Hallam kept an eye on the foreman. Armstrong was as surly as before, but at least he was keeping his distance from the visitors and not starting any fights.

Another difference in the atmosphere around the ranch was an undercurrent of excitement. The upcoming celebration was responsible for that, Hallam knew. Given the troubles that the Flying L and the other ranches in the area had been experiencing, it was likely that there hadn't been a party like this for quite a while. The word was getting around, and anticipation was growing.

Hallam was looking forward to it himself. If Eliot wasn't worried about any potential publicity, Hallam didn't see any point in bothering his own head about it.

The day of the party, Smitty Wardell started his preparations early. Several of the hands had dug a barbecue pit for him, and a good-sized steer had been picked out for slaughtering. The stove in the cookshack was working overtime as Smitty cooked beans and biscuits and cornbread. Once Smitty built his fire in the pit and started smoking the meat, there was nowhere anyone could go around the ranch house where the cooking smells weren't maddeningly delicious.

Hallam gave up trying to escape the aromas. The party was set for evening; as the afternoon went by, less and less work got done around the ranch. Everyone was in too festive a mood to worry about chores; the same mood had Eliot and Pecos and Teddy in an almost constant state of hilarity. Rae was usually with Eliot, and once Hallam saw the boy's arm go around her waist and hold her next to him. Rae didn't seem to mind.

Hallam wondered what was going to happen between them when it came time for Eliot to go back to Hollywood.

He was pondering on that as he sat on the back steps of the ranch house that afternoon, enjoying the warm sunshine, and the laughter coming from both the main house and the bunkhouse. Another sound caught his attention and made him sit up straighter. It was an engine, a loud one that was grumbling and roaring as it came closer to the house.

A truck rounded the corner from the driveway and rolled to a stop not far from the back door. The bed of the vehicle had a framework built over it, and the whole affair was covered with canvas that had been pulled tight. Hallam stood up as the truck stopped.

Two men stepped out of the cab. The driver was wearing work pants and a brown leather jacket. He had a short-billed cap pushed back on his thick, dark hair. The other man was in work clothes, too. He was burly and red-faced, with thinning blond hair. The driver strolled toward Hallam and grinned. "Howdy, Tex," he said in eastern accents. "This where the party's supposed to be?"

"That's right," Hallam told him. "Can I help you?"

The man jerked a thumb toward the truck. "We got a delivery to make. You think they want the stuff in the house or left out here?"

Hallam frowned. "What stuff?"

"The hooch, of course." The driver sounded surprised.

Hallam nodded slowly. "Why don't you just wait right here, and I'll go find out for you."

"Sure. Just don't take too long, okay? We got other places to go."

Hallam came down off the steps and started toward the barbecue pit and the cookshack. Smitty came out of the small building just before Hallam reached it. "Howdy, Lucas," he said. "What's up?"

Hallam inclined his head toward the house and the waiting truck. "You know anything about a load of bootleg whiskey?"

Smitty's eyes widened. "Damn it, they wasn't supposed to bring it right up in broad daylight like that!" he exclaimed. "Come on." He started quickly for the truck.

Hallam grinned as he fell in beside the cook, his long stride keeping up easily with the stubby-legged Smitty. "I reckon you do know a little about it, then."

"I should hope to smile. Can't have a party without a little likker." Smitty stopped in his tracks and glanced suspiciously over at Hallam. "You ain't one of them temperance types, are you?"

"Not hardly," Hallam chuckled, thinking about how freely the whiskey usually flowed back at the Waterhole. He preferred beer most of the time, but a shot of redeye every now and then didn't hurt.

"Good." Smitty started walking again.

"The bootleg stuff pretty easy to come by around here?" Hallam asked, curious.

"Oh, you got to know the right people, but it can be got," Smitty replied.

"Armstrong seems to have a steady supply, judging by that flask he carries around."

Smitty snorted. "Dan'd be better off if he slacked up a little. Too much booze muddles a man's mind. I didn't see nothin' wrong with havin' some on hand for the party, though. How about givin' me a hand takin' it down to the cookshack?"

"Sure," Hallam agreed.

As they came up to the truck, the driver looked at Smitty and asked, "You the guy who ordered this?"

"That's right. Say, how about drivin' on over there by the cookshack? Not as far to carry it that way."

"Whatever you say, Gramps." The driver and the other man got back into the truck, and its motor started up a grinding roar again.

"Glad Miss Rae ain't around right now," Smitty said as he and Hallam walked toward the cookshack again. "She don't hold much with drinkin'. She's all for Prohibition and a bunch of them other newfangled ideas. Be best if you don't say nothin' to her about this, Hallam."

"Don't intend to," Hallam said.

Within minutes, the two men from the truck had unloaded four wooden crates from the back of the vehicle and left them in front of the cookshack door. Evidently the bootleg liquor was already paid for, because the men got back in the truck and drove off while Hallam and Smitty carried the cases into the building. "Don't put 'em too near the stove," Smitty warned. "This here's potent stuff, from what I've heard. Don't want it blowin' the place up."

Hallam grinned. "Reckon that'd give us some right spectacular fireworks for the party, though."

Smitty looked aghast at him. "What a waste of good drinkin' likker that'd be!"

Hallam looked at the party and thought it was about as fine a celebration as he had ever seen.

Several tables had been carried out of the house and lined up in the front yard. They were loaded down with food until they almost seemed to sag from the weight. Beans and potato salad and greens, cornbread and biscuits, pitchers and pitchers of iced tea, pots of coffee, apple pies and chocolate cakes . . . and platter after platter of barbecued ribs and brisket. There was enough food there to feed a small army, Hallam decided, and that was just about what they had here on the Flying L tonight.

The cars and pickups had started arriving about dusk. All the families from every ranch and farm within fifty miles must have been invited, Hallam thought. The men were in their dusty black Sunday suits, and the women wore pretty cotton print dresses. There were kids everywhere, running and laughing under the oaks. Lanterns had been hung from the trees, and as night settled down, a warm yellow glow illuminated the grounds around the ranch house.

There was a warm feeling inside Hallam, too. He looked at the people who had come to this party—the cowboys, the farmers, the stockmen, the wives and children—and felt that he knew all of them, even though he had never seen most of them before. They were the kind of folks he had grown up with, hard-working and decent and one hell of a contrast to most of the people he ran into in Hollywood these days.

Lines formed on both sides of the tables as the party guests loaded their plates with the feast Smitty Wardell had prepared. Hallam found himself in line behind Pecos and Teddy and marveled at the heaps of food each of them claimed. Of course, his own plate was a little full, too, he thought.

Chairs had been brought out from the house as well, but Hallam found himself a good spot under one of the trees and sank down cross-legged. He leaned back against the tree trunk and dug in, discovering that the food tasted every bit as good as it looked and smelled.

The weather had cooperated. It was a warm evening with only a few high thin clouds floating in front of the stars. Hallam saw Eliot and Rae sitting nearby, eating and talking and laughing. Stone Riordan, Tall Cotton Jones, and Max Hilyard wandered over to join Hallam under the tree. A few minutes later, Jeff Grant, Harv Macklin, and Red Callahan also walked up. As Callahan sat down on the grass, he said, "I heard there's whiskey and beer back at the cookshack."

"The whiskey's there, all right," Hallam said. "I didn't know about the beer."

"Homemade, I reckon," Grant put in. "But there's a couple of kegs on hand."

Hallam grinned. "Reckon I'll have to look into that."

For a few minutes, all the men concentrated on their food, then Harv Macklin spoke up. "Mr. Lindsey asked us to put on a little show after while. We figured we'd do a few riding tricks and maybe put on a gunfight like they used to do in the Wild West shows."

Hallam nodded. "The folks ought to enjoy that, all right."

"Why don't you help us, Lucas?" Stone Riordan asked. "We could use another man for the gunfight."

"Sure," Hallam shrugged. "Just like bein' back on location in Bronson Canyon, ain't it?"

Hilyard laughed. "No cameras rollin' and no fancy-pants director yellin' cut."

"And no pay," Tall Cotton Jones pointed out.

Hilyard held up his plate. "What do you call this?"

The others chuckled. Hallam had to agree; a meal like this

was payment enough for any kind of performance they could put on.

When they were through eating, the men from Hollywood went into the house to prepare for the show. Hallam went into his room and dug his buckskins out of his warbag. The outfit was his own, not the property of some studio wardrobe department. The pants and the fringed shirt were old, but they had held up well to the years of wear. He put them on, then strapped the holstered Colt around his waist. The sheathed Bowie knife was tucked behind the shell belt on his left hip. He clapped his hat back on his head and went downstairs, looking every inch the frontiersman. The other cowboys emerged from the house within a few minutes, all of them in costume as well, although for most of them that consisted merely of shirts brighter and boots fancier than usual. Stone Riordan had on a fringed buckskin jacket, but it was much newer than Hallam's outfit and tan in color, in contrast to the faded brown of Hallam's attire. The trick-shot artist also wore a huge cream-colored Stetson. Two ivory-handled Colts rode in hand-tooled holsters on his hips.

"A get-up like that'd do old Bill Cody himself proud, Stone," Hallam told Riordan.

"I learned from the master." Riordan grinned.

Wayne Lindsey spotted them and came over. "Ready for the show?" the rancher asked.

"Let's get on with it," Riordan replied.

Smiling, Lindsey stepped up onto the long front porch and raised his voice. "Folks," he called, getting the attention of most of the party guests, "as some of you know, we've got visitors here on the Flying L, and this party is in honor of them. They hail from Hollywood, California, and they've been out there makin' the Western pictures that we all enjoy so much. So let's say howdy to 'em and make 'em feel welcome here in Texas!"

Applause swept through the crowd. Lindsey introduced the

men one by one, each man stepping forward and doffing his hat as his name was called. There was more applause each time. Hallam was the final one introduced, and as he swept off his hat and nodded to the crowd, he wondered where Eliot and Pecos and Teddy were. He was a little surprised they weren't getting in on this.

There was no time to worry about it, though. Several of the Flying L hands brought saddled horses from the corral, and Hallam and his friends mounted up to ride around the ranch house several times to the cheers of the partygoers. Red Callahan and Harv Macklin split off from the others then and started doing tricks, dismounting and remounting on the dead run, switching horses, stunts that looked impressive but weren't really too difficult.

While they were busy doing that, Hallam and the others split up into sides for the mock gunfight. Riordan had provided guns loaded with blanks for everyone except Hallam, who had his own revolver. He thumbed the blanks that Riordan handed him into the cylinder of the Colt, then snapped it shut. He and Riordan would be the heroes in this little performance, it was decided, and they would face down the villainous trio of Max Hilyard, Tall Cotton Jones, and Jeff Grant.

The men strolled into an open space in the front yard as Callahan and Macklin wound up their portion of the program. With his face contorted in a sinister squint, Hilyard lifted his voice and said, "I'm callin' you out, Riordan!"

"What do you mean by that, mister?" Riordan replied calmly.

"I'm sayin' you're a no-good, low-down, lily-livered skunk!" Hilyard shot back.

"And so's your partner!" Grant added.

"*And* your hoss," Tall Cotton Jones drawled.

Riordan's face set in angry lines. "Nobody talks about my hoss like that," he said in a cold voice. "Slap leather, gents!"

All five men went for their guns.

Hallam was trying hard not to laugh as he drew the Colt and commenced firing. The brief dialogue they had worked out had been ridiculous, of course, but as he glanced over at the watching crowd, he saw the rapt looks on their faces. These folks might live in Texas, but gunfights like this were a thing of the past now. They would always remember this, especially the kids.

The air was filled with the boom of shots, and a haze of powder smoke floated over the yard. Hallam and Riordan poured lead into Hilyard, Jones, and Grant—or so it appeared from the way the three men staggered back, discharging their guns into the ground or the sky, then clapping their hands to their chests and sprawling loosely. Hallam and Riordan solemnly regarded the bodies of their victims for a moment, and then Hallam holstered his Colt. Riordan went a different route, twirling both of his guns and flipping them into the air with grace and practiced ease before he caught them and slid them into their sheaths. The audience exploded with cheers and whistles and applause.

Hallam grinned, touched the brim of his hat in acknowledgment of the tribute, and strolled back into the crowd, still wearing the buckskins. The others did the same, and for several minutes all of them were busy shaking hands and talking to the other guests. The performance had been a hit, all right.

Some people were still eating and drinking, but others started to dance as the strains of music floated into the night. Three of the Flying L hands—Hallam remembered vaguely that one was named Doug—had climbed onto the porch carrying guitar, bass, and fiddle, and started playing. Hallam went back to his spot under one of the trees and sat down. His booted foot started tapping in time with the infectious rhythms.

A few minutes later, Eliot and Rae strolled up, both of

them smiling. "Hello, Hallam," Eliot said. "That was quite a show you and the others put on. Rae and I were watching from the back of the crowd. Tell me, is that what real gunfights were like?"

"Why, sure," Hallam said easily, memories flashing across his mind. Memories of pain and blood and dust and being so scared that your gut felt like it was going to push its way right out through your backbone . . . "That's what it was like, all right," he went on, still smiling.

"Well, it was very impressive," Rae said. "Thank you for entertaining. This was supposed to be a party for you and your friends, after all."

Hallam shook his head. "It's a party for everybody. We're just glad we could show the folks a good time." He looked back at Eliot. "You seen Pecos and Teddy? I noticed they weren't around durin' the performance. Sort of surprised me."

"The last time I saw them, they were heading down toward the cookshack and the bunkhouse," Eliot replied. "Say, I heard there's some liquor there as well. Perhaps they were going to get a drink."

Hallam frowned as he pushed himself to his feet, a little disturbed by what Eliot had told him. It wasn't that he didn't trust Pecos and Teddy to be able to hold their liquor, but it might be a good idea to keep an eye on them. Obviously Eliot was behaving himself tonight; the boy was too busy spending time with Rae to get into any trouble. "Think I'll take a *pasear* down there myself," Hallam mused. "Wouldn't mind tryin' some of that beer."

Rae hadn't said anything about the liquor, but he could tell from the look on her face that she wasn't thrilled with it being at the party. Hallam nodded to her and Eliot and started toward the cookshack.

The dancing was in full swing now, couples sashaying around all over the front yard while the trio of cowboys played. Most of the guests not dancing were standing on the sidelines clapping in time to the music. Everyone Hallam saw was grinning, having the time of their lives.

It had been quite a party, Hallam thought as he approached the cookshack—one of the most pleasant evenings he had spent in a long time, in fact.

"I'll kill you, you son-of-a-bitch!" somebody yelled in a loud, angry voice.

FIFTEEN

Hallam broke into a run as he recognized the voice of the man who had shouted. It was Teddy Spotted Horse, and from the thick, slurred sound of the words, Hallam figured the young Indian had been drinking.

There were quite a few men standing around the cookshack. It was darker here, since there were no lanterns hanging from the trees as there were in the yard, but enough light came from inside the shack and the nearby bunkhouse for Hallam to see what was going on. Two men were moving around in the center of the group, flinging punches at each other. Hallam heard the solid thud of fists on flesh.

One of the struggling figures was considerably larger than the other. Hallam knew the bigger man had to be Dan Armstrong. As he pounded up to the edge of the group watching the fight, he saw that he was right. Teddy and Armstrong were trading blows, and Teddy was coming off a definite second best.

Armstrong's fist smashed into Teddy's jaw as Hallam pushed his way past the spectators. The punch drove Teddy back several steps, and Armstrong was right after him, pouncing like a cat. He looped a blow into Teddy's stomach, doubling the smaller man over, then launched a right cross that would probably shatter Teddy's chin when it connected.

The punch never got there.

Hallam's left hand closed over Armstrong's wrist, stopping the blow cold. Armstrong grunted in surprise as Hallam jerked him around. The burly foreman threw a fist toward Hallam's head, but Hallam darted back, letting the punch zip harmlessly past him.

"Hold it!" he said sharply. "That's enough!"

"The hell it is!" Armstrong snapped, his breath rank with whiskey. "It won't take long to take care of you, old man, and then I'm goin' to beat the shit out of that red nigger there!"

As the last insult left his mouth, Armstrong lunged toward Hallam. Hallam was set to defend himself, poised on the balls of his feet with his fists clenched, but somebody grabbed Armstrong from behind, holding him back. "Stop it, you damn fool!" Smitty Wardell shouted. "Stop it, Armstrong!"

Armstrong was a good foot taller than the cook and considerably heavier, but Smitty was tenacious. He held on tightly, locking Armstrong's arms behind his back. Armstrong could have broken loose eventually, but after a moment of struggling against Smitty's grip, he abruptly stopped fighting. He stood there, his chest heaving.

Teddy pulled himself upright, holding one arm across his sore stomach. "Let him go!" he rapped. "Let the big bastard go! I can handle him—"

Hallam stepped over to the youngster and grabbed his arm. "Shut up!" Hallam growled. "Don't make this any worse than it already is, Teddy."

"But he was c-callin' me names, Lucas!" Teddy protested. "Said he was goin' to pound my redskin ass! I c-can't let him get away wi' that."

"You're drunk," Hallam said. "And he's a lot bigger than you. If Smitty and I let the two of you go, he'll kill you, you idiot."

Teddy lifted his head and glared toward Armstrong. "I'll

kill *him* if I ever get the chance," he snarled. His hat was gone and his raven hair was disheveled, and the way his eyes were burning with hatred at this moment, Hallam knew that he meant every word of the threat.

"Get that fool boy outta here!" Smitty snapped. "Get him outta here, Hallam, now!"

Hallam started pulling Teddy away from the cookshack. "Come on. Let's go pour some coffee down your gullet, son."

Suddenly, Teddy jerked out of Hallam's grasp. "Lemme 'lone! Tired of you playin' the mother h-hen, Hallam. By God, just lemme 'lone . . . Wanna be by myself . . ." He staggered off, pushing through the crowd of watching cowboys, and stalked unsteadily toward one of the barns.

Armstrong still hadn't moved during Teddy's tirade. Now he shook himself loose from Smitty. "Reckon it's all over," he said thickly. He glanced at Hallam. "'Less you want to dance a little, old-timer." He glared belligerently.

Hallam shook his head. "You'd better go somewhere and sober up, too," he said. He leveled a finger at Armstrong. "Just don't go lookin' for that boy. He's too drunk to fight anybody right now, let alone some big galoot like you."

Armstrong spat. "Hell, I ain't in the mood to thump him no more. Stinkin' drunk Indian. Ain't worth the effort."

"You stay away from him, you hear?" Smitty said.

"Sure, sure." Armstrong waved a hamlike hand. "Anyway, he's the one said he was goin' to *kill* me. I just wanted to hurt him a little."

A new voice said sharply, "What's this about killing?"

The crowd parted quickly as Sheriff Mart Bascomb strode up, followed by the big deputy, Roy. Several of the cowboys, who were holding mugs of beer or glasses of whiskey, started to drift away into the shadows as unobtrusively as possible.

"Just a little scuffle, Sheriff, that's all," Smitty said hurriedly. "Ain't that right, Dan?"

"Yeah," Armstrong agreed sullenly. "Nothin' to it, Sheriff."

"I thought you said somebody threatened to kill you."

"That was just whiskey talkin'," Smitty said. "The boy's an Indian, Sheriff. You know how they are about firewater."

Bascomb grunted. "So you've got bootleg whiskey out here, eh?"

Smitty grinned sheepishly. "We're right sorry, Sheriff. It's just that with the party and all, we didn't figger it'd hurt anything . . ."

Bascomb looked around, frowning balefully. Hallam met his eyes, but he was one of the few around the circle of people who did. He fully expected Bascomb to confiscate the liquor and arrest whoever was responsible for it being here. Knowing Bascomb, he'd probably blame Wayne Lindsey, Hallam thought. This had the makings of a real mess.

But then Bascomb surprised Hallam. He nodded abruptly and said, "All right, I won't haul anybody in this time. But I don't want to hear about anything like this going on around here again, you understand me, Wardell?"

Smitty bobbed his head, looking grateful. "You bet I do, Sheriff. We'll all be walkin' the straight an' narrow from now on, I guarantee it."

Bascomb grunted, obviously not believing a word of it. He turned and walked away, not looking back. The deputy trailed along behind him.

Smitty reached up and used the back of his hand to wipe the sweat off his forehead. "Whoo-ee!" he said in a low voice. "I thought we was all goin' off to the hoosegow for sure. Reckon maybe the sheriff decided he didn't have room for all of us in his jail."

"That was lucky, all right," Hallam agreed. He looked around; the crowd that had gathered to watch the fight between Armstrong and Teddy was breaking up rapidly, most of the men heading back to the front yard and the rest of the party. Armstrong was gone, too, Hallam noted. He hadn't noticed the big foreman leaving, and he wondered where

Armstrong had gotten to. He asked Smitty, "What was Bascomb doin' here, anyway? I didn't think he and Mr. Lindsey got along too well anymore after that rustlin' business."

"Reckon the boss was just tryin' to smooth some ruffled feathers by invitin' Bascomb," Smitty replied. "I hear tell the sheriff's got a soft spot for good barbecue."

Hallam grinned. "Don't we all. And that was a mighty good surroundin' you fixed up, Smitty."

"Thanks, Hallam. I just th'ow stuff together best I can."

Hallam laughed, then asked, "Have you seen Pecos? I heard him and Teddy was down here together."

"They was for a while, but then that young feller Pecos said he was goin' to find him a pretty gal to dance with. I reckon that's what he's doin'."

"Could be," Hallam nodded. "There was such a mob up there, I might've missed him."

Smitty was probably right. Pecos and Teddy were practically inseparable most of the time—until a pretty girl popped up.

"What started that ruckus between Teddy and Armstrong?" Hallam went on.

"Oh, hell, Dan just had a mite too much to drink. He was makin' cracks about Indians. The only good one's a dead one, things like that. Didn't mean nothin' by it, I don't reckon, but Teddy heard him and took exception. Can't really blame the boy, neither. Dan's got a lot of meanness bottled up inside him. He used to be interested in Miss Rae, you know."

Hallam frowned. "Nope, I didn't know that. Must've been a while back."

"It was. Before any of y'all came out here, so don't go blamin' that Tremaine feller for settin' Dan off. No, Miss Rae just weren't interested, and when Dan finally got up the gumption to go courtin', she told him so. He ain't been quite the same since. Reckon it's been just gnawin' away at him."

That would explain why Armstrong had been so hostile to them, all right, Hallam thought. It wasn't them, particularly; Armstrong was just mad at the world because a pretty girl hadn't done like he'd hoped. Hallam had seen men act like that plenty of times before. They got hurt by a gal and went looking for somebody else to take out the hurting on . . . Teddy had been handy because he was an outsider *and* an Indian.

"We'll only be here another few days," Hallam said. "Maybe we can keep the two of 'em apart for that long."

"Maybe," Smitty agreed.

"Reckon I'll go back up and watch the dancin'," Hallam said. He had lost any desire to sample the kegs of homemade beer inside the cookshack. He waved at Smitty and started back toward the front of the house.

It looked like everybody was still having a mighty fine time, and Hallam had to admit that the three cowpokes who were providing the music were pretty talented. Worry was still nagging at him, though, and it was hard to enjoy the party when he was wondering what had become of Teddy and where Dan Armstrong had gone after the fight. After twenty minutes or so, Hallam gave up and decided to try to find Teddy and make sure the youngster was still all right.

He had gotten only halfway to the barn when he heard the scream.

It was a girl's voice, and although Hallam couldn't be sure, he thought it was Rae Lindsey.

He broke into a run, his hand going to the Colt still holstered on his hip. He pulled it out, reaching behind him with his other hand to pluck some cartridges from the loops of the shell belt. These were live rounds, not blanks like those he had fired during the mock gunfight. With a dexterity born of years of experience, he slid the bullets into the cylinder of the Colt on the dead run. His bad leg was starting to hurt.

Two figures burst out of the barn, the one in the lead wearing a dress. It wasn't slowing her down much. The girl was Rae Lindsey, all right, and running just behind her was Eliot Tremaine.

Hallam slowed down and bit off a curse. It looked like Eliot had finally tried to get fresh with Rae. He figured the boy had lured her into the barn, then made advances toward her. Rae hadn't struck him as the type to scream and run, though. And she had sounded mighty upset—

"Hold it!" Hallam barked at the two of them. "What the devil's goin' on here?"

Eliot came to a stop, but Rae kept running, right into Hallam's arms. He caught her, and she gasped as she bounced off his broad chest. Hallam rumbled, "Take it easy, gal. What's wrong? This boy get a mite feisty on you?"

"There . . . there's a dead man in there!" Rae said breathlessly. "I stumbled on him and reached out to catch myself. My hand— Oh, God, it was so wet and sticky . . ."

Hallam had stiffened at her shocking statement. "Dead?" he echoed.

"That . . . that's right, Hallam," Eliot said. He was trying to catch his own breath and sounded almost as shaken as Rae. "In . . . in the barn . . ."

Hallam looked down and saw the dark stain on the girl's hand. There was blood on his shirt, too, where she had run into him. He gently put Rae behind him. "Take the girl and find her daddy," he told Eliot quietly but firmly. "The sheriff may still be somewhere around here, so you might ought to find him, too."

"What are you—"

"I'm goin' in there and take a look around," Hallam said.

He waited until Eliot had grasped Rae's arm and hurried away with her, then started toward the barn. The big double doors of the building gaped open blackly. No sound came from inside.

This wasn't the first time Hallam had walked into something not knowing exactly what he was going to find. He didn't expect anybody to shoot at him, but there was no way of knowing for sure. He held the pistol ready in front of him as he approached the barn, angling toward the doors and then going through them in a rush.

No shots rang out, and when he stopped to listen, he couldn't hear anything. Hallam stood there like that for long moments, then moved over toward the wall. He remembered that a lantern was usually kept there.

He found the lantern and lifted the chimney. There were matches in a little leather bag hung on a nail beside the lantern. It took only a second to scrape one of them to life and hold it to the wick, but he had to holster the gun in order to do so. His skin crawled a little as the flame took hold and grew. He lowered the chimney, the circle of light spreading.

Hallam turned, lifting the lantern. The glow showed him what seemed to be an empty barn at first. Hay was stored here, but no animals were kept in the stalls. Come to think of it, he realized, this was the barn Teddy had been heading toward after the fight.

Hallam spotted the dark shape on the ground, sprawled on the far side of the barn. He put his free hand back on the butt of the Colt and started walking slowly toward the fallen figure, not sure who he was going to see when he got there.

At first he had been afraid that the dead man was Teddy, but now he could see that the body was too big. Hallam grimaced. There was only one person it could be.

Hallam stopped beside Dan Armstrong's body, holding the light up. Armstrong was on his back, arms spread out, a surprised look on his face. There was a knife in his chest, plunged into his body all the way to the hilt. The rope-wrapped handle of the weapon stood straight up from the blood-sodden shirt.

There was no point in it, but Hallam knelt beside the body anyway and reached out to try to find a pulse in Armstrong's neck. There wasn't one, of course.

That's what he was doing when footsteps sounded behind him and a harsh voice said, "Don't move or I'll shoot, mister."

SIXTEEN

"That you, Roy?" Hallam asked, recognizing the deputy's voice. He stayed where he was, not even lifting his fingers from the rapidly cooling flesh of Dan Armstrong's throat.

"Just don't try anything." Roy sounded nervous. Hallam imagined the young man was holding a gun on him, and the last thing he wanted to do now was spook him.

More footsteps sounded. Mart Bascomb's acerbic tones said, "What the hell? Put that pistol down, Roy. Hallam didn't do this."

Hallam thought it might be safe to move again, so he stood up slowly and turned around, still being careful not to do anything too sudden-like. He saw Bascomb and Roy standing just inside the barn. Wayne Lindsey hurried in behind them, took one look over their shoulders, and said in a choked voice, "Oh, my Lord . . ."

"I reckon he's dead," Bascomb said, squinting at Armstrong.

"He's dead, all right," Hallam confirmed.

Bascomb nodded and stuck his hands in the pockets of his uniform pants, not looking particularly excited. "Miss Lindsey and that Tremaine fella came running up and said they'd found a dead body and that you were going to check on it, Hallam. Sort of exceeding your authority again, aren't you? Dead bodies are—"

"Are the business of the sheriff's office," Hallam cut in. "I know. I've heard the speech before."

Bascomb's pinched face tightened even more. He gestured at the gun on Hallam's hip. "That thing loaded?"

Hallam nodded. "Wouldn't do much good if it wasn't."

"Take it out with your left hand and give it to Roy. Do it slow."

Hallam hated to hand over his gun, but arguing wouldn't do any good. Bascomb had a right to ask for it, especially while he was conducting an investigation. Hallam took out the Colt, holding it by the barrel, and stepped forward to give it to the deputy.

"Trigger's a mite sensitive," he warned. "You'd best be careful."

"Unload it," Bascomb snapped to Roy. He walked forward, closer to Hallam and the body. He strode right up to Armstrong, Roy close behind him and fumbling with the pistol.

Hallam tensed and started to lift his hand, his mouth opening to say something. He had seen something on the ground next to the body, just a glimpse, an instant's flash of something white mixed in with the dirt of the barn floor. But then it was gone, lost in the shuffling of feet as Bascomb and Roy paced around the corpse.

Bascomb stopped and looked up, his eyes meeting Hallam's. "Where's that damned Indian?" he asked.

Hallam frowned. He gestured at Armstrong and said sharply, "Now you're not goin' to try to blame this on Teddy, are you?"

"I heard Armstrong say the Indian threatened to kill him," Bascomb replied. "You were there, Hallam. Did it happen or not?"

Hallam hesitated. There was no use denying it. Plenty of witnesses had heard Teddy promise to kill Armstrong if he got the chance. There had been at least a dozen men gathered around at the time. Hallam nodded. "He said it, all right. But it didn't mean nothin'. Teddy was just drunk and mad—"

"Drunk and mad enough to kill," Bascomb grated. He turned to Roy. "Go call the office and get some more men out here. Then find that Indian and bring him to me."

Roy nodded. He had stuck Hallam's revolver, unloaded now, behind his belt. "Sure thing, Sheriff." He hurried off, pushing roughly past Lindsey.

More men were crowding into the barn now. Hallam saw Smitty Wardell and several of the Flying L hands, along with Max Hilyard and Tall Cotton Jones. Hilyard and Tall Cotton both wore bleak expressions. They had heard what Bascomb had said about Teddy, Hallam knew. Like all the other Hollywood cowboys, they liked Teddy Spotted Horse, even if he and Pecos could be exasperating at times.

It was just damned hard to believe that one of their bunch could be a killer.

"See here, Sheriff," Hilyard said, stepping forward. "I heard that Teddy and this here Armstrong feller had quite a ruckus tonight. If Teddy did this, then it was because Armstrong came after him again. It had to be self-defense."

That same thought had occurred to Hallam. He didn't know whether or not to hope it was true.

"We'll see," Bascomb said. He sat on his haunches next to Armstrong's body and studied the foreman's contorted face, then shook his head. "Don't look like they was fighting to me. Looks more like somebody took Armstrong by surprise. Jumped him without warning and stuck that knife in him. That's the way it looks to me."

Hallam felt a knot of coldness in his belly. He could tell by Bascomb's voice that the sheriff was convinced the killing hadn't been self-defense. And Bascomb was the type of man whose mind wasn't easily changed once he had made it up.

There was a commotion at the entrance of the barn, and

several of the cowboys stepped aside hurriedly. Teddy Spotted Horse came staggering through the gap. His unsteady pace wasn't the result of drinking this time, Hallam saw. Instead, he had been pushed roughly into the barn by Roy.

"Here's the Indian, Sheriff," the deputy said proudly. "Found him wandering around out behind the corrals. He didn't give me too much trouble."

Hallam saw a scrape on Teddy's cheek and a slight swelling on his forehead. Chances were, Roy had slapped Teddy around a little before bringing him to the barn. Hallam tried to rein in the surge of anger that he felt. Blowing up now wouldn't do Teddy or anybody else any good.

"What is this?" Teddy demanded. "What's this crazy deputy want? I didn't do anything—"

He stopped abruptly as his gaze fell on Armstrong's bloody corpse.

Teddy stared silently at the body for a moment, then swallowed. "What . . . what the hell . . . ?"

Bascomb straightened, put his hands on his hips, and squinted at Teddy. "Why'd you kill him?" he demanded.

"Kill him?" Teddy echoed weakly. He seemed completely sober now, just frightened out of his wits. "I . . . I didn't kill anybody."

"Oh, hell," Bascomb said impatiently. "Half the men here heard you threaten Armstrong, boy. Might as well just confess and get it over with."

"But . . . but I didn't—"

Roy stepped up behind him and slammed a hand into his back. "Shut up, Indian," he said. "Shut up and answer the sheriff."

Teddy cast a befuddled glance back at Roy, then looked at Bascomb again. He didn't seem to want to look at Armstrong anymore, and Hallam could understand that. "I swear I didn't do this," Teddy said in a voice so low that Hallam could barely hear him.

Bascomb shook his head in disgust. "I know damn well you did. You got liquored up and stabbed this poor fella like some sort of savage—"

Hallam saw the warning flare in Teddy's eyes and started to leap forward, but he was too late. Teddy lunged at Bascomb, throwing himself across Armstrong's sprawled body. Teddy swung, his fist cracking into Bascomb's nose.

Bascomb howled as blood spurted. He fell back, clutching at his injured nose. Roy reacted a second later, his hand dropping toward his holstered pistol. Everyone there knew what was going to happen next. Roy was going to jerk his gun out and shoot Teddy in the back for resisting arrest.

Hallam got there first.

He slammed into Roy from the side, knocking him off balance. Hallam moved past the deputy, a knobby fist lashing out and smacking into the back of Teddy's neck, spilling him to the floor of the barn. Hallam dropped on top of him, holding him down and at the same time protecting him. Teddy was still struggling feebly, and Hallam hissed into his ear, "Be still, damn it! They'll kill you if you put up any more fight!"

Teddy stiffened for a moment, then went limp as the sense of Hallam's words penetrated his stunned brain. Hallam stayed where he was as Bascomb held a handkerchief to his bloodied nose and screamed past it, "Cuff him! Cuff the redskinned son-of-a-bitch and throw him in the car. Broke my nose, the bastard did!"

Roy put the barrel of his gun next to Hallam's head and pulled back the hammer. "Get off of him," he ordered, his voice shaking with anger.

Hallam looked up without moving. "This boy had better get to jail safe and sound," he said. He switched his gaze to Bascomb, his eyes boring in on the sheriff's. "He'd damn well better."

Bascomb made a curt gesture with the hand that wasn't

holding the bloody handkerchief. "All right, all right," he rasped. "Put your gun up, Roy, and get the cuffs on that damned Indian."

Hallam stood up slowly as the deputy holstered his pistol again. He helped Teddy to his feet and kept a hand on his shoulder to support him as Roy jerked Teddy's hands behind his back and slapped a pair of cuffs on his wrists.

"Come on," Roy growled, pulling Teddy away from Hallam and shoving him toward the door of the barn.

"Hold on," Hallam said. "Teddy, you promise me you didn't have anything to do with this?"

Teddy looked back over his shoulder at Hallam, his expression a mixture of fear and defiance. "I swear I didn't, Lucas."

Hallam nodded. "Then you just sit tight. We'll get you a lawyer and get to the bottom of this."

"You won't do anything, Hallam," Bascomb said, pushing past him, "except stay the hell out of my way. This is none of your business."

"Boy's entitled to a lawyer, Mart," Lindsey pointed out.

"You find one who's foolish enough to take the case, you just send him on down to the jail," Bascomb replied. He stalked out after Teddy and Roy.

Hallam followed along behind, just to make sure that Teddy made it to the sheriff's car safely. He didn't like the idea of the youngster being alone with Bascomb and Roy during the time it would take to drive back to Fort Worth, but there was nothing he could do about it.

If anything did happen and Teddy wound up hurt or dead, Hallam vowed, he would pull this whole county down around Mart Bascomb's ears.

Lindsey, Hilyard, and Tall Cotton Jones came up beside Hallam. Hilyard shook his head and said, "Damn. It just don't figger. I know Teddy can be a hothead sometimes, but he wouldn't hurt nobody, not on purpose."

"I don't know what to think," Lindsey said. "I liked that

boy, I really did. But my foreman's been killed. I reckon I owe it to Dan to hope that whoever killed him is brought to justice."

"Whoever," Hallam repeated. "It sure as hell wasn't Teddy, Mr. Lindsey. He wouldn't lie to me."

"You sound mighty sure of that."

"I am," Hallam said. He looked over at Lindsey. "You know where I can get hold of a lawyer tonight?"

"Matter of fact, I do. There's a good one here at the party. Name's Colonel Gilliam. I'll find him for you."

Everyone began drifting back toward the party, which was still in full swing. Some of the guests had heard rumors of trouble down at the barn, but they weren't letting that spoil their celebration.

Lindsey found the lawyer at one of the tables, filling up his plate with what, considering how long the party had been going on, had to be his third or fourth helping. Colonel Marcus Gilliam didn't show the effects of his prodigious appetite, though. He was rail-thin, with a full head of white hair and a drooping white moustache. He reminded Hallam a little of old Sam Clemens.

"Murder, you say?" he exclaimed in a resonant voice when Lindsey told him what had happened. "I'd be glad to talk to the boy and discuss representing him. We sure as hell won't let Mart Bascomb railroad him!"

"I thought that's what you'd say, Colonel," Lindsey replied. "Mart was taking the youngster down to Fort Worth, and Mr. Hallam here was a little worried that something might happen on the way."

"Hallam?" Colonel Gilliam turned toward Hallam, peering intently at him in the lantern light. "Not Lucas Hallam?"

"That's right," Hallam said. "Have we met, Colonel?"

"I was with Roosevelt down in San Antonio when he was gathering the Rough Riders. I remember how you helped him out during the business with that Mexican girl and her homicidal brothers and that lost treasure."

Hallam had to grin at the memory, but he waved it off. "Long time ago, Colonel. And we've got fresh worries now."

"Indeed. Well, I shall proceed immediately to the county lockup and insist that I be allowed to see my client."

"You sound mighty sure you're going to take the case," Hallam said.

"If the boy is your friend, sir, and you believe in him, then so do I."

Hallam extended his hand. "Thank you, Colonel. I really appreciate it."

"I must warn you, however," Gilliam said as he shook hands with Hallam. "My services do not come cheap."

"Don't worry about that. We're with one of the biggest movin'-picture studios in Hollywood. I'll just wire the boss out there to send you a retainer."

"Very well." With a nod, Colonel Gilliam hurried away toward where the cars were parked.

Hallam felt a little better now that the matter of a lawyer was settled. He was sure that the colonel would do everything he could for Teddy.

That wouldn't mean much, though, unless somebody could come up with something that would lead the way to the real killer. There wasn't much evidence in this case, and Hallam had to admit that what there was pointed straight to Teddy Spotted Horse. And Bascomb wasn't likely to do much digging around looking for any other solution. As far as the sheriff was concerned, he already had the killer in custody.

If anybody was going to find out who had really murdered Dan Armstrong, Hallam knew, it would have to be him.

"Sure glad I won't be there to see it when Mr. Darby gets that wire, Lucas," Hilyard commented. "He ain't goin' to be too happy when he finds out Teddy's in jail. Murder sure is a nasty business."

"Yep," Hallam said, thinking about the way killing sometimes seemed to follow him around, even all the way to Texas. "It sure is."

SEVENTEEN

"Oh, I admit it freely," Eliot Tremaine said. "I took Rae into that barn intending to kiss her. I certainly never thought we'd stumble over a dead body instead." He smiled, but there was little humor in his expression. "If I had, we'd have gone somewhere else."

Hallam was sitting in one of the armchairs in the living room of the Flying L ranch house. Eliot was across from him on the sofa, and the other Hollywood cowboys were scattered around the room. Pecos was sunk down in another of the armchairs, looking particularly miserable; his best friend was in the worst trouble of his life, and when it happened, Pecos had been off dancing with one of the local girls. Wayne Lindsey stood beside the fireplace. Rae had gone upstairs to try to sleep, even though she had doubted she would be able to.

The party had been over for a long time, but none of the men in this room felt like turning in just yet.

Lindsey said to Eliot, "I reckon I ought to ask you if your intentions toward my daughter are honorable, son."

Eliot looked up and met the rancher's gaze. He hesitated, then finally said, "As unusual as it may sound to those who know me, sir, I . . . believe they are. I think a great deal of Rae."

"They'd better be, because I think a lot of her, too. I don't want to see her hurt. She's had enough problems the last few months, what with the rustlin' and the ranch strugglin' and now— Well, this business with Armstrong has got her mighty upset."

"I know," Eliot said. "I'd like to do anything I can to help."

Hallam put his hands on the arms of the chair and pushed himself to his feet. "Think I'll take a walk," he said.

"If you're plannin' on lookin' around in the barn, the sheriff left a deputy there to keep everybody out," Lindsey told him. "Said he didn't want anybody disturbin' the scene of the crime."

"He wasn't that careful when him and that feller Roy were stompin' around out there earlier," Hallam grunted. "I reckon I already saw everything there was to see, though. Wasn't anything except Armstrong's body and that knife, and you said that was kept in the tack room and used for cuttin' leather to mend harness."

Lindsey nodded. "That's right. The door to the tack room wasn't locked, and it was only a few feet from where Dan was. Anybody could've reached in there and got that knife."

"Well, maybe the night air'll help me think," Hallam said. He was still wearing the buckskins, and he took his battered hat from the hook on the wall as he went to the door. He was afraid that some of the others might volunteer to come with him, but evidently all of them realized that he wanted to be alone right now. There were a lot of things to turn over in his head, and he did that best when he was by himself.

The other cowboys stayed where they were as Hallam walked outside. He settled the hat on his head, hooked his thumbs in the belt around his waist, and stepped down off the porch. He frowned as he ambled toward the corrals.

He couldn't remember how many dead men he had seen over the years, but there had been a whole passel of them, that was for sure. Quite a few of them he had made that way—too many of them, he thought. He lifted a hand, looked at it in the moonlight. It just looked like a hand, worn some by age, with long, strong fingers and knobby knuckles. You couldn't even see all the blood on it. . . .

Hallam shook his head. He hadn't been responsible for Dan Armstrong's death, and he would have wagered anything that Teddy wasn't, either. Thinking about all the dead men in the past wouldn't help him figure out who had killed this one.

He spotted the deputy lounging in the entrance to the barn. The body was long gone, of course, carried off to the morgue down in Fort Worth by some of Bascomb's men.

Hallam tried to line things up in his brain. The first thing he would have to do in the morning was talk to Teddy, or if Bascomb wouldn't allow that, to Colonel Gilliam. He wanted to find out exactly where Teddy had gone and what he had done after the brief fight with Armstrong. Once he had done that, he could start trying to find the answer to the most important question.

If Teddy hadn't killed Armstrong, then who had? The big foreman had been an unpleasant cuss, but that wasn't reason enough for somebody to kill him. Just what *had* Armstrong done that was bad enough for somebody to want him dead?

Hallam thought about that question for a long time before he finally went back to the house and tried to sleep.

Hallam wasn't surprised when the deputy at the Tarrant County jail refused to let him see Teddy. Sheriff Bascomb had left strict orders, the uniformed man told him, that no one was to be allowed to see the prisoner except his lawyer.

"And if the sheriff didn't know that Colonel Gilliam would put up a howl about it, I don't think he'd even let *him* in," the deputy went on. "Not to see a murderer like that."

"The boy's been accused," Hallam said heavily. "He ain't been convicted."

The deputy shrugged. "Matter of time."

Hallam grimaced and turned to find his way back out of the jail. The courthouse was next door, and beyond that, on the corner of Belknap and Main streets, was the building where Colonel Gilliam had his office.

Wayne Lindsey had agreed right away when Hallam asked for the loan of a vehicle that morning. He had told Hallam to take the same pickup Rae had used to pick them up at the Texas & Pacific station. That had been less than two weeks earlier, but it seemed like longer to Hallam. A hell of a lot had happened since they arrived in Fort Worth.

Pecos had followed him out of the house. Hallam had turned to look at him and ask, "Where do you think you're goin'?"

"With you, of course. I've got to see Teddy and make sure he's all right, and there's a thing or two I want to tell that damn-fool sheriff."

Hallam shook his head firmly. "You're not goin' anywhere. You'd just fly off the handle and get us all in more trouble than we already are."

"But Lucas—"

"Stay here," Hallam had told him. "I'll see that Teddy's all right, and I'll do everything I can for him." He reached out and squeezed the young cowboy's shoulder. "Hell, you're the one who keeps tellin' everybody I'm some sort of detective. Let me go do some detectin'."

"All right, Lucas." Pecos had finally nodded, grudgingly. "But if I can do anything to help—"

"I'll let you know," Hallam promised.

He hadn't had any trouble retracing the route Rae had taken from the city to the ranch. He had always had a good head for directions. The highway had eventually turned into Belknap Street, and he had followed it right downtown. Finding the massive courthouse was easy enough, since it sat up on the bluff overlooking the Trinity, and the jail was beside it.

The visit hadn't done him any good so far, though.

Fort Worth had changed some since he had been down-town last, he thought now as he walked toward Gilliam's office. Some folks still called it Panther City because some wit over in Dallas—thirty miles to the east in distance and a few hundred in snobbishness and phony sophistication—had once said Fort Worth was such a sleepy place that a panther had been spotted dozing in the middle of Main Street. Any panther foolish enough to venture onto Main Street now would have been run down in a hurry by the multitude of flivvers and roadsters and pickups that rattled and bounced along the bricks. The sidewalks were full of people, too, and Hallam didn't see many cowboy hats anymore. The place was a full-blown city now.

Lindsey had given him the address of Colonel Gilliam's office, and Hallam spotted the colonel's name painted on the front window of a two-story brick building. He went inside, gave his name to a pretty receptionist, and was shown right away into a large room lined with shelves full of lawbooks. There was a long table in the middle of the room, and Gilliam was seated at it, a thick volume open in front of him. His coat was off, and his string tie was loose around his skinny neck.

"Morning, Hallam," the colonel said as he closed the book. "I suppose you've come to see about your young friend."

Hallam nodded. "That's right. They wouldn't let me see him over at the jail. Do you know if he's still okay?"

"I saw him this morning, and he appeared to be fine—at least physically. A few bruises, but nothing serious. They haven't taken the rubber hose to him, if that's what you're worried about. The lad seems very despondent, however." Gilliam snorted. "Can't say as I blame him. He's in quite a fix."

Hallam pulled out a chair and sat down opposite the colonel. "Did he tell you what he was doin' last night when Armstrong was killed?"

• 169 •

"He claims he was simply walking around the ranch trying to sober up and cool off, as you instructed him to do. After he left the area where the skirmish with Armstrong took place, he says he went into that barn but proceeded directly through it, exiting by a rear door. From there he walked past the corrals, looking at the horses, and strolled around nearby until that deputy spotted him. That behemoth roughed him up a bit, by the way. I'd bring charges against him if I thought it would do any good."

Hallam shook his head. "Don't reckon it would. I figured Roy got in a few licks before he brought Teddy back to the barn. What do you make of the boy's story, sir?"

The colonel shrugged. "It's certainly possible that everything happened exactly as young Spotted Horse said that it did. The problem is, there's no way of proving it. He says he didn't run into anyone while he was walking around, and I'm afraid we can't call as witnesses the horses that were in the corrals." Gilliam shoved the lawbook aside, revealing his frustration for a moment. "He simply has no alibi, and the sheriff has plenty of witnesses who can testify that Teddy threatened to kill Armstrong. I must admit, I am momentarily at a loss as to how to proceed. Never fear, though. I shall come up with a defense that will ultimately win the day."

"I know you'll do your best, Colonel." Hallam stood up. "Reckon I'll do a little nosin' around of my own, though."

Gilliam lifted a bushy white eyebrow. "I'm told that you're something of a detective out in Hollywood, Hallam. Anything you can discover about this case will surely help in the boy's defense."

"I'll be in touch." Hallam quickly asked the lawyer about his fee, then nodded and asked where the nearest Western Union office was.

It was a few blocks away. Hallam would have enjoyed the walk under other circumstances. There was too much on his mind to properly appreciate the way the town had grown, though. He went into the telegraph office, picked up a message blank at the counter, and printed out the telegram he wanted to send to J. Frederick Darby. It was simple enough: TEDDY JAILED FOR MURDER STOP INNOCENT STOP NEED $500 FOR LAWYER STOP HALLAM.

"Are you going to wait for a reply, sir?" the clerk asked him after scanning the message.

"Guess I'd better," Hallam grunted. The delay would eat at him, he knew, but he needed to make sure that Darby came through with the money.

The answer took just under an hour to arrive. Hallam spent that time staring out the window of the telegraph office at the sidewalk outside, not really seeing the passersby. He was still mulling over what he knew about this case. He thought he had an idea where to start. It was farfetched, he knew, but he sure as hell hadn't come up with anything more likely yet.

"Here's your reply, sir," the clerk called to him, and Hallam went over to the window to take the slip of yellow paper.

DONE STOP RETURN IMMEDIATELY WITH TREMAINE STOP DARBY.

Hallam crumpled the message. He wasn't going anywhere, not with Teddy stuck in jail. Eliot could do what he wanted to, but Hallam had a suspicion that he wouldn't want to go back to Hollywood just yet, either.

"How would you like that money, sir?" the clerk asked.

"Can you make out a draft to Colonel Marcus Gilliam and have it delivered to his office?"

"Certainly."

Hallam scribbled out a note for Gilliam to go with the retainer and gave that to the clerk to be delivered as well. Then he stalked out of the office, impatience making his strides even longer than usual.

As he drove north out of Fort Worth on the highway,

Hallam thought about the reasons folks got killed. There were really only a few—love, money, fear, revenge. He didn't know of anybody who had a grudge against Armstrong other than Teddy, so that let out revenge. And he couldn't imagine anyone killing Armstrong over love, either. The man had tried to court Rae Lindsey, but that was over and done with. As for fear, he didn't know of anyone who had a reason to be afraid of Armstrong. The man had been a bully, but he had seemed pretty selective in his targets. He hadn't bothered anyone in the time Hallam had known him—again, except Teddy.

That left the strongest reason of all—money.

And the only thing Hallam could see that Armstrong could have been mixed up in was the rustling that had been plaguing this part of the country for months.

Once that thought had occurred to him the night before, Hallam had spent quite a while going over every event related to the cattle thefts, right from the moment Armstrong had ridden in to announce that the herd in the north pasture was gone. That was a little funny by itself, Hallam could see now. It had probably still been light when Armstrong and the hands with him had discovered the missing cows. The sensible thing would have been to follow the trail right then and there. All of the cowboys had been armed with Winchesters; they carried the rifles as a matter of course on the range, to take care of snakes and other varmints. It had been Armstrong's decision to return to the ranch house first, thus delaying the pursuit.

Of course, it was reasonable enough that the foreman might have wanted to let Lindsey and Rae know what was going on, Hallam supposed. He didn't want to read too much into what might have been simply bad judgment.

Armstrong had been opposed to him going along, though, and he had refused to take Hallam's suggestion about circling around the roughest part of the trail. Again, that could have been due simply to the man's pride . . . or it might have meant that Armstrong didn't want any outsiders along as witnesses when he lost the trail of the rustlers.

Which was exactly what had happened. Teddy's boastful statement had been right, even though Hallam didn't like to admit it. They wouldn't have caught up with the rustlers if Hallam hadn't been along to locate the trail again several times during the long chase.

All right, Hallam thought. Maybe Armstrong *was* working with the rustlers. He could have passed the word to them which pastures to hit and when to make their raids. It wouldn't be the first time a gang of crooks had had an inside man, not by a long shot. But if that was the case, how had it led to somebody sticking a knife into Armstrong?

The first thing he had to do, Hallam knew, was find some proof that Armstrong had been tied in with the rustlers. If he could do that, the trail might lead him straight to the killer—if he was lucky.

He kept driving north, passing right by the turnoff that led to the Flying L.

A little after noon, he reached the town of Denton and stopped long enough for a steak at a roadside diner before turning southwest toward Decatur. The concrete highway was narrow and winding, but there was quite a bit of traffic on it. Hallam kept his eyes open, looking for any landmarks that might be familiar.

After an hour or so, he spotted some hills to his left that he thought he recognized. If he was right, those rugged slopes were the ones he and Armstrong and the others had ridden down from as they caught up to the rustlers. He was looking at them from a different angle now, and he realized that, in just a few hours in the pickup, he had circled the area that had taken them all night and part of a day to cover on horseback.

He almost missed seeing the dirt road that turned off to the left. He had to hit the pickup's brakes and throw it into reverse, backing up until he could turn onto the narrow track. As he did, he noticed a long, low building about fifty yards up the highway, on the same side as the road. It had a sign on the roof, but he couldn't read it from where he was.

Hallam drove a hundred yards or so down the dirt road, until he was fairly sure that it was indeed the road that he had seen snaking through the valley where they had caught up with the rustlers. He pulled the pickup over to the side, onto a level patch of ground underneath some trees, and turned off the engine.

It was quiet here, Hallam discovered as he stepped down from the truck. There was the sound of traffic from the highway, but that was all.

He started walking down the road, looking intently at both sides of it as well as at the dirt surface itself. He had gone about a quarter of a mile when he came to a spot where the road widened. Off to one side, at the edge of the dirt, were tire tracks.

Hallam knelt beside them, glad that it had been dry around here lately. The marks were plain to see in the dust. It was evident from them that several trucks had been parked here on the side of the road, then driven off toward the highway. Hallam wasn't sure how old the tracks were, but he could tell they hadn't been made in the last day or so.

The trucks that had been waiting for the rustlers to arrive with the stolen stock? Hallam thought it was pretty damn likely. He became even more sure when he stepped across the bar ditch into the field next to the road and found horse tracks, coming from different directions but all leading toward the spot where the trucks had been waiting.

It made sense. The rustlers had split up during the fight with the cowboys from the Flying L, then rendezvoused here. The original plan would have called for them to load the cattle onto the trucks, but under the circumstances, Hallam imagined, they had piled their horses on instead and made their getaway in a hurry, just in case any of the posse had come after them.

He climbed back onto the road and stood there for a moment studying the truck tracks again. No one had come along here during the time Hallam had been cutting sign, but it was obvious that the road was well enough traveled to have wiped out any possibility of following the tracks. He could tell that they had started off toward the highway, but that was all. From there they could have gone in any direction.

He walked slowly back to the spot where he had left Lindsey's pickup. He had confirmed his theory about how the rustlers were operating, he thought, but that was all he had accomplished. There was nothing here to tie Dan Armstrong in with the rustling ring.

As he drove toward the highway again, Hallam tried to decide what to do next. He had to stop to wait on the traffic for a moment before pulling out onto the concrete roadway again, and as he did, his eye fell on the rather ramshackle building nearby.

It was a roadhouse, from the looks of it, a long frame building with several cars parked on the small gravel lot in front of it. The walk had made Hallam a little hot and thirsty, and some cold soda pop would taste good about now. He turned the pick-up in that direction.

The sign on the roof said "Zeke's Place," Hallam saw as he pulled into the parking lot. The building could have used a coat of paint, and some of the shingles were coming off the roof. Hallam cut the engine, stepped out of the truck, slammed the door shut. He didn't care what the place looked like as long as they had something cold and wet to drink.

He was walking toward the door when he noticed the nose of a truck sticking out from behind the far end of the building.

Hallam paused, thinking that he couldn't possibly be that lucky. It wouldn't hurt to take a look, though. Quickly, he walked to the corner of the roadhouse and peered around it.

The truck parked there was big enough to haul cattle in, all right. The back of it was covered with canvas. Hallam moved past the cab and went to the rear of the truck. There were flaps of canvas over the opening there, too, but he moved one of them aside enough to see inside. There was a slatted board gate behind the canvas, and the sides were constructed the same way. Through the gaps in the gate, he could see the bed of the truck was clean—maybe a little too clean, as if it had recently been washed out. Hallam put his nose close to the opening and sniffed.

Some odors didn't wash out well. Hallam nodded. There had been cattle in this truck, all right.

"Hey! Get away from there, mister!"

Hallam straightened and looked past the truck, toward the corner of the building. Two men had stepped around it, and now they were coming toward him, angry expressions on their faces. Both of them wore range clothes and Stetsons, and the outfits looked like they had had a lot of wear. One of the men demanded, "What are you doing messing around with that truck?"

"Just takin' a look," Hallam said coolly. "It belong to you?"

"No, but we don't like to see people messing around with other people's stuff," the second man said. Hallam could tell that he was the one who had told him to get away from the truck.

The two men looked alike, not the way brothers resemble each other but rather the way men in the same business look. One had a brown moustache while the other was clean-shaven, but they were both unmistakably ranch hands, at least at first glance. Hallam dropped his gaze to their hands and wasn't so sure. The palms seemed a little soft for men who worked with horses and cattle.

Maybe they drove trucks instead, Hallam thought. Maybe they were lying about this one not belonging to them.

He held up his hands in a conciliatory gesture. "Didn't mean to cause any trouble, gents," he said. "I've been thinkin'

• 176 •

about buyin' a truck, and I was just lookin' this one over. You got any idea where I might could find the owner?"

The one with the moustache shook his head. "Nope. None of our business and none of yours, either. Why don't you move along?"

"I was thinkin' about goin' in here for a drink," Hallam said. "That all right with you boys?"

The other one shrugged. "It's a free country."

"Last time I looked," Hallam commented dryly. He walked past them toward the front of the building, ready to move in a hurry if they tried to jump him. They didn't, and he turned at the corner and went to the entrance of the roadhouse.

He pushed through the door into the dim interior. The inside of the place didn't look quite as dilapidated as the outside. A bar ran along the back wall of the building. There were stools in front of it, indicating that the business might have begun life as a diner. Narrow booths lined the side and front walls, and there were round tables scattered through the center of the room. Only a few of the tables were occupied, a desultory poker game going on at one of them. There were several couples sitting in booths, and Hallam had a feeling that the only reason a man and a woman would get together in a place like this in the middle of the afternoon was that they weren't married—to each other. The stools along the bar were doing the briskest trade; most of them were full.

There were a few empty seats, though, and Hallam headed for one of them. As he walked across the room, he saw in the sparse illumination from a couple of lamps behind the bar that the customers all had either mugs of beer or shot glasses in front of them. If this was a speakeasy, it was even more of an open secret than the ones in Hollywood.

A big bald-headed man wearing a greasy apron was behind the bar. He watched Hallam closely, and Hallam could feel other eyes on him, too. He was a stranger here, after all, and for all these people knew, he might be a revenue agent come to close the place down and arrest all of them.

Of course, any revenuer foolish enough to walk into somewhere like this by himself might not come out again, not in one piece, anyway.

Hallam settled himself on one of the vacant stools and nodded to the bartender. "Hot day out there," he said.

The bald-headed man just grunted.

"Could sure use a cold beer about now," Hallam went on.

"Beer's illegal," the bartender said flatly. "Haven't you ever heard of Prohibition, mister?"

Hallam looked pointedly at the mug full of foaming liquid in front of the man sitting next to him. "What about that?" he asked.

The bartender shook his head. "I don't see any beer." He raised his voice. "Anybody in here see folks drinking beer?" There was a negative mutter from the patrons of the roadhouse. The bartender faced Hallam again and went on, "You want a Dr. Pepper or a Nehi, buddy, we can fix you up. Otherwise maybe you better move on."

Hallam shrugged. He was about to order a Nehi so that he could stick around long enough to ask a few questions about the truck parked outside when someone said behind him, "Lucas? Lucas Hallam? Is that you?"

The voice wasn't familiar. It seemed like all he had been doing since he got back to Texas was running into people who remembered him. When he turned around on the stool and studied the face of the man who had spoken, though, he found to his surprise that he recognized him.

"Johnny Clark?" Hallam grinned. "How the hell are you, Johnny?"

The man was short and lean, with a shock of red hair that was shot through with gray now. He stuck out his hand and pumped Hallam's, smiling broadly as he did so. "I'm just fine, Lucas," he said. "Never expected to run into you around this neck of the woods again. Last I heard of you, you were out West somewhere."

"Still am, most of the time," Hallam told him. "I'm just back for a visit."

The bartender leaned forward and said, "I reckon you know this fella, Johnny. He all right?"

"Sure," Clark said, waving a hand. "We went to school together, 'bout a hundred years ago, seems like. He's all right. Give him whatever he wants, Junior."

The bartender smiled, reached under the hardwood counter for a mug, and started filling it from a tap that was also underneath the bar. Evidently Johnny Clark's recommendation carried enough weight to justify a cold beer.

The beer was cold, all right, and good, Hallam discovered as he sipped it. The man who had been sitting next to Hallam relinquished his stool to Clark, who set his own mug down on the bar and chattered excitedly. "Lucas Hallam," he repeated. "Never thought I'd see you again after what happened. Say, I'm real sorry about your pa. You ever catch up to those men?"

Hallam nodded. "I did." His tone of voice made it clear that he didn't want to discuss those old memories. He changed the subject by asking Clark, "You live around here now?"

"Naw, I'm still down in Azle, still on the old home place. I work up here at a dairy just outside Decatur, though."

Hallam grinned. "Still milkin' cows, I reckon."

Clark wiggled his fingers. "A man does what he's good at."

Hallam lowered his voice a little and said, "They seem to know you pretty well in here."

"Shoot, I stop in most every day for a drink after work. Man gets up in the middle of the night, drives twenty miles, and milks cows for six hours, he needs a beer afterwards. Honey don't mind. She says a man needs his relaxin' time."

"Honey?"

Clark's voice was proud as he answered, "That's the little woman. I married Honey Edwards. Don't know if you remember her or not, Lucas. She's a couple years younger than us."

Hallam shook his head. "Sorry. I don't recall her. The two of you have any kids?"

"Five. And twelve grandkids. What about you, Lucas? You ever get married?"

"Been too busy, I reckon," Hallam said. He might have married Liz, if things had worked out differently. . . .

"No wife for all these years? Man, you're in desperate need of some home cookin', then." Clark downed the rest of his beer. "You're coming home with me for supper. That is, if there's nowhere else you've got to be."

Hallam thought it over for a moment. They were probably wondering about him back at the Lindsey ranch; he had planned on being back by the middle of the day. But if Johnny Clark was telling the truth about being a regular customer here at this roadhouse—and there was no reason for him to lie about it—he might be able to tell Hallam who owned the truck outside. Since he worked in the area, in fact, he might know all sorts of things about what went on around here. One thing about Johnny, he had always liked to talk.

"All right," Hallam said, making up his mind. "I'd be glad to go with you, Johnny. Just let me finish this beer."

"Sure. You got a car, I reckon?"

Hallam nodded.

"You can follow me," Clark went on. "I generally take the back roads and cut down through Boyd. Closer that way. You might get lost after all these years, though, if you weren't going to be following me."

"Reckon I would," Hallam said. He polished off the rest of the beer and tried to pay for it, but Clark insisted that the bartender put it on his tab. As he and Clark started toward the door, Hallam noticed that the two men who had confronted him outside had come in and taken seats in one of the booths. They had shot glasses in their hands, and they gave him hard looks as he and Clark went by.

He would have to ask Johnny about those two, he thought. Every instinct he had was telling him that they were mixed up somehow in the case that had brought him here.

"Homeward bound," Clark called out, cranking a ten-year-old Studebaker into noisy life.

That was right, Hallam thought as he was getting into the pickup. He was going back to a place he hadn't seen in too long a time.

He should have known, should have known that he couldn't come to this part of Texas and not wind up back home again.

Blood always drew a man back.

EIGHTEEN

Hallam followed Johnny Clark's old Studebaker along twisting country roads, across plank bridges covered with wrought-iron frameworks, through small communities with names like Rhome and Aurora and Boyd. Hallam remembered them all, recalled the names anyway. The towns just looked like any other small town to him now. The closer they came to Azle, though, the more familiar the countryside became to him. Flat Rock and the ranch where he had been born were only a few miles south of the town, and he had ridden into Azle with his parents plenty of times when they went to pick up supplies. Hallam had ridden in the back of the buckboard, anxious to reach MacDonald's general store so he could talk his father into getting him a stick of candy. John Hallam was a tough, hard man, everyone knew that, but somehow the little boy had usually wound up with that stick of candy. He would suck on it while he sat in the wagon and watched the cowboys swaggering in and out of the town's lone saloon across the street. It was a low building made of stone and sporting a bright red roof, and Hallam had thought that the laughing, gun-hung young men who drank there were about the most impressive things he had ever seen in his young life.

God, he thought, that was a whole other world. Had he ever been ten years old? Had things ever been that simple?

Or had life really started when he saw his own father gunned down over something that he hadn't even understood?

Maybe coming back here hadn't been such a good idea after all.

Everybody had their own private tragedies, though, he thought. And it would sure as hell be a tragedy if Teddy Spotted Horse was convicted of murdering Dan Armstrong. *That* was what he needed to be thinking about now, Hallam told himself, not ancient history.

He drove down the road from Boyd, still following Johnny Clark, past the two-story schoolhouse where he had received his first book-learning. They came up to Main Street and turned left, and Hallam saw that most of the things he remembered about downtown Azle had changed. The red-topped saloon was still there, but it was a café now, he saw. The old drugstore building was still next to it, but that was the only other structure Hallam recognized. Everything else was new.

Clark hung a right on South Stewart. Hallam stayed behind the Studebaker, crossing over Ash Creek and passing the Baptist church that was named for the stream. Hallam recalled attending a few services there as a youngster, remembering especially the way the circuit rider had preached with his six-guns lying on the pulpit so they'd be handy in case the Comanches tried to pull one of their frequent horse-stealing raids.

The old Clark homestead was less than a mile past the church. Johnny brought his car to a stop in front of the old whitewashed frame house, and Hallam parked beside him. As Hallam got out of the pickup, he could look to the south and see the heavily wooded ridges rising to the plateau called Flat Rock.

Honey Clark met them at the door, seemingly not surprised that her husband was bringing someone home with him. Johnny had always been a friendly sort, so Hallam imagined they had company pretty often. Honey was a white-haired, buxom woman, still handsome, and Hallam didn't have the slightest recollection of her. She seemed to remember him, though, and she took his hand and shook it enthusiastically when Clark told her who their visitor was.

"Why, Lucas Hallam!" she exclaimed. "I'll swan. I never thought we'd see you around these parts again. Come in, come in."

Hallam tried to apologize for joining them unannounced, but Honey wouldn't hear of it. She told the two men to sit down and talk over old times. Dinner would be on the table in just a few minutes.

Hallam told himself that this was just marking time until he had a chance to pump Clark about what went on at the roadhouse called Zeke's Place, but he found himself enjoying all the reminiscing. He spoke about himself as little as possible, letting Clark carry the conversation. Johnny had no trouble with that, telling Hallam about all the things that had happened in Azle since he had left and bringing him up to date on everyone they had gone to school with, most of whom Hallam had no memory of whatsoever.

"Come and get it," Honey called from the dining room.

Dinner was fried chicken and mashed potatoes and biscuits and gravy. Honey wasn't the cook that Smitty Wardell was, but Hallam had to admit that the food was good. Honey beamed when he told her as much. When the meal was finally over and Hallam and Clark had carried their glasses of iced tea back into the living room, Hallam knew the time had come to get on with the real reason he was here.

Hallam glanced toward the kitchen. Honey had retreated out there to clean up the supper dishes. In a low voice, he asked, "Tell me, Johnny, what kind of place is that roadhouse where I ran into you?"

Clark grinned slyly. "Zeke's has got the coldest beer and the smoothest whiskey you're likely to find around here, Lucas."

"How do they get away with serving it right out in the open like that?"

"Well, I never really stopped to think about it," Clark shrugged. "If I had to guess I'd say they probably pay the local cops to look the other way."

"What about the federal men? I hear it's hard to bribe them."

Clark waved a hand. "Shoot, them revenuers got better things to do than come down here to Texas. They're too busy up in Chicago and New York and places like that, from what I read in the paper. They pretty much leave things down here to the Rangers and the local law."

Hallam grunted. The Rangers were even less likely than the federal men to take a payoff, but unless their situation had really changed, the Rangers were probably still spread pretty thin. County sheriffs were a different matter. Hallam had known good ones and bad ones, but most of them were politicians at heart, rather than lawmen. It was pretty common to find one with his hand out, ready to be greased.

He wondered suddenly about Mart Bascomb. According to Lindsey, Bascomb had been ineffective at tracking down the rustlers.

Maybe he was being paid not to track them down.

This was getting more complicated than Hallam had expected. Pretty soon, he was going to be suspecting that everybody in the whole damn county was part of the rustling ring.

He changed the subject. "Say, I noticed a truck parked up there next to Zeke's. You have any idea who it belongs to?"

Clark shook his head. "Nope. Those cattle trucks park there a lot, though, sometimes just one, sometimes two or three. I imagine the fellers who drive them know Junior or something and got his permission to leave them there."

"Junior's the bartender?"

"Yeah, but he owns the place. There ain't no Zeke, not now anyway. I think he was the one who built it in the first place."

Hallam nodded. "I was lookin' at that truck and two fellers came out and told me to leave it alone." Hallam described them quickly and added, "You reckon maybe they own it?"

"I don't think so. I've seen those boys around, the ones you're talking about, and I never saw them driving any of the trucks that are left there. I think their names are Kerr and Garrett, something like that. They've been just sort of hanging around the place for the past few weeks, but I don't know what their business is. They ain't too friendly."

"I noticed," Hallam grunted.

Clark's brows drew down in a frown. "Why all the questions about that roadhouse, Lucas? It's just a place where a man can get a drink."

Hallam hesitated, trying to decide just how much of the truth to tell his old friend. He trusted Clark, he supposed, but at the same time he didn't want to get the man involved too much in this case, either. After a moment, he said, "Well, actually, I'm sort of lookin' for a feller, Johnny. I was told he might have some connection with that roadhouse. I need to talk some business with him."

"Lucas, Lucas," Clark said, that sly grin coming back. "Don't tell me you've gone and turned bootlegger!"

"Well . . ." Hallam let his voice trail off noncommittally. Clark could think whatever he wanted as long as it kept him talking.

"Like I told you, I know most of the regulars there. What's this guy look like?"

"He's a big man, dresses like a ranch hand, has curly brown hair and a jaw that looks like a slab of rock." Hallam was prepared to give Dan Armstrong's name to Clark, but he wanted to see if Clark came up with it on his own first.

"Oh, sure. That sounds like a feller named Armstrong. Comes into Zeke's pretty often."

Hallam felt his pulse speed up a little. There were no definite connections yet, but he was starting to weave a pattern. "Seen him there lately?"

Clark shrugged again. "He was there a couple of nights ago. I stayed sort of late that night, because Honey was over in Weatherford visiting her sister that evening. Junior cooked me up a steak for supper."

"Did you talk to this Armstrong?"

Clark shook his head. "Don't reckon I've ever said more than a dozen words to him, maybe not that many. He ain't real friendly. He hangs around with some other cowboys most of the time. Every now and then some guys in suits come in and talk to him." Clark looked puzzled. "I never really thought about it before, but it seems to me that Armstrong just comes in to talk to those folks. He never drinks much while he's there. Always carries a flask with him, though."

Hallam started to say something, but Clark's eyes lit up with another memory, and the man went on, "Now that I think about it, when I saw Armstrong night before last, he was talking to those two men you asked me about earlier, that Kerr and Garrett."

"He ever talk to them before?" Hallam asked quickly.

"Not that I recall. And he didn't seem too happy about talking to them then, either. Acted like they were bothering him." Clark sipped his iced tea and narrowed his eyes. "How about telling me what this is all about, Lucas? You been pumping me like you're some sort of cop."

"Not hardly," Hallam said honestly. "Like I said, it's about a business deal I'm tryin' to set up. I'm not out to make trouble for Armstrong." That would be difficult now, he thought.

"Well, good. You and me are old friends and all, but I don't need anybody holding any grudges against me."

"Nobody will ever know you told me any of this, Johnny," Hallam promised.

"Thanks. Some of those fellas in the liquor business are a mite touchy about folks talking about them."

"I understand," Hallam said, not bothering to tell Clark that he was interested in rustling, not bootlegging.

He still had no proof of anything, but it looked like the rustling ring was using the roadhouse as its headquarters. The fact that Dan Armstrong had been a frequent customer indicated that he might indeed have been working with the cattle thieves. His meetings with other cowboys and with strangers in suits could point that way. But who were the strangers named Kerr and Garrett, and how did they tie in with everything? If Armstrong had not wanted to talk to them, it could mean that they were trying to move in and cut themselves a piece of the action. They had certainly looked hardboiled enough to pull something like that.

Honey came bustling in from the kitchen, putting an end to the discussion, but Hallam figured he had already gotten all the useful information he was going to get out of Johnny Clark. He was still a long way from finding out who had killed Armstrong, but he thought he was at least moving in the right direction now.

After a little more conversation about the old days, Hallam stood up and reached for his hat. "Reckon I'd better be going," he said. "Got a long drive back to the place I'm stayin'."

"We'd be glad to put you up for the night, Lucas," Clark offered.

"Thank you kindly, Johnny, but there are folks expectin' me." He turned to Honey. "Thank you for supper, ma'am. I really enjoyed it. And it was good to see you again after all this time."

"Likewise, Lucas. You take care of yourself, hear, and come back to see us."

"Next time I'm through this way, I sure will," Hallam promised.

Johnny followed him out into the yard. Night had fallen,

and Clark asked, "You sure you can find your way back in the dark, Lucas?"

"Sure. I can get back to Fort Worth from here, and I know where I'm goin' from there." He held out his hand. "Thanks, Johnny, for the supper and for the talk and for . . . well, for bein' an old friend."

"Sure thing, Lucas." Clark took Hallam's hand. "Be seein' you."

Hallam got in the pickup and turned it around, heading back toward Azle and the highway running through town that led to Fort Worth. He slowed down before he got there, though, looking at a road that turned off to the right.

He couldn't leave just yet, couldn't be this close to Flat Rock and not take a look at it. He wheeled the pickup into the turn.

There were a couple of creeks to ford on the way, but they were low at this time of year. Then the road began to climb. The grade was steep in places, but the pickup was able to make it. In a few minutes, Hallam reached the flatland and turned toward home.

The light from the moon and stars was enough for him to recognize the spot when he came to it. He braked the truck to a stop, turned off the headlights and engine and stepped out. The night was incredibly quiet. He could hear the chirp of insects and the rustle of small animals in the woods bordering the huge open field that had once been his father's horse pasture. The house had been down at the far end in the trees.

Hallam walked out into the field. Off to his left, he could make out the low hump of an Indian mound. Ten years or so before his family had settled here, the place had been a regular camping spot for the nomadic Comanche bands. As a kid, he had found plenty of arrowheads and cooking implements in this pasture. Most of them were gone now, he imagined, picked up as souvenirs during the last forty years.

He had learned to ride here, learned how to shoot a gun. He had fished in the creeks that ran through the bluffs at the edge of the plateau. When he was a little older, his younger brothers and sisters had played here, and he could remember their squeals of happy laughter. His mother had laughed, too, at the antics of her children. Hallam could not remember his father laughing much, but he recalled the times he had seen John Hallam looking out from the front porch of the house, surveying the place he had made for himself and his family. There had been a smile on his father's lips then—but still something unsatisfied lurked in his eyes. They had left this place eventually, trying to find whatever it was that gnawed at John Hallam's insides, and then come back. Come back to death and the splitting of a family . . .

Hallam shook his head. No matter how it had ended, there had been good times here, plenty of good memories. And he was glad he had come here tonight to see it one last time.

He knew he would never be back. Something in his bones told him that.

He turned and went to the truck, glancing at the glow in the sky that came from the lights of Fort Worth, to the southeast. He had taken this job from Darby to escape the recent past. He was done with memories, good and bad, he had thought. But by coming here he had plunged into older memories. Now it was time to go back to the present and stay there.

Hallam got into the pickup and drove away from Flat Rock.

NINETEEN

Pecos was waiting for him when he pulled up next to the ranch house a couple of hours later. The young cowboy ran up to Hallam as he got out of the truck and said anxiously, "Where the hell have you been, Lucas? I thought you'd be back by afternoon. Is Teddy all right?"

"Teddy's fine," Hallam told him. "Sorry I'm so late gettin' back. I got to thinkin' about the case and decided to look around a little. I told you I was goin' to do some detectin'."

"You find out anything that could help Teddy?"

"Maybe," Hallam said. He didn't want to go into any of the details yet, not until he had something besides a theory that was pretty shaky on the surface of it. Hallam's gut told him he was on the right track, though, whether he could prove it yet or not.

"Well, we've had a few things happen around here today," Pecos said. "Eliot said he wanted to talk to you in the house if you ever showed up again."

Hallam frowned. It sounded like Eliot was taking on some responsibility, but Hallam didn't know whether it was the result of the actor's growing maturity or of his desire to be in charge of things.

"Might as well go see what he wants," Hallam said. He started toward the house, Pecos falling into step beside him.

Eliot was waiting in the living room of the ranch house with Rae Lindsey and her father. As Hallam walked in, Eliot looked up and said, "Well, we were beginning to think that you had abandoned us, Hallam."

"Not hardly." Hallam hung his hat on one of the hooks. "Pecos said you wanted to see me."

"I just wanted to tell you that Darby called here on the telephone this morning. He seemed rather upset." Eliot smiled thinly. "Something about a wire you sent him asking for money."

"Had to pay Teddy's lawyer," Hallam explained. "I figured the studio would want to pick up the tab, since Teddy's workin' for them and all."

"I don't think it was the money that had Darby upset. He wanted you to bring me back to Hollywood immediately. Said we couldn't afford the bad publicity that might result if it was known that I was involved in a murder case, however indirectly."

Hallam thought about the telegram he had crumpled and left in the Western Union office. "He wired me the same thing. I didn't give him an answer."

"I did." Eliot's smile grew broader. "I told him to go jump in the lake."

Despite the seriousness of the situation, Hallam had to chuckle as he imagined what J. Frederick Darby's reaction to *that* had been. He said, "I figured you might be anxious to get back to Hollywood."

"Not hardly, as you're fond of saying." Eliot nodded toward Rae and Lindsey. "We can't desert our friends in their time of need. Armstrong's death has thrown the whole ranch into an uproar."

"Several of the hands have quit, Mr. Hallam," Rae put in. "They were the ones closest to Dan. I suppose they didn't want to work here now that he's dead."

Hallam nodded slowly. That was possible. Or it could be that they had been in on the rustling scheme with Armstrong and hadn't known what to do next after his murder.

"At any rate," Eliot continued, "the Flying L is short-handed at the moment, so I decided that all of us should help them out. I talked to Riordan and the others, and they're all agreed. We're going to be ranch hands, Hallam."

Hallam grunted. "You came out here to learn to be a cowboy, all right, but I don't reckon this is what Darby and your pa had in mind."

Eliot shook his head. "I don't care about that. I just want to help keep the ranch going until things settle down somewhat."

That was noble of the boy, but it also gave him an excuse to stay here longer, Hallam thought as he saw Eliot reach over and slip his hand into Rae's. Whatever Eliot's motivation was, though, Hallam didn't want to leave yet, either. He couldn't, not as long as Teddy was in jail and the real killer was still on the loose.

"I reckon we'll stay, then," he said.

"I don't know how to thank you boys," Lindsey told them. "You've taken on our troubles like they were your own, and we appreciate it."

"Did you find out anything today, Hallam?" Eliot asked.

"Not enough to do any real good," Hallam replied. He stretched, feeling the pull of weary muscles. "It's been a long day. Reckon I'll turn in."

He could tell that Pecos was champing at the bit to find out exactly what Hallam had learned, and he wasn't surprised when the youngster started to follow him up the stairs.

"I can help you, Lucas," Pecos said. "Just tell me what you've been doin'—"

"Lookin' around and askin' questions," Hallam said. "That's what most detective work is. You'll hear about it when the time's right, son."

Pecos stopped and glared up at Hallam. "You don't *want*

anybody helpin' you, do you?" he accused. "You figure you can handle everything yourself, solve all the problems and catch all the killers."

Hallam shrugged. "Just don't want to rope anybody into trouble unless I have to," he said.

"The day'll come when you need help, Lucas. Everybody does sooner or later."

"I reckon you're right," Hallam told him. He grinned. "I'll know who to yell for, won't I?"

He left Pecos there on the stairs and went on to his room, aware that for the first time since Hallam had known Pecos, the boy was mad at him. But there was nothing he could do about that.

Nobody else was getting killed if Hallam had anything to say about it.

By the time he had spent another restless night going over the facts of the case, he had figured out what he wanted to do next. The two strangers called Kerr and Garrett were nagging at him, and it was time to find out what their connection was with Dan Armstrong. The only way to do that, as far as he could see, was to keep an eye on them and see what they were up to.

After breakfast, he asked Lindsey if he could borrow the pickup again, and the rancher readily agreed. Eliot, Pecos, and the other visitors from Hollywood were already at work, pitching in to make sure the ranch's chores got done. For men like Max Hilyard and Tall Cotton Jones, who had spent most of their lives working on ranches, this had to be like old times. Riordan, Grant, Callahan, and Macklin had done their share of cowboying, too. Wayne Lindsey was getting a whole passel of top hands to replace the ones he had lost.

Pecos had been quiet during breakfast, and Hallam knew the boy was still resentful because Hallam had refused to include him in the investigation. He had just been a loner for too long, Hallam thought; the idea of someone else working with him made him uncomfortable.

He drove from the ranch to the highway and turned north toward Denton again. There was probably a closer way to reach Zeke's by cutting through the back roads, but Hallam didn't know the route and didn't want to get lost. When he reached Denton, he turned onto the Decatur highway again and followed it.

It wasn't noon yet when he reached the roadhouse, but already several cars were parked in front of the run-down building. Hallam drove past it and up a hill about a quarter of a mile farther on. When he had topped the rise, he swung the pickup in a circle and stopped with it pointing back the way he had come, the nose of the truck just edging past the crest of the hill. He wouldn't be very noticeable up here, but he would be able to keep an eye on the place. Kerr and Garrett might already be inside, in which case he would have to wait for them to leave, or they might show up later. Either way, he intended to see where they went when they left Zeke's.

The cattle truck was still parked beside the building, Hallam saw. If anyone tried to leave in it, he would follow them, postponing his plan to trail Kerr and Garrett. Of course, there was always the chance that the two strangers would drive off in the truck.

He slumped down in the seat of the pickup. He could still see the roadhouse, but he wouldn't be as visible from the highway. Several cars had passed him already. If anyone was curious, he would look like he had just pulled over at the side of the road for a snooze.

By the time an hour had passed, half a dozen more cars and trucks had pulled up to the roadhouse, but none of them contained the two men he was looking for. Hallam felt himself getting sleepy for real. Several restless nights in a row had left him a little weary. He sat up a bit and shook his head, trying to dislodge some of the cobwebs. There was a breeze blowing, and he lowered the window next to him so that he could feel it a little better.

There was a sound beside the pickup, the scrape of a foot. Hallam started to turn his head. A gun barrel came in the window of the truck along with the breeze and stuck itself in his face.

"Don't move, you son-of-a-bitch," the man holding the gun said.

Hallam stayed still except for his jaw. His teeth grated together in anger. He *was* getting too old for this business. Either that, or the stranger was damn good. Hallam didn't know whether the man was Kerr or Garrett, but there was no mistaking the barrel of a Colt .38. Not when it was only a couple of inches away from his nose.

The passenger door of the pickup opened, and the other man reached in, patting Hallam down as best he could. It was a quick, professional job. "Nothing," he grunted a few seconds later. The door slammed shut again.

The man with the gun backed away from the pickup, but the muzzle was still lined up on Hallam's head. "There's too much traffic along here," he said coldly. "Get out of the truck, mister. You're coming with us."

Hallam wondered if he could yank the brake off, throw the truck in gear, hit the starter, and start rolling downhill before the man could shoot. The thought lasted a couple of seconds before he threw it out. That would be a good way of getting a bullet in the brain, he decided. For the moment, all he could do was play along.

But he was damned if he was going to let them take him off into the woods and shoot him in the back of the head, not without putting up a fight. He would wait for a better moment to make his move, though.

He opened the door and stepped out of the truck. "You boys are pretty smooth," he said. "When'd you spot me?"

"Chuck saw you parked up here and recognized the truck when we drove by before. We were going to stop at Zeke's,

• 196 •

but we went on past and came back on foot. You should have had somebody with you, watching your back, mister."

That would have been a good job for Pecos, Hallam thought wryly, if he had let the boy help out. Too late for that now, though.

The man with the gun gestured with it. "Go on across the ditch. There's some trees over there where we can talk."

Hallam figured talking was the last thing they had on their minds. He walked around the front of the truck, moving fairly quickly. He was going faster than the gunman had anticipated, in fact, and for an instant, the hood of the pickup gave Hallam some cover up to his chest.

He threw himself at the other man.

The gun blasted, a bullet spanging off the metal of the truck's hood. The second man was standing at the edge of the ditch, and Hallam slammed into him. Both of them fell, landing heavily, but Hallam was on top. He could feel the hard jut of a pistol grip under the man's shirt. His fingers closed around it and jerked, tearing cloth and popping buttons. The gun came free from where it was tucked behind the man's belt.

Hallam rolled to the side, banging up against the other bank of the bar ditch. He brought up the pistol, noticing that it was a .38 like the one the other man carried. His thumb eared back the hammer and he stared over the sights at the first man, who had just rounded the front of the truck. "Hold it!" Hallam rapped.

The man already had his own gun lined up, but he didn't shoot. He froze for a second, then called, "Chuck! You all right?"

The second man had banged his head when Hallam tackled him, but he lifted himself on an elbow and replied, "Yeah! I'll get him, Fred!"

The man was only a couple of feet from Hallam, and he could hear the words plainly as Hallam growled, "You just stay still, mister. You move and I'll plug your pardner there."

"You can't stop me from shooting you, too, old man," Fred snapped.

"Then we'll both be dead, won't we?" Hallam asked calmly. "Why don't you tell me what the hell this is all about, and then maybe nobody'll have to die."

"That's all we wanted to find out from you, you idiot!" the one called Chuck said hotly. He had to be angry about the way Hallam had jumped him and taken away his gun.

Hallam was starting to feel awkward, lying here in a ditch like this. He didn't believe for a second that the two men had only wanted to ask questions of him, but they couldn't stay here like this forever, either. He said, "How about we all put up the guns and talk this over peaceable-like?"

"Now you're talking sense," Fred said. "You're going to be in one hell of a lot of trouble otherwise."

Without looking over at Chuck, Hallam said, "Move away, mister. I ain't puttin' anything down until you're on the other side of that ditch where I can see you."

Chuck hesitated, and Fred ordered, "Do what he says."

Slowly, Chuck got to his feet and walked into the narrow strip of grassland between the ditch and the trees. Once he was there, Hallam was able to get his free hand under him and push himself into a sitting position without lowering the gun. A moment later, he was on his feet.

"I thought we were going to end this Mexican standoff," Fred protested.

"I'll put this peashooter down when you get rid of yours," Hallam said.

Fred shook his head. "I can't really do that."

Hallam could see Chuck out of the corner of his eye; the man was standing very still, waiting to see what was going to happen next. After a moment of tense silence, during which Hallam and Fred kept staring at each other over the barrels of the Colts, Chuck abruptly said, "Oh, shit. This is stupid, Fred. Tell him who we are. Then maybe he'll realize he can't mess around with us."

Hallam had to grin. "Figure I'll be impressed, do you?"

"That depends on who you really are, mister," Fred said. After a moment's hesitation, he went on, "Maybe you're right, Chuck." To Hallam, he said, "Now don't get edgy on that trigger finger; I'm just reaching into my pocket for something."

"Slow and easy," Hallam warned.

Carefully, Fred slid his free hand into the back pocket of his jeans and brought out a small leather folder. He flipped it open and held it where Hallam could see what was inside. The midday sun bounced brightly off the badge pinned to the leather. Hallam's eyes narrowed in surprise. He knew that badge, had carried one just like it a lot of years earlier.

A silver star in a silver circle—the emblem of the Texas Rangers.

TWENTY

Hallam didn't lower the gun in his hand immediately. "Rangers, huh?" he grunted. "Folks can steal badges."

"Not these," Fred snapped. "Show him yours, Chuck."

Chuck pulled out a similar leather folder and opened it to reveal another badge, identical to Fred's. "These are the real thing, mister," he said to Hallam, "and you're going to be in a lot of trouble for resisting arrest and interfering with a couple of lawmen."

"You boys never told me I was under arrest," Hallam pointed out. "And how the hell was I supposed to know you were Rangers?" He looked at both of the men and sensed that they were telling the truth, however. He let down the hammer of the Colt and allowed the barrel to tip slightly toward the ground. Even if the two men tried something funny, he could still get a couple of shots off by double-actioning the pistol, he thought.

"You know it now," Fred said. "I'm Sergeant Fred Kerr, and this is Ranger Chuck Garrett. Who are you?"

"Name's Lucas Hallam. I used to be a Ranger myself."

Both of them looked at him in surprise. "Hallam," Fred Kerr echoed. "I've heard the name before. There was a

Hallam who rode with McNelly into Mexico. I've seen his picture at headquarters."

"That was my father, John Hallam."

"And his son was a Ranger later on, or so I've heard."

Hallam nodded. "You boys startin' to believe me now?"

"Maybe. Tell us why you were poking around that truck yesterday and why you were watching the place today."

"Well, believe it or not," Hallam said, smiling slightly again, "I was looking for you two boys. Never figured *you'd* come to *me.*"

"What's your interest in that cattle truck?" Garrett prodded.

"I'm lookin' for rustlers," Hallam said, his face grim now. "I reckon that's what you're doin', too. I was just thinkin' the other day that we'd have sent in somebody undercover, back in my time, to try to bust up the ring that's operatin' around here."

"What do you know about a rustling ring?" Kerr demanded sharply.

They were asking all the questions and not offering any information of their own, Hallam thought, but he was willing to play along for a little while. He said, "I know they've been hittin' all the ranches over in the next county and that they had an inside man on at least one of the spreads."

"And who would that be?"

"Dan Armstrong," Hallam said.

Kerr and Garrett exchanged a glance. "That's what we thought," Kerr mused, "after we saw him talking to some of the other men we suspected. We got a tip that they were using that roadhouse as a meeting place. Armstrong wouldn't talk to us when we tried to sound him out about it, though."

"Appears to me that the feller who owns the place might be in on the scheme," Hallam said, "the way he lets them park those trucks there."

"That makes sense." Kerr finally lowered his Colt and

stroked his moustache, peering intently at Hallam. "Now, just what got you mixed up in all this, mister?"

"I'm lookin' for a killer. Somebody stuck a knife in Armstrong over on the Flyin' L. The boy they arrested for the killin' is a friend of mine, and I'm certain sure he didn't do it."

Garrett laughed harshly. "What makes you think you can come in here and conduct an investigation of your own, Hallam? This is business for the law."

Hallam thought about how much he sounded like Mart Bascomb, then said, "This ain't the first time I've gone after a murderer. I'm licensed by the State of California as a private detective."

"Wait a minute," Kerr snapped. "What's a hawkshaw from California doing in Texas?"

Hallam sighed and let the Colt drop to his side, convinced now that the two men were on the level. "It's a long story, boys," he said.

They moved into the shade of the trees while Hallam told it. He gave the pistol back to Chuck Garrett. The Ranger had a sullen expression on his face as he took the gun, and Hallam knew that Garrett was still put out that he had been able to grab the weapon. Kerr seemed more interested in what Hallam had to say at the moment, though.

Hallam explained about Eliot Tremaine and the job that had brought him from Hollywood to Texas, going over that part quickly so that he could get to the situation on the Flying L ranch. Kerr nodded when Hallam told them about the raid by the rustlers and the pursuit that had resulted in the recovery of the stolen herd.

"We heard about that," he said. "I take it you're the one who chased them down."

"I helped," Hallam said. "Armstrong was supposed to be in charge. Now that I look back on it, I don't figure he ever intended for us to catch up to those rustlers. Once we did, though, he had to go along with the rest of us or risk exposin' himself as one of the gang."

"Why would Armstrong help the rustlers?" Garrett asked.

Hallam shrugged. "Money was most of it, I reckon. But he could've been carryin' a grudge against Rae Lindsey, too, for the way she told him she wasn't interested in him. Don't suppose we'll ever know for sure, since Armstrong's dead now."

"And you think someone connected with the rustling killed him?" Kerr mused.

"That's the way I've got it figured. I know Teddy Spotted Horse didn't do it." Hallam told the two Rangers about the clashes between Teddy and Armstrong, leaving nothing out. He could tell that neither one of them was convinced of Teddy's innocence, but they didn't know the boy. Hallam did.

"All right, I think I've got all of this straight," Kerr finally said. "When we saw you messing around that truck yesterday, we thought you might be one of the gang. I guess we were just working at cross-purposes." The Ranger sergeant's mouth tightened. "There won't be any more of that. You're going to have to stay out of this investigation from now on, Hallam."

Hallam bristled. "You intend to find out who really killed Armstrong, do you, so that Teddy can be cleared?"

"That's not our job. We were sent in to find the men responsible for the rustling, and we don't need to be tripping over you while we're trying to complete our assignment."

"That won't help Teddy," Hallam pointed out.

"It might. We might uncover something in our investigation. But we can't worry about that now. Like I said—"

"It ain't your job," Hallam finished bitterly.

"It's not," Kerr snapped. "If you used to be a Ranger, you know what it's like to try to cover the whole state with a handful of men. We can't handle everything at once, and right now the only thing Chuck and I can concentrate on is that rustling ring."

Hallam snorted in disgust. "It sure as hell wasn't like that in the old days," he said, forgetting for the moment his vow not to dwell on the past.

"This ain't the old days, Pops," Garrett said scornfully. "In case nobody told you, the Old West is dead and gone."

Hallam shook his head and turned away. He started toward the pickup.

"Don't forget what I told you, Hallam," Kerr called after him. "We could arrest you right now, but we're not going to since you're a former Ranger. Just don't get in our way again. Go back to Hollywood, damn it!"

Hallam got into the truck, slammed the door, ground his foot against the starter. The engine roared to life. He jerked the pickup into gear and started down the hill, well aware that Kerr and Garrett were watching him.

He could stop at the roadhouse, he thought, but he wasn't sure what good it would do now, other than to irritate the two Texas Rangers. They had been his best lead, and that hadn't panned out at all. He drove on past Zeke's, heading back toward Denton.

Stay out of it, they had told him. Go back to Hollywood. The Rangers had sure changed since his day, all right.

But he hadn't. And today's Rangers sure as hell didn't know Lucas Hallam if they thought he was going to turn tail and run. No, sir . . .

For all his muttering and grumbling, though, Hallam had to admit to himself that he wasn't sure what to do next. The roadhouse had been his only starting place, and now Kerr and Garrett would be watching for him. If they saw him hanging around the place again, he had no doubt they would arrest him in order to get him out of their way. That wouldn't do Teddy any good.

He wanted to talk to the boy again, he decided. It could be that Teddy had seen something useful on the night of

Armstrong's death, something whose importance hadn't even occurred to him at the time. It was worth a try.

Hallam stopped and had a late lunch in Denton again, then headed toward Fort Worth. It was mid-afternoon when he got there, and the streets around the courthouse and jail were just as busy as before. A different deputy was in charge at the jail, but he, too, refused to let Hallam see Teddy at first.

"Sheriff Bascomb said that Colonel Gilliam could see the prisoner, didn't he?" Hallam asked.

"That's right. The colonel is the kid's lawyer, after all," the deputy said.

"Well, I'm workin' for the colonel." That was stretching the truth a little, Hallam thought, but Gilliam *had* said that anything Hallam could turn up might help in Teddy's defense. "Seems like that permission ought to apply to one of the colonel's investigators, too."

The deputy looked doubtful, but he said, "Well, I suppose you could be right. I'd check with the sheriff, but he's out of the office right now. . . ."

That was a lucky break, Hallam knew. If Bascomb had seen him, there would have been no chance in hell he'd get in to talk to Teddy.

"All right," the deputy said abruptly. "Just make it quick, okay? If the sheriff doesn't want you around here, it'll be my rump that gets chewed out."

"Thanks," Hallam said.

The deputy summoned one of the jail guards to take Hallam back to the cells. Their steps echoed hollowly in the stone corridor leading to the cell block. The guard opened several barred doors, then led Hallam down another corridor between cells. Teddy was near the far end.

"I'll be watching you, mister," the guard warned. "Don't try anything funny, and keep some distance between you and those bars."

Hallam nodded.

Teddy looked up from where he was sitting on the bunk inside the cell. Surprise was the first expression on his face, followed closely by relief. "Lucas!" he exclaimed. "You've come to get me out of here!"

"I wish I had, Teddy," Hallam said solemnly. "I'm afraid things haven't changed much, though. I've been doin' some pokin' around, but I still don't know who really killed Armstrong."

Teddy's features fell. He was wearing a jail uniform and hadn't shaved, and he looked like he was about ready to give up. "I thought you might have found something," he muttered.

Hallam reached up and took off his hat, then sleeved beads of sweat from his forehead. It was fairly cool in the jail, but he felt hot anyway. "I wanted to ask you about the night Armstrong was killed," he said. "You sure you didn't see nobody while you were out walkin' around?"

"That lawyer Gilliam's asked me that same question over and over, Lucas," Teddy replied dully. "I didn't see anybody who could give me an alibi."

"Maybe not, but what about somebody you saw who didn't see you?"

"What?" Teddy looked up again, puzzled this time.

"If there was anybody else lurkin' around them barns and corrals, they might be the one who killed Armstrong."

Teddy shook his head. "There was nobody. Everybody was up at the party."

"There were folks around the cookshack. It's not that far from there to the barn where Armstrong was found."

"That's right," Teddy said, frowning in thought. "I suppose somebody could have slipped around the other side of the house from the party, too. There was so much celebrating going on that he probably wouldn't have been missed."

"So you see, it's possible," Hallam said. "Now we've just got to figure out who had a reason to kill Armstrong."

"Nobody but me, as far as I know." Teddy sighed.

"Yep, but I don't reckon anybody's told you that Armstrong was mixed up with that rustlin' ring."

Teddy glanced up sharply and then came to his feet. He stepped up to the bars and gripped them. "You mean he was a crook?"

"It sure looks like it."

"Then his death could have been connected to that," Teddy mused.

The door at the end of the corridor opened again. Hallam looked over his shoulder, figuring that the guard was coming back to tell him that he had to leave. Instead, three familiar figures came through the door, followed by the same guard.

Colonel Marcus Gilliam was in the lead, and Pecos and Smitty Wardell were with him. Smitty was carrying a basket with a cloth draped over it.

"Good day, Mr. Hallam," Gilliam said. "When that deputy told me one of my investigators was already back here, I knew it had to be you."

Pecos pushed past the colonel, rushing toward the cell and reaching through the bars to grab Teddy's hand and pump it. "You old redskinned heathen!" he exclaimed. "How the devil are you, Teddy?"

Teddy had to smile slightly at Pecos's enthusiastic greeting. "I'm getting by," he said. "Been better, though."

"Shoot, we're goin' to have you out of there before you know it!" Pecos turned to Hallam. "Ain't that right, Lucas?"

"Here's hopin'," Hallam replied.

"Howdy, Teddy," Smitty said as he came up with the covered basket. "Brought you some good ranch-cooked food. There's some fresh doughnuts in here, too, if them guards ain't pawed 'em all to pieces goin' through the basket." He shook his head. "Durned if they didn't act like they thought I was tryin' to smuggle in a Gatlin' gun to you."

"I encountered these two gentlemen on the sidewalk outside as I was coming to see my client here," Gilliam explained. "I was able to persuade the authorities to allow all of us in. A most fortuitous meeting, I must say, especially if we can prevail upon Mr. Wardell to bring out those doughnuts."

Smitty glared at the lawyer. "I brung these sinkers for Teddy."

The young prisoner laughed. "Go ahead and share them with everybody, Smitty. Give the guard one; maybe that way he'll quit glaring at all of us."

"Just stay back from that door," the guard cautioned. "I'll unlock it long enough for you to hand in that basket, but don't try anything. You'd never make it out of here."

"I assure you, my good man, we are all law-abiding citizens here," Gilliam told him.

Hallam could tell from the look on Pecos's face that the boy wouldn't have minded trying to pull off an escape attempt, but the guard was right. There wouldn't be a chance of it succeeding. "Take it easy, son," Hallam murmured to Pecos.

The guard unlocked the cell door and pulled it open just long enough to take the basket of food from Smitty and pass it in to Teddy. Then the barred door shut with a slam, locking automatically. Teddy set the basket on his bunk, lifted the cloth covering, and inhaled the aromas that drifted up from the fried chicken and homemade bread and doughnuts. For the first time in a good while, Hallam saw a genuine smile on his face.

"Here," he said, passing some of the doughnuts back through the bars. "Might as well enjoy them."

Smitty didn't take one. "I got to be goin'," he said. "I got to go to the store and stock up on provisions. Pecos asked if he could come along with me and see Teddy, and I said sure."

"Thanks, Smitty," Pecos said, slapping the cook on the shoulder. "I'll catch up with you before you head back to the ranch. I want to talk to Teddy for a while."

"Sure thing, son. So long, y'all." Smitty waddled back down the corridor to the cell-block door. The guard on the other side of the door let him out.

"I've filed a motion for bail, Teddy," Gilliam said, then took a bite off the doughnut in his hand. He brushed some powdered sugar off his moustache, the white stuff falling in a little shower to the jail floor, and went on, "I don't expect it to do much good, but we have to at least make the attempt. Other than that, I'll push for a delay in the trial. I know it's hard on you, just sitting here and waiting, but the more time we have to investigate, the better the chances we'll be able to clear you."

"And if you can't find any evidence that I didn't kill Armstrong . . . ?"

"We'll do the best we can, son," Gilliam said quietly. "I'd better be going now. Mr. Hallam, you and Pecos stay as long as you like. I'll tell the deputy in charge that you are indeed working with me."

"Thanks, Colonel."

The lawyer went back down the corridor, still munching the doughnut. Teddy swallowed the last of his and then said, "Well, tell me what's going on up at the ranch? Eliot still trying to learn how to be a cowboy?"

"He's convinced he is one." Pecos grinned. "All of us have been helpin' out since some of the hands quit."

"Some of the Lindseys' men left?"

"That's right. They were Armstrong's pards. I suppose they were pretty shook up by what happened to him."

Teddy nodded. "I guess I can understand that."

Hallam frowned, deep in thought, as Pecos continued telling Teddy about the activities on the Flying L. Some of the stories about Eliot's determination to be a real cowboy now might have been funny if Hallam had been paying any real attention to them.

He was wondering, instead, about the men who had drawn their time and left the ranch. He was going to have to find out their names and where they had gone. If one or more of them had been part of the rustling ring with Armstrong, there was a good chance that the foreman's killer might be one of them. There could be a lead there he had overlooked until now. Something else was bothering him, too, but he couldn't quite pull it out of the back of his head. Something he had seen or heard—

"Hallam!" The voice was as cold as ice, and just about as sharp. "What the hell are you doing here?"

He turned to see Sheriff Mart Bascomb striding down the corridor, the worried-looking guard behind him. The lawman's face was flushed with anger. Bascomb went on, "I gave strict orders that no one except his lawyer was allowed to see that murdering savage, and now I find some sort of goddamn picnic going on back here!"

"I'm workin' for Gilliam," Hallam told the sheriff calmly. "Figured I had a right to talk to the colonel's client."

"You figured wrong," Bascomb snapped. "I want you and this friend of yours out of here—right now! And if you try to come back, I'll see that you stay a while!"

Hallam reached out and put a hand on Pecos's arm. He could tell that the youngster was aching to take a swing at Bascomb. Hallam could understand that; he felt the same way himself. But at the moment, they were just about Teddy's only hope. If they got thrown in the hoosegow, that would probably destroy any chance of clearing Teddy.

"We're goin'," Hallam said. "Just give us a minute to say good-bye to our pard."

Bascomb put his hand on the butt of his holstered pistol, and the guard followed his example. "I said now," Bascomb grated.

Hallam grimaced, glanced over his shoulder at Teddy, and said, "So long, son. We'll be seein' you."

"Take care of yourself, Teddy," Pecos said through the bars. "Don't worry, Lucas'll find out—"

"Move!" the sheriff rapped.

Hallam almost had to drag Pecos away from the cell.

Bascomb and the guard followed them along the corridor, and the lawmen didn't take their hands away from their guns until the little group had reached the lobby of the jail. Hallam turned to the sheriff and said, "You know, Bascomb, I'm sort of glad we run into you. I never did get my gun back after that big deputy of yours took it off me the other night."

"And you won't until you're ready to leave Texas," Bascomb replied. "It's been temporarily confiscated."

Hallam's mouth twitched. There were no grounds for the sheriff's refusal to return the old Colt—other than the fact that Bascomb was a chickenshit son-of-a-bitch. Pointing that out probably wouldn't help, though, Hallam decided.

"When I get ready to leave, I'll let you know," he said.

"You be sure and do that," Bascomb returned coolly.

Still hanging onto Pecos to make sure that the boy didn't fly off the handle, Hallam pushed through the doors of the lobby and onto the sidewalk outside. Afternoon sunlight washed the stone walls of the big courthouse next door, striking pretty glints from the flecks of granite, but Hallam was in no mood to appreciate the sight. He stood on the sidewalk for a moment, trying to figure out what to do next, and was vaguely aware of someone coming out of the jail behind him.

"Hey, cowboy," a voice said. "Talk to you for a minute?"

Hallam looked around and saw a short, slight man in a suit and tie. The stranger had a fedora tilted back on his dark-haired head. His eyes studied Hallam and Pecos.

"What do you want, mister?" Hallam asked.

"I saw the way the sheriff escorted you and your pal out of the building. What did you do to get him so mad at you?"

"What business is that of yours?" Hallam wanted to know.

"I'm a newspaper reporter, work for the *Star-Telegram*. Bascomb's not one of my favorite people in the world, and I suppose the feeling's mutual." The man shrugged his narrow shoulders. "I just thought you looked like you might have an interesting story to tell."

Hallam shook his head. He didn't feel like having a reporter jabbing questions at him. "I reckon we'll keep our dealin's to ourselves."

"Suit yourself, bud. I just thought maybe it had something to do with all the rustling."

Hallam had started to turn away, but he stopped at the reporter's words. "You know about the rustlin' that's been goin' on around here?"

"Sure," the man said. "I work the police beat. You hear things, sometimes things the cops don't want you to hear." He stuck his hands in his pockets and angled his head toward downtown Fort Worth. "Looks pretty peaceful, doesn't it? Let me tell you, mister, it ain't. We've got that rustling ring operating around here, we've got illegal gambling, we've got more moonshine being trucked out of this area than anywhere else in the state. When it comes to crime, Chicago and the boys back east don't have much of a lead on Fort Worth."

The reporter sounded almost proud of that fact, Hallam thought. And he obviously liked to hear the sound of his own voice. "Listen, mister," Hallam said, "if you know anything about that rustlin', I'd sure appreciate it if you'd tell me."

The reporter chuckled humorlessly and shook his head. "Something for nothing? I don't think so."

"Listen, goddamn it," Pecos said, stepping forward with his fists clenched. "Lucas asked you a question—"

"Hold on there, Pecos," Hallam said sharply, putting out an arm to block the youngster's advance. "We don't want to go startin' trouble right in front of the jail. Bascomb'd love to have an excuse to jug us. Besides, this feller's got a right not to talk to us if he don't want to."

The reporter had started to look a little nervous, but now he relaxed and pulled a crumpled cigarette from his pocket. As he stuck it in his mouth, he said, "I just figure the conversation might go two ways. I spill what I know, and you do likewise."

"Come on," Hallam said. "Let's get a cup of coffee."

TWENTY-ONE

The reporter's name was Mickey Springstead, and it was obvious from the way he talked about Sheriff Bascomb that he liked the sheriff about as much as Hallam and Pecos did—not at all.

"I can't come right out in the paper and say he's a crook," Springstead told them over coffee in a nearby diner. His voice was pitched low, in case any of Bascomb's cronies were in the place. "But he sure hasn't gone out of his way to find those rustlers, just like he hasn't done anything about all the bootlegging around here. And most of the gambling houses run untouched. The city cops have closed down most of the places in town, but criminals seem to have a free hand out in the county."

"You sound like that bothers you," Hallam said.

"Why shouldn't it? I don't like seeing corruption in our elected officials."

"Maybe Bascomb's just incompetent instead of on the take," Hallam suggested.

Springstead sipped his coffee and cocked an eyebrow. "Could be—but I don't think so."

Hallam nodded thoughtfully. After a moment, he said, "So

there's lots of folks brewin' 'shine around these parts, is there?"

"I don't know," the reporter replied. "Even though it pains me journalistically to admit that. There are either a lot of small-time bootleggers in this part of the country, or somebody's got one big operation. One thing's for sure, though: Not only is enough liquor being produced to stock all the speakeasies around here, but I've heard rumors that it's being trucked out to places all over the state. Hell, some say the supply for most of the Southwest comes right out of north Texas."

"That's interestin'," Hallam mused.

Interesting might be all it was, he thought. But there was a chance it might be more than that. The pieces he had been trying to fit together in his mind over the last few days hadn't formed a complete picture yet, but that might have been because he didn't have all of them.

If a man was mixed up in one crooked scheme, Hallam knew, he might be mixed up with another.

"Seems to me that I've been doing all the talking," Springstead said. "That's not the way it was supposed to be."

"We're friends of one of the prisoners Bascomb has in there," Hallam told him. "The sheriff didn't want us visitin' him. That's all there was to it."

Springstead shook his head. "Sorry, I don't believe that. You were asking about Bascomb and his connection to the crime around here for a reason. I want to know what it is." After a moment of silence, he went on, "Look, I won't put it in the paper, if that's what you want. Strictly off the record . . . for now."

"Meanin'?"

Springstead smiled. "Meaning that when the story breaks, I get first crack at it."

Hallam had to grin at the eagerness in the man's voice. Springstead reminded him of a friend of his named Drake who was a reporter on one of the Los Angeles papers. The two men were nothing alike physically, and Drake had a lot of years on Springstead, but they shared the same desire to break a big story. Drake had helped Hallam out on the Elton Forbes case a few months earlier; maybe Springstead had now done the same.

"As long as it's off the record for the time bein'," Hallam said, "I reckon it won't hurt to tell you the story."

Quickly, he gave Springstead some of the details of the Hollywood group's visit to Texas, leaving out Eliot Tremaine's status as a rank amateur when they had arrived. When he reached the murder of Dan Armstrong and the arrest of Teddy Spotted Horse, he told Springstead only the bare facts of the case, leaving out all of the detective work he had been doing and the speculations it had led him to.

"So you see, we were just interested in the rustlers because they hit the ranch where we're stayin'," Hallam concluded. "And I told you why we don't get along with Bascomb."

"You think this Indian friend of yours is innocent? I've read the reports, Hallam. It sure sounds to me like he must have done it."

Hallam shook his head. "You won't never convince us of that. We know the boy too well."

"Damn right," Pecos added in a growl. He had been silent for the most part, still regarding Springstead with suspicion.

"Well, if you happen to stumble over anything that might clear the Indian—not that you'd be trying to conduct some sort of investigation of your own"—Springstead grinned as he spoke, and Hallam knew that the reporter hadn't been completely fooled—"you'd probably do better to bring it to the newspaper than to Bascomb. He'd probably just bury it."

"Could be you're right," Hallam said noncommittally. He put some coins on the table to cover the coffee and stood up. "Been nice talkin' to you, Mr. Springstead. Maybe we'll run into each other again."

"I'd count on that if you're going to stay around here," Springstead said.

As Hallam and Pecos walked out onto the sidewalk, the younger man frowned and said, "I don't think I trust that fella, Lucas. He was a mite too curious."

"You know how them newspaper reporters are, Pecos. They ain't happy 'less they're diggin' around in something. Sort of like private eyes, I reckon."

"Maybe," Pecos grunted, but he didn't sound convinced.

"I suppose we'd best find Smitty, so's you can ride back to the ranch with him."

Pecos looked at him in surprise. "You're not goin' back to the Flyin' L?"

Hallam shook his head. "Nope. Got to go see a man about a dog."

Pecos couldn't get any more out of him, despite the questions the youngster asked. Hallam climbed back into the borrowed pickup and motioned for Pecos to get in as well. Smitty had planned on going to a market a few blocks away from the courthouse, Pecos told him, and when Hallam pulled up in front of the store, the ranch cook was just waddling out with his arms full of sacks.

"Good timin', men," Smitty grinned as he saw Hallam and Pecos. "They's more supplies inside to load up." One of the Flying L's other trucks was parked at the curb.

"Pecos'll help you," Hallam told Smitty through the open window of the pickup. "I've got to be goin'."

"You be back at the ranch for supper?" Smitty asked. "Ain't goin' to be nothin' fancy, just steak and taters and homemade bread."

Hallam thought about the bread Smitty baked, the way wisps of steam rose from the warm, floury loaves when you sliced into them, bringing with them one of the best smells known to man. He smiled but shook his head. "Sounds mighty temptin', Smitty," he said. "But there's things I've got to do."

"Well, be careful, then," the cook told him. "We'll be

lookin' for you later. Might save you a plate, if there's any left."

"Now, I'd appreciate that," Hallam said. He put the truck back in gear and pulled away from the market.

He drove north on Belknap Street, thinking about what Mickey Springstead had told him and about the idea that had occurred to him while he was talking to the reporter. It was possible that whoever was behind the rustling was also involved with the bootlegging that Springstead had mentioned. The roadhouse in the country between Denton and Decatur might be the headquarters for more than one criminal operation.

The two Rangers, Kerr and Garrett, hadn't said anything about bootlegging, though. According to them, their only objective had been to find the rustlers.

These days, there was more money in brewing and running booze than stealing cows, Hallam thought. But rustling might prove valuable in other ways. . . .

He had no proof of anything, that was for sure. And it seemed to him that there was only one place he might find any.

It looked like he was going back to Zeke's Place after all.

Dusk was settling down when Hallam pulled into the gravel parking lot in front of the roadhouse. He cut the engine, then paused for a moment before getting out of the pickup. Reaching underneath the seat, he pulled out something he had placed there earlier before leaving the ranch.

He might not have his Colt, but the bowie knife in its leather sheath was as sharp and deadly as ever.

Hallam pulled up the leg of his pants and slid the sheathed blade down into his high-topped boot. The end of the handle was just below where the boot ended. It was handy enough there to get to in a hurry, but it wasn't likely to be noticed. He would limp a little when he walked, but he did that anyway because of the knee hurt years earlier.

He pushed down his pants leg and reached for the handle of the truck's door. At that moment, the door of the roadhouse opened, and Hallam settled back in the seat, sliding down so that he wouldn't be as easy to see. He wanted to know who was coming out of the roadhouse before he went in. If it was Kerr and Garrett, still working undercover, he would wait until they were gone. Of course, there was a chance that they would be inside the place when he went in, but he was just going to have to risk that.

One man emerged from the roadhouse and turned toward the Flying L's pickup. Hallam didn't move as the man got into a Model T parked several cars away. There was still enough of a glow in the western sky for Hallam to get a good look at the man's face.

The last time he had seen those lean, dark features, the man had been on horseback, trying to get away from Eliot Tremaine.

Hallam's pulse beat faster. It made sense that if the roadhouse was being used as a base of operations for the rustlers, he would spot someone he recognized sooner or later. This man was definitely one of the bunch that had wide-looped the herd from the Flying L's north pasture.

The rustler started the Model T, backed out of the parking lot, and headed west toward Decatur. As soon as he was out of earshot of the place, Hallam hit the pickup's starter again. Leaving his lights off, he backed up as well, then waited until the Model T had topped the hill where Hallam had been surprised by the two Texas Rangers. Then Hallam fed gas to the truck and sped after him.

The most important thing about detective work, Hallam had learned, was keeping your eyes open and remembering what you saw. But being in the right place at the right time was a big part of it, too, along with knowing how to accept good luck when it came your way.

He was on the rustler's trail now, and he didn't intend to lose it.

The man stayed on the highway for several miles. Hallam hung back, keeping at least a quarter of a mile behind him. There was less traffic on the road now, with night not far away. Finally, the Model T swung to the right, and when Hallam reached the spot, he found a dirt road leading in the direction the rustler had gone.

He turned off the pickup's headlights and wheeled the vehicle into the dirt road. There was still barely enough light to see to drive. Conditions were worse now than they would be later, once the moon and stars were out. On the other hand, Hallam thought, that might be a blessing. He was sure the truck was kicking up some dust as he drove along the dirt surface. Maybe this way it wouldn't be spotted if the man in the Model T was watching his back trail.

Hallam saw the flare of brake lights; then the taillights of the Model T vanished as the rustler stopped and killed them. Taking his foot off the accelerator, Hallam switched off the engine of the pickup and let it coast to a stop. He was still a couple of hundred yards short of the place where the Model T had halted.

The evening was quiet as Hallam slipped out of the truck and eased the door shut. He started down the side of the road, wishing he had his gun with him. The Bowie would have to do if he ran into any trouble. With luck, he would be able to sneak up and see where the rustler had gone, then get back to the pickup and go look for some help. His instincts told him that he was about to find the real headquarters of the rustling ring.

It was more than that, he saw a few minutes later as he crouched behind a bush, not making a sound.

The Model T was parked in front of an old, run-down farmhouse. Judging by the way the place had fallen into disrepair, it had probably been abandoned several years earlier. It was not vacant at the moment, though: There were four cars parked in front of it, and Hallam saw the noses of two trucks that were backed up into a large barn behind the house. He could see a tendril of smoke curling from a makeshift vent at the back of the barn's roof.

Folks normally didn't start a fire in a barn. There didn't seem to be any animals around here, however, and Hallam doubted very seriously that the structure was now being used for the same purpose as it had been built.

There were lights in the house and in the barn, but as Hallam looked around the surrounding countryside, he couldn't see any other telltale glows. This farmhouse was in a little valley, and from the looks of things, it was the only place around here. The people who had taken it over could do just about anything they wanted without being observed unless by accident.

Or unless somebody trailed one of them out here, Hallam thought.

He wondered if there were several stills set up in the barn or just a single large one. Either way, the bootleggers probably kept the fires burning nearly all the time as they distilled the homemade whiskey. It was likely stored in kegs, which were then loaded on the trucks and carried away. Zeke's probably got the first delivery, since the roadhouse was only a few miles away. From there, the trucks would go on to who knows where, carrying their loads of contraband liquor.

Hallam had never been much of a believer in Prohibition; any fool could see it wasn't working. The Waterhole, back in Hollywood, was a speakeasy and there was no denying that. He couldn't hate the men who had set up this bootlegging operation simply because they were violating the Volstead Act.

But when they went to killing people and a friend of his got the blame . . . well, that was different, Hallam thought.

He edged away from the bush, ready to head back to the pickup. Now he wanted to find Kerr and Garrett, instead of avoiding them. With the support of the Texas Rangers, Hallam knew he could get the Wise County authorities to do something about this place.

Out of the corner of his eye, he saw a shadow move.

Hallam threw himself forward and to the side, heard the swish of something whipping past his head. He whirled around, saw a man lunging at him out of the gathering darkness, flung up an arm to block the blow coming at him.

He had figured that there would be guards out, but he thought he had avoided all of them. It was plain as day now that he had been wrong.

Hallam drove a punch at the other man and felt it connect. Before he could follow it up, someone else landed on his back. Whoever it was wrapped an arm around Hallam's neck and bellowed, "Help!"

That tore it. He had to get away from here in a hurry now. There were probably eight or ten men around the farm, and he wouldn't have a chance if they got into this fight.

He reached up, grabbed hair, and pulled as hard as he could, bending sharply forward. The man on his back screeched and let go, flying over Hallam's shoulders and falling right into the path of the first man. They both went down in a heap.

Hallam leaped over them and started to run toward the spot where he had left the pickup. Another shape suddenly came out of the brush at the left side of the road, and Hallam tried to stop as he saw the figure swinging something toward him.

He had just enough time to think that the thing felt like a two-by-four as it crashed into his head. His feet went out from under him, dropping him to the road. He seemed to taste dust in his mouth for an instant, and then there was nothing, no taste or smell or sight, nothing but blackness.

TWENTY-TWO

The Bowie was gone. That was the first thing Hallam realized when he woke up. The second thing he became aware of was that somebody had trussed him up like a bulldogged calf. His arms had been yanked behind his back, and ropes were tied around his wrists and ankles.

He stayed still, listening for a long moment. There were faint sounds coming from the darkness surrounding him, but none too close. The floor underneath him was made of rough planks, and he would have been willing to bet that he had been tossed into one of the rooms in the abandoned farmhouse after his captors got through tying him up.

Hallam tried to lift his head to look around, and that was a mistake. A groan came involuntarily from his lips as thunderclaps of pain went off inside his skull. A second later he heard the rasp of a match and knew he hadn't been alone after all.

Somebody had just been waiting for him to wake up.

"I figured you'd wake up before morning," a voice said. "That head of yours is too thick for a crack with a board to keep you out more than a couple of hours."

The flickering yellow glow of a lantern welled up and filled the room. As Hallam had thought, he was inside the farmhouse. A 1922 calendar, probably left there by the previous tenants, was still hanging on the wall. Under the calendar, sitting in an old rocking chair, was Sheriff Mart Bascomb. The lantern was on a small table next to the chair. The sheriff's legs were crossed casually, and nestled in his lap was a double-barreled shotgun. The twin barrels were pointed straight at Hallam, and there was nothing casual about them.

"You were just too damn stubborn to leave it alone," Bascomb went on. "That was your mistake, Hallam. Reckon it's going to cost you your life, come morning."

There was no gag in Hallam's mouth. It took him a minute to get his throat working, but then he said, "Why wait that long?"

"You might come in handy later on," Bascomb said, "in case somebody gets the idea of rushing this place. They might be a little less eager when they find out we've got you in here."

Hallam shook his head. "Nobody's comin'. Nobody knows I'm out here."

"I was going to ask you about that." Bascomb smiled thinly. "Funny thing is, I'm not sure I believe you. No, we'll keep you around just in case there's any trouble before Noonan takes that load out before dawn."

Hallam didn't know any Noonan. His head hurt something fierce and his muscles were starting to cramp up some from the awkward position he was lying in, but it was plain that Bascomb didn't intend to kill him right away. Might as well keep the sheriff talking, he thought, find out as much as he could about what was really going on around here.

"The Wise County sheriff might not like it if he found out you're brewin' 'shine and runnin' stolen cattle over here in his county," Hallam said. "Could be he'd want to be paid off, just like you."

Bascomb chuckled humorlessly. "I doubt it. He seems to be honest, the damn fool."

"Must've been pretty profitable for you, takin' payoffs to

look the other way from the rustlers *and* the bootleggers. 'Course, I reckon that's all the same bunch, ain't it?"

Bascomb's eyes narrowed. "Just how much do you know?"

Hallam wished he had something to drink. It wasn't likely Bascomb would oblige him, though, so he went on. "Seems to me the rustlin' was pretty much a smokescreen. The fellers runnin' this show would clear a little profit from it, but not much. The real reason they kept it up was so the Rangers would stay busy tryin' to find out who was stealin' cattle and not pay any attention to the whiskey comin' out of these parts. There's always been bootleggin' around here, I suppose, but it's only lately that it's been turned into a major operation. That right?"

"Close enough," Bascomb muttered. "Noonan and Jenkins were brought down here from Chicago to set it up. It's been growing like a house afire ever since."

"That your idea, was it, to import some real-life gangsters from up north to show you how it's done?"

"I don't run things, Hallam. I just take my cut and make sure that snoops like you don't ruin things." Bascomb jerked the muzzle of the shotgun slightly. "You're asking questions like you think you're going to be getting out of here, Hallam. You can forget that. As soon as the next load leaves and we're sure that everything is still covered, you're a dead man."

"Wouldn't hurt to tell me who's really behind this, then would it?"

Bascomb just leaned back in the rocking chair and smiled. It was about the ugliest expression Hallam had ever seen.

It was funny how time could pass so quick and so slow at the same thing, Hallam thought. As he lay there hog-tied, with one hell of a headache and a mouth that felt like cotton, the minutes seemed to drag. At the same time, there was a good chance this might be the last night of his life, and that seemed to speed things up.

Bascomb said very little over the next couple of hours, and then he was relieved by another man who took the shotgun and said even less. Hallam hadn't seen this man before, and he wondered if the guard was normally a rustler or a bootlegger. For that matter, the members of the gang could take turns, he supposed.

He had been in more uncomfortable spots, he told himself. And sometime long after midnight, he even managed to doze a little.

He figured it was a couple of hours before dawn when Bascomb and two other men came into the room. One of the strangers was stocky and wore a suit and hat, and his face seemed almost like it was divided in half by a large black moustache. Hallam recognized the other man; he had been driving the truck that had delivered the bootlegged whiskey to the Flying L before the party.

"This is him, Ike," Bascomb said to the man in the suit. "Name's Lucas Hallam. He's some sort of cowboy actor from Hollywood."

"What's he doing messing in our business?" the man called Ike asked harshly.

"Getting himself dead," Bascomb said.

For somebody who hadn't shown much of a sense of humor up until now, the sheriff was getting downright witty, Hallam thought.

Bascomb went on, "I think he's just too damn nosy for his own good. He's not working with the Rangers or anybody else, as far as I know."

"Good," Ike grunted. He pulled a watch from his pocket and flipped it open. "Vince will be leaving in a few minutes. As soon as he meets the boss and finds out for sure where this load is going, we'll be that much closer to being rich men, Sheriff." He snapped the watch shut. "Wait a little while, then take this yokel out and kill him."

"I'll do it, Mr. Jenkins," the other man said. He sounded excited by the prospect.

"All right, Dirk, that'll be fine."

This Ike Jenkins was one of the men Bascomb had spoken

of, Hallam thought. Vince would probably be the other one. Noonan, that was the name Bascomb had mentioned. Ike Jenkins and Vince Noonan . . . Hallam would try to remember those names for when he got out of here.

Damned if he was going to give up yet.

Bascomb, Jenkins, and Dirk went out of the room, leaving on guard the same man who had been there for the last several hours. In the silence, Hallam heard the sound of night birds singing in the trees outside.

A few minutes later, the birds were drowned out by the rumble of a truck's motor. That would be Noonan leaving with the load of illegal liquor.

Another twenty minutes went by, and then the trio who had been there earlier reappeared. Jenkins was smiling now, as were Bascomb and Dirk, but that didn't make any of them any prettier, Hallam thought. "Get him on his feet," Bascomb ordered.

Dirk and the silent guard stepped forward, Dirk leaning over to slash the ropes around Hallam's ankles with a clasp knife. They grabbed his arms and hauled him up, grunting with the effort it took to lift his massive frame. Hallam could see unshaded windows now on two sides of the room. The sky was just beginning to get gray with the approach of dawn.

"What about his hands?" Dirk asked.

"Leave them tied," Bascomb ordered. "I don't trust the son-of-a-bitch." He held up his hands. "Take a look at these, Hallam. I think I'll keep them, sort of like trophies."

Hallam's eyes narrowed as he saw that Bascomb held his Colt and his Bowie. The big knife was still sheathed. The revolver was loaded; he could see the leaden noses of the cartridges in the cylinder.

"Or maybe I should just give the gun to Dirk and let him use it on you," Bascomb went on. "That seems appropriate."

"Those weapons are old friends of mine, Bascomb," Hallam said slowly. "I surely do hate to see a man like you with his hands on them."

The sheriff's face tightened with anger. "Well, that's just too damn bad, isn't it? You don't have much say in the matter." He thrust the Colt at Dirk, who took it eagerly; then Bascomb tucked the knife under his arm, reached out, and took the shotgun from the guard. "Let's go, Hallam," he grated. "Time to get this over with." He pulled back both hammers on the scattergun.

"Throw out your weapons and come out of the house with your hands up!" a voice shouted. *"This is the Texas Rangers! You are surrounded!"*

"Goddamn!" Jenkins exclaimed, digging inside his coat for a gun. "They must have followed the old bastard after all! Get over to the window and tell them we've got Hallam and we'll kill him if they don't back off!"

Hallam had stiffened at the sound of the shout, thinking he recognized Fred Kerr's voice. He didn't know how many men were out there, didn't know how they'd react when they heard that he was a prisoner in here. But there was a chance that Bascomb and Jenkins might be successful in their plan to use him as a hostage. They might put a gun to his head and bargain their way out of here.

Lucas Hallam wasn't going to allow that.

He lunged as Bascomb started to turn toward the front window. Hallam's foot came up, slamming into the shotgun in the sheriff's hands and knocking it violently to the side. Bascomb's finger was through the trigger guard, and the jolt touched off both barrels.

The shotgun roared, the double loads of buckshot tearing into the guard and all but cutting him in half. He died without making a sound, just as he had passed the night.

"Damn it!" Bascomb had time to howl. He knew, just as Hallam did, that the blast of the shotgun would be all the prodding the men outside needed to open up.

The next instant, what sounded like the chatter of a Gatling gun ripped through the early-morning air. The glass in the room's front window shattered into a million pieces, the shards flying through the air. Bascomb jerked abruptly, red patches suddenly flowering on his uniform shirt. The slugs threw him back against Hallam.

Hallam felt himself falling and didn't try to stop it. He sprawled on the floor, Bascomb's bullet-riddled body half on top of him, as a hail of slugs tore into the farmhouse. The old, rotten wood of the building's walls offered no resistance to the flying lead. The roar of pistols and rifles and automatic weapons seemed to go on forever. Hallam saw the man called Dirk clutch at his middle as a line of slugs stitched across his body. He crumpled lifelessly.

The lantern suddenly exploded as a bullet hit it. It was still burning, and flames whooshed up as the blazing kerosene splashed over the dry wood of the floor.

Hallam heard more shooting from the other rooms and knew that some of the gang must have been inside the house. Now they were trying to return the Rangers' fire, but it was a lost cause, especially with the place about to go up in flames around them. Hallam twisted out from under the body of Sheriff Mart Bascomb.

He had to get out of here in a hurry, or he would burn up with the rest of them. His gaze fell on the Bowie knife, lying nearby where Bascomb had dropped it when the shooting started. Rolling over so that his back was to it, Hallam reached behind him and grasped the handle of the blade, shaking the sheath off it. This wasn't the first time he had used the Bowie to cut himself free. It was chancy—you could slash your own wrists just as easily as the ropes that bound them—but there was no time to worry about that now.

He sawed with the sharp blade and felt the ropes fall from his wrists. Rolling again, Hallam started to come to his feet. There was another window in the far wall of the room, and there didn't seem to be as much gunfire on that side of the house; he might be able to dive out through it without getting shot.

But Ike Jenkins was in his way.

The gangster's coat was stained with blood, but he was still on his feet and still had a pistol in his hand. His face contorted in hate as he saw Hallam. He jerked the gun toward the big man.

Hallam's muscles were stiff from his long captivity, but they worked well enough. He brought his arm up and released the Bowie without aiming. Instinct did that for him.

Flames flickered on the blade as it flew across the room. It thudded into Jenkins's chest, staggering him as the point sliced all the way into his heart. He managed to get off one shot before he fell, the bullet whining wildly past Hallam.

All the walls of the room were on fire now. Hallam leaped over Jenkins's body, reaching down to snag the Bowie and rip it free of the dead man's chest. Slugs still sang through the air. He would have yelled for the fools outside to quit shooting, but there was no way they could hear him over the blasts, Hallam knew. He paused one more time, to scoop up the Colt that had fallen from Dirk's lifeless hand, then he hurled himself toward the window. Just before he hit it, he noticed that only one of the panes was broken. The other three had somehow managed to escape being hit by the rain of bullets.

Hallam crashed into the window, catapulting through it in a shower of shattered glass. It seemed to take him a long time to fall to the ground outside. As he spun through the air, he thought that if the Rangers tried to shoot him, then, damn it, he might just shoot back.

He hit the ground hard and rolled over, aware suddenly that silence had dropped over the place. Spotting movement out of the corner of his eye as he came up, he raised the Colt, ready to fire.

A man holding a machine gun was running toward him through the shadows and the early morning mist. Hallam let the barrel of the Colt sag toward the ground. The man wore a silver star in a silver circle, and Hallam knew his face.

"What the hell took you so long, Hallam?" Fred Kerr asked. The glow from the blazing farmhouse reflected redly on his badge.

Hallam reached up to take the hand the Ranger extended toward him. "Reckon I could ask you the same thing," he said.

TWENTY-THREE

Hallam had a bullet burn on his left forearm and another on his right side, just below his ribs. He hadn't noticed either one during the hectic few minutes while he had been trying to escape the inferno inside the farmhouse.

One of the Rangers patched up the minor wounds as Hallam said to Fred Kerr, "You boys been followin' me all along, haven't you?"

Kerr nodded, then said, "Well, not from the first, just since that run-in we had with you over by the roadhouse. We figured you were too stubborn to leave things alone. Sometimes the quickest way to crack a case is to let somebody else stir things up."

"Reckon that's what I did, all right." Hallam looked at the smoking ruins of the farmhouse. The sun was starting to come up, and the black haze of smoke that had been produced by the fire was stark against the lightening sky.

He could hear plenty of racket coming from inside the barn. More Rangers were there, busting up the stills they had found in the old structure. Four members of the gang were sitting in the backseats of official cars that had been brought up. The bootleggers were all handcuffed, and a couple of them had bloodstained bandages on their heads.

All the rest of the bunch were dead, a few sprawled around the farmhouse where they had fallen as they attempted to shoot their way out, the others still in the ruins. Blankets had been spread over the bodies on the ground. The Wise County coroner had plenty of work waiting for him.

"We would have gotten here earlier, but Chuck had trouble finding a telephone," Kerr said.

"I was the one following you last night," Garrett put in. The Ranger was leaning against the fender of a nearby car. "I didn't know what the hell you were doing when you took off from the roadhouse without even going in, but you seemed to know where you were heading."

Hallam shook his head. "I was just followin' a feller I spotted comin' out of there. Recognized him as one of the bunch that stole those cows from the Flyin' L."

"That's where your knowledge came in handy," Kerr told him. "We'd probably seen the same guy around the place several times, but we never would have recognized him as one of the rustlers. You and those friends of yours were the only ones who were ever close enough to recognize any of them."

"Thanks, pard," Hallam said as the officer finished his rough first-aid job. As he shrugged back into his bullet-torn shirt, Hallam went on, "I had a feelin' the rustlin' and the bootleggin' was tied in together. Looks like the same bunch was doin' all of it and usin' this place as their headquarters."

"That's what we figure, too," Kerr agreed. "I'm sure that when we get a chance to sift through the ashes of the house, we'll find some evidence to that effect. At any rate, we can jail the survivors on attempted murder charges, and the ring is certainly busted up now." The Ranger grinned. "All in all, a pretty good morning's work."

"I wish I could have gotten you out of there, Hallam," Garrett said. "No hard feelings about that tangle we had the other day. But once I found a telephone and called the alarm in to Fred, I had to wait until he showed up with reinforcements. I saw those guards clout you and was going to pitch in then, but they hauled you off too quick. I couldn't risk getting caught myself until I had gotten hold of Fred and passed the word about this place."

Hallam waved a hand. *"De nada.* Shuttin' this operation down was more important than savin' my hide. Anyway, I came out all right." He pointed to the remaining truck parked in the barn's entrance. "Did you see another truck like that leave just a little while before all hell broke loose?"

Garrett nodded. "Fred and the other boys hadn't gotten here by then, so there was nothing I could do about it. I got the license number, though, and we've radioed out a good description of the truck. Somebody will pick it up sooner or later."

"It's loaded down with whiskey," Hallam said, "and the feller drivin' it is Vince Noonan. Him and another feller named Jenkins came down from Chicago and set all this up."

"What happened to Jenkins?" Kerr asked.

Hallam nodded toward what was left of the farmhouse and didn't say anything.

Kerr grunted. "Looks like this wraps everything up. At least it will once we grab Noonan and that truckload of booze. Too bad we couldn't have taken Bascomb alive." The Ranger's eyes were hard as he went on, "There's nothing worse than a crooked lawman. I'd have liked to see him go to prison."

"Reckon it's a little hotter where he is than it ever gets down at Huntsville," Hallam commented. Kerr started to turn away, but Hallam stopped him by saying, "What about Armstrong?"

"What about him?" Kerr asked. "It looks like he may have been working with the gang, but we'll never know that for sure. Like Bascomb and Jenkins and the others, he's dead now. He can't be punished anymore."

"Teddy Spotted Horse can," Hallam said grimly.

Kerr shook his head. "That's out of our hands, Hallam. We appreciate everything you've done, but there's still no evidence to indicate that that boy didn't kill Armstrong. That murder doesn't necessarily have anything to do with all of this. You'll have to talk to whoever takes over for Bascomb. Maybe he'll be willing to reopen the investigation."

Hallam supposed Kerr was right—at least as far as the Ranger knew. But Kerr was dead wrong about one thing. This case wasn't wrapped up, not by a long shot.

The sun was climbing steadily in the sky as Hallam drove the pickup back toward the Flying L. The Rangers would want to talk to him again later, Kerr had said, but for the time being he was free to go.

As he drove, the warm morning air blowing freshly in his face, Hallam thought.

He hadn't told Kerr and Garrett about the fact that someone else besides the two gangsters from Chicago was really behind the combined bootlegging and rustling scheme. They could think that if they wanted, but Hallam knew better.

Bascomb had been in the pay of whoever was running the ring. Bascomb had been adamant that Teddy was guilty of Armstrong's murder, and he had done everything in his power to make sure that any further investigation was quashed. Could be, Hallam mused, that Armstrong had really been killed by the ringleader of the gang, who had then given orders to Bascomb to see that no suspects except Teddy were considered.

That would mean that the man who was behind all the trouble was right there on the Flying L.

Hallam sent his mind back to the night Armstrong had been killed, thought through all that had happened, reconstructed in his memory the way things had looked in that barn.

His big hands tightened on the steering wheel of the truck.

He knew who the killer was, all right. He should have known all along.

A bitter curse wanted to come out of his mouth, but he swallowed it. No sense in cussing himself now. It was too late for that. But maybe it wasn't too late to really end things.

He pressed down harder on the truck's accelerator, sent the vehicle rattling faster down the highway.

It was mid-morning when Hallam got back to the Flying L. The pickup must have made enough noise to warn everyone that he was coming, because there was a crowd waiting for him. Pecos led the way, but Eliot was there, too, with his arm around Rae Lindsey. Rae's father was close behind, followed by Stone Riordan, Max Hilyard, Tall Cotton Jones, Red Callahan, Harv Macklin, and Jeff Grant. All of them gathered around Hallam as he climbed out of the pickup.

Out of the welter of questions thrown at him, Hallam heard Pecos demand, "Where the hell have you been, Lucas?" The others were echoing pretty much the same thing.

Hallam held up his hands to silence them. "I'll explain it all later, but for now I want to tell you, Miss Rae, and you, Mr. Lindsey, that you won't be havin' no more trouble with rustlers. The Texas Rangers killed most of them and captured the rest early this mornin'."

That only brought on another clamor.

Hallam looked at the people surrounding him. When they quieted down, he asked, "Where's Smitty?"

Several of the group looked around, as if just realizing that the cook was not with them, but Rae said, "I saw him saddling up a horse a little while ago. He said he was going to take a ride around the place before he had to start lunch."

"Does that every now and then, does he?" Hallam asked.

Rae shrugged. "Sometimes. He used to be a cowboy, he told me. I think he misses riding the range."

"Hallam, what's this all about?" Eliot demanded. "You come in here looking like you've been in some sort of battle, say something about Texas Rangers and rustlers, and now you start asking questions about the ranch cook. This is starting to sound like the script from one of my father's pictures."

"Nope," Hallam said. "This ain't make-believe." He pushed past them and headed toward the corrals.

Pecos, Eliot, and Rae caught up with him while he was saddling a horse. "Damn it, Lucas, what are you doin' now?" Pecos wanted to know.

"Got to go see a man about a dog," Hallam grunted as he tightened a cinch.

"That's what you told me yesterday, and then you up and vanished!" Pecos grabbed at his arm. "We just want to help—"

Hallam shook off the grip roughly. "I got to do this by myself, Pecos!" he snapped. He turned to Rae. "Which direction did Smitty go?"

"Northeast, I think," Rae replied, pointing in that direction. She was frowning worriedly. "Is he in some sort of danger, Mr. Hallam?"

"Not sure yet," Hallam said honestly. "I sure need to talk to him, though."

"Let us go with you," Eliot said. "It will only take a moment to saddle more mounts—"

Hallam swung up on the back of his horse, ignoring Eliot's request. He touched the brim of his hat and, nodding to Rae, said, "Much obliged for the help, ma'am." Then he heeled the horse into motion and rode away from the ranch house, heading northeast. As he rode off, he thought he heard Pecos mutter, "Stubborn old bastard."

He cut Smitty's sign within minutes and started following the trail. He couldn't be sure that Smitty's horse had made the tracks, but they were fresh and they led in the right direction. It was a gamble worth taking, Hallam thought.

He hadn't been up to this part of the ranch, but the route he was taking now led in the general direction of the highway between Fort Worth and Denton. There were probably gates in the fences and rutted roads winding up into these rolling, brushy, isolated hills. It would be easy enough to meet someone without being observed.

There had been plenty of time for Vince Noonan to get over here with the truck. Hallam pushed the horse hard, getting as much speed out of the animal as he could. He wanted to reach the rendezvous before Noonan left; otherwise it was going to be hard to prove anything.

He reined in at the top of a rise. In the valley below, the truck he had last seen parked inside the barn at the abandoned farm was sitting on a rough road with its motor idling. Hallam could hear it plainly in the quiet morning. A man in a flashy cap and jacket was sitting on its running board, talking to another man who wore an apron and stood nearby holding the reins of a horse.

Hallam had never seen the man in the cap before, but he had to be Vince Noonan. He was here to get his orders for the delivery of the bootlegged whiskey from the man who was really in charge of the operation.

Smitty Wardell.

Hallam slid down out of the saddle and tied the horse to a slender tree. There was enough brush between him and the truck to give him cover part of the way, and then there was a shallow gulley that would take him even closer. Close enough, he thought. Hallam started catfooting his way down the hill.

In his earlier days, he had been told that he moved so quietly he could sneak up on an Apache. Hallam had always known that was an exaggeration, but Smitty and Noonan weren't Apaches, either. The gangster from Chicago wasn't used to the outdoors, wouldn't know what to listen for. And Smitty was probably convinced that no one had any idea of his connection with the bootlegging ring. He wouldn't be as alert as he should have been.

At least, Hallam *hoped* he was right about both of those things.

He slipped into the gully and crawled the last forty yards on his belly. The Colt had been tucked behind his belt, but it was in his hand now as he took off his hat and lifted his head enough to peer over the lip of the gully. Smitty and Noonan were only about twenty feet away from him.

"You take care now, you hear?" Smitty was saying to the gangster. "And take care of this load. It's goin' to bring a right smart payoff."

"Sure, boss," Noonan grunted. "I'll see you again in a few days."

Hallam stood up, lined the Colt on them, said, "Don't neither one of you move."

Smitty and Noonan both jerked around. Noonan started to reach under his coat, but he froze when he saw the rock-steady barrel of the Colt pointing at him.

"Hallam!" Smitty exclaimed. "But I thought— I mean, what the hell you doin' here, old son?"

"Reckon you are a mite surprised to see me, Smitty," Hallam said grimly. "You figured Bascomb and Jenkins had me dead and buried by now. The Rangers got there first, though. Your pards are dead, the farmhouse's burned to the ground, and them stills are busted into kindlin' by now. It's all over, Smitty."

He could see both men pale as the news hit them. Smitty opened his mouth a couple of times like a fish out of water, then finally managed to say, "I don't know what the hell you're talkin' about, Hallam."

Hallam shook his head. "I just heard this fella from up north call you boss. I know all about how the rustlin' was just a cover-up to keep the Rangers from lookin' into the bootleggin', and I know you're behind all of it, Smitty." He paused, then grated, "I know you killed Dan Armstrong, too."

"What the blue blazes . . . ! Killed Armstrong? You're havin' delusions, Hallam." Smitty licked his lips as he tried to talk his way out of this.

"Look at your apron, Smitty," Hallam told him. "Don't

reckon I ever saw you without it 'cept for that time in the jail. Brush your hand over it."

Smitty started to shake his head. "You've gone plumb crazy—"

"Do it!" Hallam eared back the hammer of the Colt as he rapped the order.

Smitty lifted a shaking hand and passed it over the front of the apron. A dusting of flour sifted down from it.

"The same thing happened when you stuck that knife into Armstrong," Hallam said. "I reckon you were tryin' to talk him out of something, and when he wouldn't listen to reason, you took that knife from behind your back and stabbed him 'fore he knew what was happenin'. Your arm probably brushed across the apron when you did it, because there was flour on the ground beside where he fell. I just caught a glimpse of it before Bascomb and that deputy of his tromped it into the dust. Reckon that was an accident, but it served its purpose anyway. I never did get a chance to check that white powder, and afterwards it slipped my mind. Didn't seem like anything important, I reckon. That was my mistake. That, and trustin' you."

Smitty's upper lip curled in a sneer. "Hell, that ain't no kind of proof. A little bit of flour that might've been there and might not have been. Gone now, anyway, that's for sure. No cop's goin' to pay attention to that."

Hallam nodded toward Noonan. "No, but they'll pay attention to your pard there, once he starts singin' to save his own skin. You're caught, Smitty. It ain't goin' to hurt you now to admit you killed Armstrong and save Teddy's hide."

"Hell with that!" Smitty spat. "Armstrong was a scared, greedy, stupid fool. Got all shook up when you almost caught them boys who was doin' the rustlin'. He said he had to have a bigger share, or he wasn't goin' to take the risk of helpin' us no more. Like you said, the bastard wouldn't listen to reason, and I was tired of his troublemakin' anyway. Reckon I felt sorry for Teddy, 'cause I knew he'd get the blame, but it just seemed like the time had come to get rid of ol' Dan." The cook laughed. "But you can't prove a lick of what I just said, and Vince here ain't goin' to talk. He knows I got too many friends on the inside. If I go to prison, so does he—and he won't never come out if he don't keep his mouth shut."

Noonan's features were even more ashen than before, and Hallam knew that Smitty's threat had struck home. Hallam looked at Smitty and said, "Ex-con, are you?"

The man's mouth spread in a gap-toothed grin. "Best damn cook the Huntsville pen ever seen, Hallam."

"The contacts you made there helped you get in touch with Noonan and Jenkins."

Smitty nodded. "Reckon you've got it all figured out, all right. Won't do you no good, though. We ain't goin' nowhere."

Hallam started to frown.

Smitty and Noonan moved at the same instant.

The cook went one way, the gangster the other. Smitty dove behind his horse, using the animal for cover. Noonan twisted, reaching into the cab of the truck. Hallam knew he had to be grabbing for a gun, and he triggered the Colt. The slug smacked by Noonan's head and went through the open door of the truck, burying itself in the upholstery of the seat. Noonan had a tommy gun in his hands by then and was bringing it to bear.

Hallam had seen automatic weapons in pictures about the Great War and knew how much damage they could do. He had seen a vivid example of that damage a few hours earlier, too, as the Texas Rangers stormed the farmhouse. He snapped off another shot and then threw himself backward into the gulley as a burst of fire from the tommy gun chewed up the ground at his feet.

"I'm hit!" Noonan howled, the machine gun falling silent. That second quick shot must've gone home, Hallam thought.

"Get in the truck!" That was Smitty. Hallam poked his head up. He saw the cook grabbing the shoulder of the wounded Noonan, shoving him into the cab and across the seat behind the wheel. Smitty snatched up the tommy gun from where Noonan had dropped it and piled into the truck behind him.

Hallam had caught a glimpse of blood on Noonan's coat but didn't know how badly the gangster was hurt. Not enough to keep him from driving, though, Hallam saw as the truck roared to life and lurched into motion. He scrambled up out of the gulley and fired again, aiming for the tires, but he saw the bullet kick up dust a few inches away from its target.

The truck was rolling faster now, the door on the passenger side still flapping open. Through it Hallam could see Smitty struggling with the ammunition drum on the machine gun. The cook was probably unfamiliar with the weapon, and he was having a hard time getting it to work.

Hallam grimaced, turned, started running up the hill to the spot where he had left his horse. The truck was almost out of range already. The only chance he had of bringing Smitty and Noonan to justice, let alone saving Teddy from a murder charge, was to catch up to the speeding vehicle.

His bad knee was throbbing by the time he reached the horse. He jerked the reins loose and vaulted into the saddle like a man thirty years younger. He felt all of his own years as he landed, though. No time to worry about aches and pains now, he thought. He pulled the horse's head around and kicked it into a gallop.

The truck rounded a big curve and was out of sight. Hallam headed for the hill that the road circled around. It was rough and brushy, but the horse took it gamely. From the top of the slope, Hallam could see the whiskey truck again as it careened around the sharp turns in the winding road.

If he could keep cutting across country instead of following the road, he might be able to catch up to the truck. He had to try.

As if sensing his rider's desperation, the horse put every bit of its gallant strength into the pursuit. Hallam rode up and down hills, some of the slopes so steep that the horse slid rather than galloped down them. A broad, deep gully opened up in front of them. Hallam had only a split second to judge it with his eyes, and then he was urging the horse toward it at full speed. He leaned forward over his mount's neck.

The horse leaped, sailing up and out for what seemed like minutes instead of instants. Then its front hooves thudded down on the far side of the gap and it was galloping again, scarcely breaking stride. The jump would have done Red Callahan—or any other stuntman in Hollywood—proud.

He had gained on the truck, Hallam saw. With a surge of excitement, he realized that he could angle in front of it now. He sent the horse pounding toward the road again. Once he reached it, he could face the truck and blast out its windshield if he had to. He was going to stop the damn thing, one way or another.

Smitty suddenly leaned out the door of the speeding vehicle, and the machine gun in his hands sprayed bullets toward Hallam.

He felt the tug at his pants leg as a bullet passed by, heard the horrible thud as the slug smashed into the horse beneath him. The animal broke stride, stumbled, started to go down. Hallam kicked his feet free of the stirrups.

The horse went head over heels, throwing Hallam from the saddle. The whole world turned upside down, then something smashed into him. He had time to realize he had hit the ground before an incredible weight slammed into his right leg. Hallam screamed as the horse rolled over him.

There was dust in his mouth. He spat it out, realized that the Colt was no longer in his hand. His right leg was a mass of agony. Hallam lifted his head and saw the horse kicking out the last of its life a few yards away. The gun was nowhere in sight.

But through the red haze of pain that had dropped over his eyes, he could see the truck, could see the way it veered off its course. He hadn't quite reached the road, but the ground here was level enough for the truck to negotiate it without any trouble.

Noonan was hunched over the wheel, Smitty beside him with the tommy gun. And they were coming right at him.

Hallam tried to lift himself with his arms. He couldn't drag himself out of the way, he knew that, but he at least had to try. He wasn't going to lie there and watch them run him down.

A flash of movement caught Hallam's eye. A man on horseback came galloping down out of the hills, the animal racing toward Hallam. Hallam blinked the dirt out of his eyes, saw Eliot Tremaine crouched over the horse's neck. Eliot was coaxing the horse to run harder and harder. . . .

The boy wasn't going to try—

Even if he was, the truck was too close. He'd never make it, Hallam thought.

A grin pulled his lips back. There were more riders right behind Eliot. He saw Pecos and Stone Riordan, Max Hilyard and all the others. So they had followed him after all. Some of the Flying L hands were with them. Hallam heard the crackle of gunfire and knew it wasn't blanks this time. There was nothing phony about this gunfight.

The truck loomed up in front of him. Over the roar of its engine, he heard the sound of hoofbeats, heard Eliot Tremaine cry, "Hallam!"

Hallam threw up his arm, felt Eliot's strong fingers close around his wrist. The jolt pulled his arm right out of its socket, but suddenly he was moving, being jerked out of the path of the speeding truck. Eliot's horse flashed in front of the vehicle as the actor leaned far over from the saddle and pulled Hallam to safety with inches to spare.

Eliot released Hallam's arm, letting him fall to the ground again as the truck roared on past. Hallam hardly felt the pain of the dislocated shoulder. Compared to what had happened to his leg when the horse rolled over it, this new injury was nothing. He used his remaining good arm to lift himself slightly as Eliot reined in and leaped from the back of his horse to come running toward him.

"Hallam!" Eliot exclaimed as he dropped to one knee next to him. "Are you all right?"

"Best . . . best damn stunt I ever seen . . . ," Hallam whispered.

He looked past Eliot, saw the other cowboys closing in on the truck. The machine gun chattered again, but the shots went wild as both front tires blew, hit by the gunfire from the cowboys. The vehicle careened wildly back and forth, completely out of control as it angled toward the edge of a bluff.

It plunged over, dropping out of sight. Hallam heard the crash an instant later, followed by the *whump!* of an explosion. Flames and smoke shot up as the bootleg whiskey burned, turning the wrecked truck into a fiery coffin for the two men inside.

"Sorry, Teddy," Hallam muttered.

Then he closed his eyes and went away from the pain for a long time.

TWENTY-FOUR

"Got another visitor for you, Lucas," Pecos said from the doorway of the room in the Fort Worth hospital.

"Another one?" Hallam tried not to groan as he shifted his leg, which was encased in a cast from ankle to hip. His shoulder hadn't required a cast, just a lot of taping up to keep it still for a while, but the smashed knee was going to keep him laid up for a long time.

"You'll want to see this one," Pecos promised him.

Hallam wasn't sure about that. He'd had plenty of visitors already, and he'd only been awake a few hours. There had been cops waiting to talk to him, for one thing. Lots of cops, including Fred Kerr and Chuck Garrett. The authorities had wanted first crack at him, and he had told the story to them over and over, including Smitty's confession. Smitty and Noonan were both dead, though, so there was nothing to corroborate Hallam's claims.

Kerr and Garrett had been talking in low, intense voices to the acting sheriff as they all left. Hallam had tried to take that as a hopeful sign.

Once the cops were through with him, everyone from the Flying L had crowded into the room. There were so many of them, in fact, that the doctor had threatened to have them all thrown out. Stone Riordan had taken the man aside for a personal talk, however, and after that no one had disturbed them.

It was good to see all of his friends, Hallam had to admit, and there had been a heap of explaining to do to them, too. When Hallam finished the story, Rae Lindsey just shook her head and said, "It's so hard to believe. Smitty was such a good friend . . . I thought . . ."

"Reckon everybody who knew him thought that," Hallam told her. "It's a waste, all right. He was a damn fine cook."

He had tired out quickly, and Wayne Lindsey had ushered everyone out of the room to let him get some rest. Now, though, Pecos was back, and he had brought somebody with him.

"All right," Hallam said. "Let's get it over with."

Pecos grinned, reached out into the hall, and pulled Teddy Spotted Horse into the room. Eliot Tremaine entered right behind him, grinning just as widely as Pecos.

Hallam sat up straighter, ignoring the twinge of pain in his shoulder. "Teddy!" he exclaimed. "They let you out!"

"They sure did," Teddy agreed. He was unshaven and tired-looking, but his eyes were shining with excitement. "Those two Ranger friends of yours went to the district attorney, along with that new sheriff who took Bascomb's place, and they told him everything you said, told him they believed every word of it. Once he heard that, he said they might as well let me go. Wasn't a jury in the State of Texas that would argue with the Rangers, he said. Shoot, Bascomb had never even charged me with the killing. According to the Rangers, the district attorney was mighty embarrassed by the whole thing."

Hallam leaned back against his pillows. "I'm right glad they had that much sense. I tried to find enough evidence to clear you, but after that truck crashed and burned up—"

"It's a good thing you and Teddy both have friends, isn't it,

Hallam?" Eliot said. "Pecos told me how stubborn you are about accepting help, but it can come in handy sometimes."

Hallam thought about how Eliot had risked his own life to snatch him from in front of that speeding truck, thought about how the others had pitched right in to stop Smitty and Noonan. They had waited a few minutes after he rode off from the ranch house before following him at the insistence of Pecos and Eliot.

Without those two, he would be dead now, and Smitty and Noonan would have escaped.

Hallam held out his good hand to Eliot Tremaine. "Thanks," he said simply.

Eliot shook with him, and then Pecos and Teddy did the same. They were right, Hallam thought as he swallowed hard. It was damn good to have friends.

The doctor came bustling in, frowned slightly when he saw that Hallam still had visitors. He said, "You really should get some rest now, Mr. Hallam. As soon as that leg heals, we're going to do surgery on it."

It was Hallam's turn to frown, this time in confusion. "What do you mean, Doc? Do surgery on it when it heals? That don't make sense."

"As soon as the broken bones above and below the knee have knitted properly, I want to do some work on the knee itself. When we were putting you back together, I noticed that you'd had some injuries to the knee in the past."

Hallam nodded. "It's been banged up some, all right. I took a slug in that leg, too, right close to the knee."

"But you never had the knee itself repaired, did you?"

"Never had time," Hallam shrugged. "It always mended up well enough for me to get around."

The doctor smiled. "Well, I think we can fix it so you can get around a lot better. I'm fairly certain not all the damage is irreversible."

Eliot clapped Hallam on his good shoulder. "That's wonderful, Hallam!" he said. "You'll be doing those Running W's again before you know it."

Hallam took a deep breath. "I'll be laid up for a long time. Don't much like the sound of that. And who's goin' to pay for all this fancy surgery?"

"I don't think you have to worry about that," the doctor told him. "We received a wire from a man named Darby in Hollywood, instructing us to send all the bills to him."

Hallam glanced at Eliot, saw the smile on the actor's face. "Reckon you must've had something to do with that," he grunted.

Eliot shrugged. "I called Darby and had a talk with him. I spoke to my father, too."

"They're probably anxious for you to get back out there and start makin' movies."

Eliot shook his head. "I told them to recast my part in *Sagebrush*."

"You're not goin' back?" Hallam stared at him in surprise.

"Oh, I will sooner or later. I think I'm going to enjoy making Western pictures. But that can wait until you're back on your feet, Hallam. Besides, the Flying L can still use a few extra hands while the ranch is recovering from the damage done to it by Wardell and his cohorts. Right, lads?"

Pecos and Teddy both grinned and nodded.

"So you see, we'll be able to visit you quite often while you're recuperating," Eliot went on.

"That's fine. Just be sure and invite me to the weddin'," Hallam muttered.

"Wedding?" Eliot echoed. "I'm sure I don't know what you mean."

"You will," Hallam told him. "Once you figure out Rae Lindsey's the kind of gal who usually gets what she wants, you will."

Eliot laughed. "We'll see. For now, though, I just want to live the carefree, happy-go-lucky life of a cowboy for a while longer."

Hallam looked at Pecos and Teddy and shook his head. "Go educate this boy," he said. "He's got a heap of learnin' to do yet."

Pecos laughed, but before he could say anything, the doctor put in, "I really wish all of you would leave now and let Mr. Hallam get some rest. You can come back later, of course."

Eliot nodded. "You're right, Doctor." He turned to Hallam. "So long, pard."

"So long," Hallam said. He nodded to Pecos and Teddy, and the three young men filed out of the room, talking and laughing among themselves. It was a good sound, Hallam thought. The doctor followed them out and shut the door behind him, leaving Hallam alone.

Only alone for the time being, he thought as he settled down in the bed and closed his eyes. They would be back. Pals of the saddle, that was what they were. Men to ride the river with, every one of them . . .

Lucas Hallam went to sleep.